S0-BBC-893

"WHY HASN'T SOME WOMAN JUST SNAPPED YOU UP?"

Faye's eyes were full of mirth as she gazed up at David from the safety of his arms. "You do like women, don't you?"

"Definitely," he said, his eyes gleaming. He ran one hand tantalizingly over her hip. "But I'm just not the marrying kind. In my line of work I have to be free to travel a lot—Europe, Africa, the Mideast. Marriage just hasn't been in the cards."

"There's got to be more to it than that."

There was, but David saw no reason to tell her his life story at that moment. He had more ardorous concerns on his mind. "Maybe I just haven't met the right woman," he finally murmured.

Faye's smile was enigmatic. *But now you have,* she silently told him.

ABOUT THE AUTHOR

It was Jane Silverwood's love of animals that made her decide to set her latest romance at a zoo. A former teacher, Jane started writing after grading what she estimates as her ten thousandth English composition. This seasoned author has now written or cowritten more than twenty-five romances under her own name, as well as the pseudonyms Anne Silverlock and Alexis Hill Jordan. Jane lives in Columbia, Maryland, with her professor husband and two children.

Books by Jane Silverwood

HARLEQUIN TEMPTATION
46–VOYAGE OF THE HEART
93–SNOW MELT
117–A PERMANENT ARRANGEMENT

Don't miss any of our special offers. Write to us at the following address for information on our newest releases.

Harlequin Reader Service
901 Fuhrmann Blvd., P.O. Box 1397, Buffalo, NY 14240
Canadian address: P.O. Box 603,
Fort Erie, Ont. L2A 5X3

Jane Silverwood

THE TENDER TRAP

Harlequin Books

TORONTO • NEW YORK • LONDON
AMSTERDAM • PARIS • SYDNEY • HAMBURG
STOCKHOLM • ATHENS • TOKYO • MILAN

Published November 1987

First printing September 1987

ISBN 0-373-70282-5

Copyright © 1987 by Louise Titchener. All rights reserved.
Philippine copyright 1987. Australian copyright 1987.
Except for use in any review, the reproduction or utilization of
this work in whole or in part in any form by any electronic,
mechanical or other means, now known or hereafter invented,
including xerography, photocopying and recording, or in any
information storage or retrieval system, is forbidden without
the permission of the publisher, Harlequin Enterprises Limited,
225 Duncan Mill Road, Don Mills, Ontario, Canada M3B 3K9.

All the characters in this book have no existence outside the
imagination of the author and have no relation whatsoever to
anyone bearing the same name or names. They are not even
distantly inspired by any individual known or unknown to the
author, and all the incidents are pure invention.

The Superromance design trademark consisting of the words
HARLEQUIN SUPERROMANCE and the portrayal of a Harlequin,
and the Superromance trademark consisting of the words
HARLEQUIN SUPERROMANCE are trademarks of Harlequin
Enterprises Limited. The Superromance design trademark
and the portrayal of a Harlequin are registered in the
United States Patent Office.

Printed in Canada

CHAPTER ONE

"OH, DR. O'NEILL, thank God you're here!" Miss Prior, the fiftyish secretary to whom David had just introduced himself, seized his wrist and urged him toward the door. "We've been just frantic waiting for you."

"I came as fast as I could, but the traffic was heavy and quite a few cars were backed up at the bridge."

"Oh, I know, I know. It couldn't have happened at a worse time." The gray-haired little woman teetered down a set of concrete steps and then along a gravel path that led past a collection of empty cages. "Normally we would have called Dr. Zuckerman, but he retired to Florida a couple of months ago. None of the other vets in the area were willing to come." She clucked. "I can't say I blame them. Gorillas give me the shivers."

Ignoring that, David asked, "Dr. Zuckerman was Wilderness Worlds' veterinarian?"

"Yes, he's been taking care of the farm stock around here ever since I can remember."

"I see." Actually David wasn't surprised that they'd been employing a domestic animal vet not specifically trained to handle exotic animals. Small out-of-the-way zoos commonly relied on a local practitioner who knew more about horses and cows than lions and tigers. On the other hand, from what he could see of the construction going on around him, Wallace Gaffey's operation might be out-of-the-way, but it certainly wasn't going to be small.

"The children's zoo is the only section of Wilderness Worlds that's been open to the public as yet," Miss Prior explained a little breathlessly. "Mr. Gaffey doesn't plan to open the main park until this July."

Not commenting, David studied the low building toward which they were headed. Like everything else in Wilderness Worlds, it was so new that it looked as if the mortar holding its bricks together was barely dry. "Is that the ape house?"

"Yes. You'll find Mr. Wallace Gaffey in there along with Roy Hubbard. Roy's in charge of maintenance around here and is Mr. Gaffey's right-hand man. They're standing guard just in case Kong should try and rip off Miss Johnson's head or something."

David raised an eyebrow. "Kong?"

Miss Prior clucked again and then for good measure, tch-tched. "Her first name is Faye, you see. So Mr. Gaffey thought it would be a good joke to call her gorilla Kong. Now I suppose he doesn't think it's so funny."

"No, I don't suppose he does," David agreed. "Well, I'll certainly do my best to see that she doesn't lose her head over him." He immediately regretted the joke, which was certainly out of place in this macabre situation. But Miss Prior didn't seem to have noticed and rattled on toward the ape house without missing a beat.

When they were inside the building, David was impressed by its size. He'd arrived in Baltimore after Christmas to spend a semester as a visiting professor teaching comparative pathology to postgraduate students at Johns Hopkins. During the three months he'd been on the east coast, he'd heard quite a lot about the zoo Gaffey was building—both good things and bad.

The good was that it was very well equipped. Four years earlier Wallace Gaffey, the eccentric multimillionaire real estate entrepreneur and king of the Eastern Shore crab industry had opened a children's zoo near his hometown of Haverton. Like everything he touched, it had succeeded beyond all expectation and become a popular stop for families vacationing at the nearby beaches on the Delmarva peninsula. A year later he'd acquired a large parcel of adjoining land and begun planning an elaborate animal park. It was to have everything, including an aviary filled with exotic birds, a tropical jungle and an African range where giraffes, zebras, antelopes and ostriches would live together just as they do in the wild.

Unfortunately, as David had been warned by his colleagues at Hopkins and as today's incident proved, Gaffey was staffing his fledgling zoo with well-meaning locals who still had a lot to learn about the management of exotic animals. David knew only too well the sort of tragedy that could lead to.

Following Miss Prior across the ape house's quarry-tile floor, he glanced around. Apparently Gaffey was still in the early stages of stocking, for all the compartments had been lavishly landscaped with plants, rocks and trees for climbing, yet they appeared empty except for the chamber on the far right. Just outside it two men turned and watched his approach. Though they were physical opposites, one being elderly and heavy while the other resembled the Jughead character of the old comic strip, they both wore the same anxious expression.

"Dr. O'Neill is finally here," Miss Prior sang out to the older and more substantial of the two.

He hurried forward and held out a hand. "I'm Wallace Gaffey and this—" he pointed at his associate, who clutched a high-powered rifle "—is Roy Hubbard."

While he shook the elderly millionaire's fleshy hand, David frowned at the firearm. Then he looked back at Gaffey. "He's not going to use that, is he?"

"Only if it becomes absolutely necessary. Faye Johnson is my niece but she's like a daughter to me. If we have to kill Kong to save her, then so be it."

"I see." David took his hand out of Gaffey's. "I'm afraid the story I got was pretty garbled. Just exactly what's going on?"

"Have a look for yourself."

Gaffey pointed at the Plexiglas wall behind him and David peered in. Sitting on the floor in the far corner with her back against the wall was a fragile-appearing young woman wearing blue jeans and a shredded blouse. She had a cap of white-blond hair and an up-turned nose sprinkled with vivid freckles. She also had a worried expression. Despite that, she was talking in calming tones to a half-grown gorilla. The gorilla, David noted, was developing the auburn shock of hair on his forehead characteristic of the mature male of the species. His arms were wrapped around the young woman's waist and he was looking up into her face lovingly.

Indeed, at first sight their pose struck David as a bizarre travesty of the Madonna and child. On closer inspection, however, it was obvious that the adolescent gorilla squatting on her lap had Miss Faye Johnson pinned against the wall.

"We've tried everything we can think of," Gaffey said. "We even tried buying him off with his favorite food. But he wouldn't let us get anywhere near him. He's made up his mind that she's going to stay put."

David repressed the oath he felt like muttering and turned to face the man. "How did this happen? What was she doing in there with him?"

Behind his spectacles, Wallace Gaffey's faded brown eyes were filled with worry, and with his pug nose and wrinkled jowls he looked more like an aging bulldog than the crabs who'd made him so rich.

"Faye is Kong's keeper," he explained, wringing his hands. "She always goes in daily to check on him."

"Is this the first time he's refused to let her out?"

The old man turned to Hubbard. "He hasn't done anything like this before, has he, Roy?"

Hubbard pushed up his baseball cap and scratched behind his left ear. "He never liked it when she left, that's for sure. Always tried to stop her. But this is the first time he's got real nasty about it." He shook his head. "I warned her not to go on treating him as if he was still a baby, but she wouldn't listen."

"Well, she should have," David said flatly. "May I have a look at your rifle?" He took the firearm out of Hubbard's hands and quickly and expertly removed its ammunition.

"Hey!" Hubbard protested. "What if he gets violent?"

David handed back the unloaded weapon and then started to take off his corduroy sport coat. "Believe me, Miss Johnson and I will be safer in there without a gun at our backs. Take me around to the door and unlock it for me, will you, please? I'm going in."

FAYE WAS FEELING distinctly cramped. Rubbing the back of Kong's neck where she knew he liked to be tickled and humming a soothing lullaby, she tried once again to dislodge him. But Kong would have none of it. As soon as she managed to remove one of his hands from her shoulder, its place would be taken by a foot, or more menacingly, by a strong pair of jaws digging in not quite hard enough to break the skin. For half the day now Faye had struggled and cajoled, but it was useless. Sighing, she gave up and patted his shoulder until the innocent expression returned to his face and he closed his shiny black eyes in a pretended snooze.

"You know you can't keep me here forever," she remonstrated.

But Kong only snuffled in her ear and cuddled closer.

"This is really silly. How am I going to fix your dinner if you won't let me up?"

Kong shifted his considerable weight and dug his iron-hard nails into her arm just deep enough to let her know who was boss.

At that moment Faye sensed she was being observed and glanced up at the window on the opposite wall. Of course she knew that Wally and Roy were out there, but this was different. Sure enough, her gaze met the steady gaze of a pair of gray eyes. The eyes were behind silver-framed aviator style eyeglasses and deep-set in a rugged masculine face that was unfamiliar to her. She knew Uncle Wally had contacted some hotshot animal specialist who was new at Hopkins. Was this the man?

A moment later the heavy door to Kong's room slid open and the stranger walked in. His self-possession made her guess him to be somewhere in his late thirties, though he looked younger. He was not particularly tall—no more than five feet ten inches—yet his lean, athletic build suggested a jogger's regimen or regular workouts in a gym.

Just inside the room, he stopped and waited a moment, obviously gauging Kong's reaction.

Faye held her breath. The gorilla aimed a suspicious look at the intruder and tightened his grip on her. Otherwise he didn't react, which was surprising. Even as an infant Kong had had definite opinions about the humans with whom he'd come in contact. From the first he'd disliked Roy, and lately had become so demonstrative about his dislike that Roy had refused to enter his compartment.

Faye peered up at the stranger and smiled. "You must be giving off good vibrations or carrying a lucky charm. Kong doesn't seem to mind you."

The newcomer smiled back at her. "I usually get along pretty well with animals, but just to be on the safe side I carry a four-leaf clover."

He had a baritone voice with a faint British accent that Faye liked. "Have you come to rescue me, by any chance?" she inquired.

"Yes, or at least I intend to try. I'm Dr. David O'Neill."

"How do you do. I'm Faye Johnson, but I guess you already know that."

"Yes." David set down his medical bag. It was open, and inside there was a syringe filled with a tranquilizer and a dart gun loaded with the same substance.

"Just how do you intend to manage this rescue?" Faye asked.

"Carefully." Fixing his gaze on Kong, David took another step forward. "First I'd like to talk a bit while your friend gets used to me."

Faye's brow puckered. "Then what? You're not planning to use drugs, are you?"

"I may have to tranquilize him." David took another step and waited for Kong to object. So far nothing.

Faye's frown had deepened. "Kong has a very delicate stomach. Doping him might make him sick. And really, it's not necessary. I didn't want Wally to drag you here all the way from Baltimore. Honestly, this isn't as bad as it looks."

"Isn't it?" David fixed her with a speculative look. Behind her abundant freckles, she was pale and there were blue shadows under her eyes. Yet with that last statement she'd managed a brave little smile. It lit up her face and suddenly he realized that she was quite pretty. Her eyes were a lovely, if rather feline, shade of green. How old was she, he wondered. Twenty-four? Twenty-five? Surely no more than that. And she certainly had guts. Most women trapped in a situation like this would be hysterical by now.

"Sooner or later Kong's bound to fall asleep," she reasoned.

"Yes, but if he takes a snooze while he's wound around your body, you won't be able to just tiptoe off."

"I suppose you're right." She sighed. "Still I really can't believe he would hurt me."

"I don't want to alarm you, but I don't want you to do anything foolish, either. Left undisturbed, gorillas are usually pacific creatures. But adolescent males can have mercurial tempers." David had once seen an escaped gorilla rip off the ear of its keeper.

"I raised him from a baby," she argued. "When he was tiny, I practically lived with him. I fixed his special diet, boiled his milk, measured out his vitamin drops, whipped up his Ovaltine nightcap."

"And you probably played with him."

"Well, yes. He was very boisterous. He loved games of tag."

"I'll bet he loved being cuddled, too. Baby gorillas are a lot like human infants."

"Oh, they are." She patted the top of Kong's head and he grunted. "He still loves to be cuddled. That's the trouble, I guess. I've spoiled him."

Though it wasn't just that, David nodded and made a mental note that later he'd give her and her employer a proper lecture on where they'd gone wrong. "Yes," he said. "It was fine to pick him up and hold him when he weighed twenty pounds. Now it's a different story." He took another step forward, but quickly retreated when Kong started to growl.

"Very different," Faye commented glumly.

David stood still. Now that he'd backed off, Kong no longer appeared threatening. Indeed, his expression was one of angelic contentment.

"What happens when you try to get away?"

"I'll show you." Faye looked down at Kong, muttered, "Naughty boy!" and attempted to push him off. Instantaneously, the animal transformed himself from a hairy angel to an imp from hell. He bared a sharp set of fangs, dug in his nails and snarled menacingly.

"That's enough," David warned.

But Faye didn't stop struggling soon enough. In a twinkling, Kong wound his fingers through her short blond locks and tugged. With the other hand he grabbed the sleeve of her partially torn blouse. Before the little fracas was ended, she had lost some of her hair and most of her blouse, but she still had a one-hundred-pound adolescent gorilla wound around her like a python.

"Don't do that again!"

"Not to worry. I won't!" Gasping and trembling, Faye looked down at herself. If Kong weren't covering her like a fur coat, she would be virtually naked above the waist. Distractedly, she rubbed at her head where he'd ripped out several tufts. "Before this is over, I'll be bald."

"It'll grow back. Even without it, you'd still be prettier than most women," David told her.

The unexpected compliment made her glance up at him in surprise. Suddenly she found herself wondering if he was married. There were no rings on his long, capable-looking fingers, but you couldn't always tell from that.

Despite the exigency of her situation, she *had* noticed that he was a very attractive man. And he seemed to be as nice as he looked, too. Faye trusted her intuition. It was true that she tended to make snap judgments, but those judgments almost always turned out correct. Ever since Dr. David O'Neill had come into the room her spirits had begun to lift. She trusted him when he said he was going to get her out of this.

"Well," David said. "I'm afraid there's no other option. He'll have to be tranquilized."

Resignedly Faye nodded. "How do you intend to do it? With a dart gun?"

"Possibly." Hesitating over his plan of action, David glanced down into his open medical bag and then back up at the pretty young woman who was all but submerged in a loving mound of young gorilla. How would Kong react to the prick of a dart gun? These animals could bite hard and rip viciously, and they could be so unpredictable. What if in the moment or two before the tranquilizer began to work he took out his displeasure on his keeper. No, David decided, it would have to be done without inflicting even a tiny amount of pain. And that meant the drug would have to be administered by mouth.

"How long since he's been fed?"

"Oh, quite a while," she answered over the top of Kong's head. "He wouldn't accept any food from Wally or Roy, so he must be getting pretty hungry."

David closed his medical bag and picked it up. "We'll see what we can do about that. Hang in there. I'm going to leave for a few minutes."

"Oh, must you?" The words were out before Faye could stop them, and she was immediately embarrassed by the tone of her voice—all trembly and pleading. She'd been alone with Kong almost all day, so why should it bother her to be left alone with him a few more minutes? Yet, whether or not it made any sense, she knew that she didn't want David O'Neill to go.

"I won't be gone long," he assured her.

"No, of course you won't. I'll be fine."

Once more David found himself admiring her spirit. Saluting, he turned and strode back out through the door. On the other side of it, Roy Hubbard and Wallace Gaffey accosted him.

"What do you think?" Gaffey pressed.

"I'll tell you what I think," Roy Hubbard interjected. "If this gun were loaded, Kong would be dead meat by now. I would've plugged him when he started pulling out Faye's hair."

Out of pure survival instinct, David had long ago learned to control his Irish temper. But for a second or two it flared very hot and he had a struggle. "That would have been completely unnecessary," he finally said. "Kong didn't harm her seriously and by taking potshots with that rifle, you might have."

Hubbard looked insulted. "I'm one of the best shots in the county. There's not a chance I would have hit Faye."

"And what if you'd injured Kong enough to make him really see red while he had her in his clutches?"

"I would have plugged him right between the eyes."

Gaffey silenced his subordinate with an impatient gesture and looked anxiously at David. "What are you planning to do?"

Instead of answering the question directly, David turned his back on Hubbard and inquired politely, "Where can I get a bunch of bananas?"

A short time later, he reentered the gorilla's compartment. Looking so pale and drained that her freckles stood out against her white skin like cinnamon, Faye leaned back against the wall, trying to doze. Kong was still stuck fast to her.

"Faye?"

She opened her eyes. They widened with relief when she focused on David. "Oh, I'm so glad to see you."

"Well, I''m pretty happy to see you." It was true, too. During the few minutes he'd been gone, he'd been worried about her.

Faye swallowed and murmured, "It's funny, isn't it? We hardly know each other, but while you were away I missed you as if you were the only friend I had in the world. Am I beginning to lose my grip?"

"A state of affairs like this throws everything out of perspective," David counseled gently. "But I'd like it if you did think of me as your friend and ally."

She was right, he thought. It was probably just the situation, but he, too, was aware of the peculiar intimacy that had developed between them. David brought one hand out from behind his back and raised a bunch of plump bananas. "I've brought the key to your rescue."

Faye glanced at the fruit and tried to quiet Kong, who'd started to lick his lips at the sight of it. "Are you going to feed those to him?"

"No, you are." David squatted on his haunches. "Listen, Faye, the one with the sticker is a Trojan banana, so to speak. I've injected a knockout dose of phencyclidine into its pulp."

She eyed the banana in question. "It's a good thing you didn't take off the skin. Kong likes to peel his own."

"I figured that. When I slide the doped banana across the floor to you, I want you to offer it to him. But first I'm going to shoot over one that hasn't been tampered with."

She looked almost as interested as Kong. "Why?"

David grinned and suddenly his square Irish face was full of charm. "There's a rule about giving doctored food to suspicious animals. First offer the real thing. Then, when you've established your true-blue credentials, it's easier to put one over."

"You sound more like a con artist than a doctor, Doctor."

His grin widened and his gray eyes crinkled at the corners. "Believe me, when your job is outsmarting elephants with toothaches and hippopotamuses with upset stomachs, you learn to be devious."

"You've done a lot of this sort of thing, then?" Though this was hardly the time for chitchat, Faye was truly curious.

"I've worked with all sorts of animals in zoos all over the world," he told her. "Take my word for it, this is the way to go."

"Okay, doc, send me the first banana and I'll see what I can do."

"Good girl." He broke a piece of fruit off the stem and skimmed it across the tile floor directly into Faye's outstretched hand.

Kong, whose bright dark eyes had been observing the interaction between David and Faye with close attention, grunted excitedly.

"Time for a snack," she said as she proffered the fruit.

Kong gazed at it for a moment, then grabbed the banana. He peeled it with one hand and his teeth, the other hand maintaining a hold on Faye's neck. After eating the pulp with relish, he licked the skin and threw it down. When he was finished, he turned and gazed expectantly at David.

"So far so good," David said. "Time for our trick banana." Casually, he picked off the one with the sticker and sent it skimming across the tile floor. Faye fielded it just as easily as she had the first.

"How about another little treat?" she asked Kong brightly, and raised the banana to his lips.

The animal seemed to actually smile. Grunting, he accepted this second offering, peeled it and prepared to thrust it into his mouth. Then, at the last instant, he paused. It was as if out of the deep recesses of his mind he were having a new thought. He stared consideringly at Faye. Whether it was a generous impulse or one of suspicion, she and David would never know. But suddenly, making a soothing cooing sound, Kong pulled her head back and jammed the banana firmly between her teeth.

"Aaargh!" she gurgled.

David watched in horror. "Don't eat it!" If she swallowed the doped banana pulp, she would be unconscious within minutes. It was also possible that she might suffer from some distressing side effects.

"Spit it out, for God's sake!" he commanded.

Desperately, Faye tried to follow his order. She spluttered and gulped. But when she ejected the pulp, Kong seemed not only surprised by this ingratitude, but quite irritated. Clucking like an impatient parent, he poked the bits of mashed banana back between her teeth. With one powerful set of fingers he held her mouth shut, all the while cooing solicitously and shaking his massive head in remonstrance.

Helplessly, David watched. If he attacked the animal now, that would probably make things worse. Nevertheless, he took the dart gun out of his bag, ready to use it if Kong got any rougher.

For a full minute Faye resisted Kong's ministrations. There was banana pulp all over her chin and neck, but a lot of it was still in her mouth, and her face turned bright red with the effort not to swallow. Then she gave up and her throat worked convulsively. Satisfied, Kong released his hold. She continued to gag and moan. Then she gazed miserably over at David.

"That was awful," she half whimpered.

"God, I'm sorry."

"What's going to happen to me?"

"In a couple of minutes you'll go to sleep."

"Is that all?" She gazed at him worriedly.

Before answering, he hesitated. She hadn't swallowed the whole banana, he told himself. Probably she had ingested no more than ten milligrams. Still... "You might be sick for a day or so," he finally said, "but you'll get over it."

Faye's unhappy gaze lingered on his face, and she wondered if there was something he wasn't telling her. But then she couldn't think about it anymore. Her eyelids felt heavy and she yawned. Already the phencyclidine was taking effect. "You won't leave me, will you?" she whispered.

"No, I won't. Just relax. When you wake up, you'll be safe in your own bed. I promise."

David watched while her eyes closed and her head slumped back. So did Kong. Agitatedly the ape shook her shoulders. But she was completely knocked out. Her head bobbed limply. Letting out a yelp, Kong shook her again, but with the same result. He made a whimpering noise deep in his throat and used his fingers to wipe her face and throat clean of the lingering traces of mashed banana. Then he turned his head and gave David a long, thoughtful stare. What sort of connections were being made in Kong's brain? It was impossible to really tell what the animal was thinking, but David had his suspicions. If he knew anything at all about gorillas, that look boded ill—not for

Faye, but for him. He tightened his grip on the dart gun and waited to make his move.

For the first time since early that morning, Kong disengaged himself from his blond keeper. Laying her carefully on the floor, he shambled to his feet and turned to face David.

"That's a good boy," David told him. "Leave her alone and come after me. I'm the one who drugged the banana, not her."

"If I had the use of my gun I could shoot him now," Hubbard shouted through the window.

"Forget the gun and leave this to me, please," David said tightly, all the while keeping his gaze pinned on Kong.

Frowning mightily and growling, the ape flexed his muscles like an Olympic weight lifter. *How many rounds can I go with an enraged gorilla,* David wondered. After he'd used the dart gun, it might be several minutes before the animal succumbed. David knew that if Kong were full-grown, he'd have no chance whatsoever. A mature male had the strength of three men. Fortunately, the creature glowering at him was not mature. But he was still a daunting sight.

When Kong had taken several steps toward David and away from Faye, David aimed and fired the gun. The dart hit him squarely in the chest and he paused for several seconds, blinking in surprise. Then, bellowing in fury, he reached down and pulled out the small missile. After hurling it to the floor, he bared his teeth, thrust out his arms and rushed straight at his assailant.

David had been a wrestler in college and was proficient at karate. At the last possible moment he sidestepped, while aiming a kick at Kong's knees.

Shrieking, the animal fell to the ground and lay there for a moment, apparently dazed. Was the tranquilizer beginning to make its way to the brain? But at last Kong sat up, shot David a murderous glare and surged to his feet.

"I'm doing this for your own good," David informed him. "It would never have worked out between you and Miss Johnson."

As he spoke, he took a defensive stance and waited for the beast's next charge. Emitting fearsome, warlike shrieks, Kong came boiling across the room. Though David once again managed to dance out of his path, one of the ape's flailing arms hit him in the chest with the force of a baseball bat and he went down. Fortunately, he too had managed to land a solid blow. Gasping, Kong reeled backward several steps.

"O'Neill, get to your feet quick," Gaffey yelled. "You're closer to the door than he is. I'll open it so that you can run out."

But David only shook his head and got up. He couldn't leave Faye in here. Somehow he had to hold out until the phencyclidine took effect. He knew that the dosage had been correct. Why was Kong still looking so damned alert? Then, mercifully, it happened. As he started to barrel forward again, the animal suddenly staggered. His eyes rolled and he reeled to one side. Then his lids came down and his heavy head sagged. Slowly he crumpled to the floor.

"Thank God," Gaffey shouted from the window.

Silently seconding that, David counted to ten and approached the ape. Gingerly he prodded him. Then, still wary, he took his pulse. He was sound asleep and would be unconscious for the next couple of hours.

"Is it safe to come in there?" Gaffey asked from the window.

"Yes." David turned and looked toward Faye. She, too, was crumpled on the floor. During the past few minutes he'd been too busy watching Kong to notice her state of undress. Now he took in the fact that other than her jeans and sneakers she wore nothing but a half-torn bra. Up until that minute Faye Johnson had given David the impression of being a boyish type. Now he realized how very unboyish she really was.

As he crossed to her he unbuttoned his own shirt. It, too, had seen better days, but at least it was still in one piece. He was just draping it over her when Gaffey and Hubbard came into the room.

"How's Faye?" Gaffey demanded.

"Out like a light." David knelt and took her pulse. "She'll be that way for quite some time."

Casting a nervous glance at the prone Kong, Wallace Gaffey made his way across the room, closely followed by Hubbard. "Will she suffer any ill effects?"

David studied Faye's pale face. "She might be sick for a little while. Side effects from phencyclidine have been reported in humans."

"What sort of side effects?"

"They vary."

"How do you mean?"

David glanced up. "She'll just be feeling rocky," he said. "But don't worry. I'll see to it that she comes out of this all right."

CHAPTER TWO

RUBY PRIOR PURSED her lips. "Miss Johnson should be seen by a real doctor, don't you think?"

"I'm real enough." David smiled as he took out his stethoscope. "I have an M.D. as well as a degree in veterinary science." He didn't add that he was a full professor of comparative pathology and had written the definitive text used by all the top medical schools.

While he examined Faye Johnson's limp body, carefully monitoring all her vital signs, Wallace Gaffey and his secretary hovered at the foot of the tufted leather couch where she lay. After the debacle in the ape house, Roy Hubbard had stayed behind to see to Kong while David had carried Faye to Gaffey's office. When he completed his examination, he turned toward the two anxious onlookers.

"Is she going to be all right?" Gaffey asked.

"Yes, though she may need a day or so to recuperate."

"That nasty ape ripped the shirt right off her back." Averting her eyes from David's naked chest, Miss Prior came forward holding a yellow keeper's jacket. The garment was emblazoned with a red and white logo dominated by a palm tree whose drooping fronds formed the words, Wilderness Worlds. When she had slipped Faye's limp arms through the jacket and covered her decently, David retrieved his shirt and corduroy sport coat. Fortunately the weather outside was warm for March.

"Does she live with her family?" he asked. "Is there someone who ought to be called?"

Wallace Gaffey shook his head. "The poor girl lost her folks a few years back. Right now, I'm the only family she's got."

"You're related? I think I heard you say you were her uncle."

Gaffey scratched his head. "Well, more like a great-uncle. Around this part of the Eastern Shore we're all related. Her dad was a nephew of mine. When she lost her mother and then her father died in a fire at one of my hotels, I took her under my wing."

David closed the last button on his shirt and began tucking the garment into his waistband. "She's going to need someone to look after her for the next couple of days."

"You can bring her over to my place," Gaffey offered. He looked vague for a moment. "I'm a busy man," he added, emphasizing the word "busy" as if there were some special meaning attached to it. "So I won't be there all the time to see to her myself. But my housekeeper will make sure that she's taken care of."

"Addy Hawkins quit last week," Miss Prior reminded him, "and you haven't found a replacement yet."

"Oh, yes." Gaffey seemed startled by this information, then looked at David as though expecting a suggestion.

David hesitated. He was thinking about the symptoms that Faye Johnson might experience when she came to. On apes phencyclidine worked very effectively and had almost no side effects. With humans, unfortunately, it was not so ideal. Reactions varied widely. There was no way to tell how she might respond when she regained consciousness. She might be perfectly all right. On the other hand, there could be periods when her behavior was abnormal.

As these thoughts ran through his head, he gazed down at her pale features. She looked so young and vulnerable lying there that he was pierced by a sharp stab of guilt. What had happened wasn't his fault, but still he felt responsible. If he'd sent the doped banana first . . .

"Miss Johnson should be watched by someone with medical qualifications who knows about the effects of phencyclidine," he finally said. "If you'll show me where she lives, I'll stay with her long enough to be sure she comes out of this okay."

Gaffey beamed. "Excellent. I'll pay you for your time, of course." A calculating look had come into the older man's eyes. "Oh, and I wonder, as long as you're going to be around for a while, O'Malley, would you mind having a look at my other animals—just to be sure everything's copacetic, if you know what I mean?"

"Sure, but my name's O'Neill," David answered gently.

FAYE JOHNSON LIVED in Haverton, a historic little town only a few miles north of Wilderness Worlds. As David drove toward it with Faye stretched out in the backseat of his sedan and Miss Prior sitting next to him, the older woman explained that Wallace Gaffey owned about half the real estate in the community. Sixty-eight years ago he had been born on one of its shady streets.

"Oh, he's a remarkable man," she exclaimed, patting her tight gray curls, though the warm breeze wafting through the window hadn't disarranged them in the least. "He started with nothing but a few crab pots and a broken-down boat, and now he's one of the richest men in the country, maybe even the world."

"He would have to be," David agreed. "Putting together your own private animal park is an expensive hobby."

"Yes, but what you've seen today is only the beginning. Wallace intends to reproduce all the exotic wilderness of the world. They'll be exactly like the originals in every detail, including the animals."

"Really?" David was amused by the extravagance of the idea and a bit surprised at the enthusiasm he heard in Miss Prior's voice. It was obvious that she worshipped her boss. "But that's out of the question, you know," David told her. "There are ecologies that can't be reproduced and animals that can't be acquired, no matter how much money you have to spend."

"Oh, excuse me, Mr. O'Neill, but I think you underestimate what can be done when you have resources like Wallace Gaffey's and an imagination to match. That's the secret of his success, you know— he's always possessed a bold imagination and the daring to turn his ideas into realities."

"Yes, I've heard some of the stories about him." David thought of Gaffey's flamboyant advertising campaigns, his penchant for risk taking, his decisions to acquire oceanfront hotels and expand his fishing business into fast-food crab cake franchises that now dotted the landscape from coast to coast. He had done these things in the teeth of recessions and just when his competitors were pulling in their horns.

"I know that your boss is a remarkable man," David said. "But he can't perform miracles. To give you an example of what I mean by animals virtually impossible to acquire, there's the mountain gorilla and the snow leopard, which are both very close to extinction. Then there's the giant panda. That animal inhabits vast wilderness areas in China and can't be purchased at any price."

"But there are pandas in the National Zoo," Miss Prior objected.

"Exactly. Those animals were donated by the Chinese government to our government as a goodwill gesture. They were a politically motivated gift. No private person could legally import such a rare creature."

Miss Prior shrugged bony shoulders. "All I know is that Wally Gaffey is a man who gets things done and who usually doesn't let red tape stand in his way." Dismissively she pointed at a narrow side street to the right. "Faye lives down there."

A couple of minutes later David pulled to a stop in front of a neat white cottage. "Cute little place," he commented as he got out and opened the door to the backseat. Carefully he lifted his unconscious patient and carried her up the flagstone walk.

"It belonged to Faye's grandmother," Miss Prior informed him. Then she turned her attention to a fat old golden retriever dozing in a sunny spot on the porch. "Out of the way, Missy, shoo." Stepping over the animal, who did nothing but thump her tail and lift one eyelid, she opened the front door and then stood aside with a slightly disapproving air while Da-

vid carried Faye in. He took her through the small
living room, furnished with comfortable-looking
pieces slipcovered in faded chintz, to the back of the
house where he found a pretty bedroom. There, after
Miss Prior dislodged three napping marmalade tabby
cats, he laid Faye carefully in the center of an old-
fashioned brass bed and sat down on the edge so that
he could unlace her shoes.

Miss Prior hovered at the foot of the bed, eyeing the
proceedings nervously. "Faye has always been crazy
about animals."

"So I see. How many pets does she have?"

"Only the cats and the old dog now, but there was
a time when this house was filled with everything from
gerbils to a parrot." When David didn't comment, she
asked, "Do you think you'll be spending the night
here?"

"Possibly."

"Where will you sleep?"

"On the couch in the living room, I expect." David
set the first of his unconscious patient's shoes on the
floor and began working on the second. "Miss Prior,"
he said, looking up, "I'd like to get Faye into a nightgown and under the covers. But I'm a man and a
stranger to her. Would you prefer to undress her while
I wait in the living room?"

The woman flushed slightly and took a step backward. "Oh, my, no. I have to get home, actually. I'm
expecting some relatives for dinner. And since you're
a medical doctor and all, it doesn't mean a thing to
you to undress a woman, does it?"

"Not a thing," David agreed with a perfectly
straight face. "You can take my word for it, Miss

Johnson will be safe in my hands. Do you need a ride?''

"My house is only three blocks away. The walk will do me good.'' Miss Prior bobbed her head, made a few fluttery movements and turned to go. "Don't forget to feed the cats.''

"I'll manage.''

"My number's in the phone book. Just call if you need my help.''

"Oh, I will. Don't worry about a thing.''

Very shortly after that, David heard the front door shut and breathed a sigh of relief. He had removed both Faye Johnson's shoes. Now it was time to do the rest. But before divesting her inert body of any more clothing, he crossed the room to an oak bureau and began opening its drawers one by one in hopes of finding a clean nightgown.

It was certainly a little strange for a confirmed bachelor like himself to be rummaging through a young woman's underwear this way, he thought. A silk half-slip caught on the callused undersides of his fingers and he paused, staring down at the delicate fabric. The fragrance of violets wafted up to his nostrils, doubtless a result of the tiny packets of sachet that Faye had scattered through her drawers. Resolutely David pushed the clinging silk away from his hands and continued his search.

Since coming to Baltimore, he'd led a rather solitary existence. He'd been a loner most of his life, so he didn't really mind. But there were times when he missed Grace, a colleague back in California with whom he'd had a casual relationship.

Grace Palmer was a research biologist, a very high-powered person who definitely had a mind of her own.

Three years older than he, she was divorced with two grown daughters. Once, early in their liaison, she'd said very plainly that the only reason to marry was to have a family, and she had no interest in doing either as she already had children and was committed to her career.

David hadn't seen any reason to try to talk her out of what appeared to be a very sensible attitude, and when this visiting professorship at Hopkins had come up, he and Grace had agreed to part for a while with no floods of tears on either side. If the grant they'd applied for came through, they'd be spending the next year in England together, anyway. Yet the past three months in Baltimore had been lonely—long hours in a lab and then returning to an empty apartment where he'd spent restless nights in an even emptier bed.

The notion made him glance over his shoulder at the bed behind him. Looking rather like a modern-day Sleeping Beauty, Faye Johnson lay stretched out on it. She really was pretty, he thought. With her incredible white-blond hair spread in a halo around her small head, she appeared positively angelic. That might be because those green eyes of hers were closed. Where had he seen eyes like that before? Not on another woman, or he would have remembered.

David opened the last drawer of her bureau and found what he was looking for. It was a floor-length white cotton nightgown with a high neckline and long sleeves. Somehow it seemed more appropriate for the situation than the other more revealing nightwear he'd come across in her other drawers. Shaking it out and then draping it over his arm, he turned toward the bed.

It was true that when he was in a medical mode, undressing a woman shouldn't disturb him and usually didn't. After all, he knew as much about anatomy as most any man alive and where there was no mystery there shouldn't be any excitement. But as he bent to unsnap the waistband of Faye Johnson's jeans, he realized that rule was not going to hold true with this particular female. Somehow, knowing how this young woman was put together didn't make her any less intriguing.

Instead of pulling open her zipper, he stood a moment, gazing at the way her jeans snugly encased her slim hips and long legs. Except for her breasts, she did have a boyish build. Perhaps, he told himself wryly, if he just pretended she was a boy... Bending over, he gently slid the zipper open. But when he'd tugged her denim pants around her thighs, he realized that pretending Faye Johnson was anything but all female would be quite impossible.

Though her outer clothing was practical in the extreme, what she wore beneath it was seductively feminine. Faye had on a pair of high-cut white lace bikini panties that left absolutely nothing to the imagination.

When David had removed her jeans, he began to unbutton the white keeper's jacket that covered her upper torso. Through it all Faye lay completely limp. Even when he lifted her to a partial sitting position so that he could dispose of the jacket and unsnap her ruined bra, she didn't stir. A moment later he laid her back down again. Except for her panties, she was completely naked.

Quickly David reached for her nightgown. But when he had it in his hands, he made no further move. He couldn't keep himself from staring at Faye Johnson's body. He'd decided before that she was pretty. Now he realized that she was beautiful. She was made like one of those fairy-story princesses, delicate and perfect with everything in ideal proportion. In sharp contrast to her slim, lightly tanned limbs, her creamy white breasts were full and round. Their pink tips seemed to beg for a man's touch, and involuntarily one of David's hands strayed toward her.

Then he caught himself and, feeling ashamed, he turned away. It wasn't right to stand here ogling the poor girl. He'd offered to stay with her only because he wanted to protect her. Was he going to have to protect her from himself as well? Neither Gaffey nor Ruby Prior had said so, but surely she had a boyfriend. No female as pretty as this would lack for lovers.

Abruptly David opened the nightgown from the bottom. Then he turned toward Faye and, resolutely avoiding looking at her breasts, he levered her up into a partial sitting position and maneuvered the gown over her head. She was so limp it was like handling a rag doll. With one hand supporting the small of her back, he pulled her close so that he could put one of her arms through the sleeves. Of necessity, her face was very near his and he was conscious of her breasts pressing against his chest. Through the thin cotton of his shirt, his skin suddenly felt alive.

Trying not to think of his own increasingly disturbing reactions, he put her other arm into the nightgown and focused on her face. Her head was tipped back and her pink lips were slightly open so that he could see her small, white teeth. She had a very soft, kissable-looking mouth. David found himself wanting more than anything in the world to know what those lips of hers would feel like against his.

I've obviously been alone too long, he thought and laid her down again. The bunched-up nightgown covered only her arms and shoulders, leaving everything else in plain and tantalizing view. Hurriedly David attempted to pull the cotton garment down. That, unfortunately, necessitated putting his hands under her bottom and lifting so that he could maneuver the white cotton material over her torso.

Though he worked as quickly as possible, he couldn't help noting how round and soft her buttocks felt in his hands. Nor could he ignore his own strong response. *If Miss Prior could see me now,* he thought wryly. At that moment there was nothing detached and coolly professional about Dr. David O'Neill. He felt as if his blood were on fire.

Hurriedly David pulled Faye Johnson's nightgown around her ankles. Then he got to his feet and strode out of the room. In the kitchen he stood staring out the back window taking long, deep breaths. After a moment he fixed himself a tall glass of ice water and drank it in three rapid gulps. Just how would Faye Johnson react to the drug she'd swallowed, he wondered. He hoped that when she woke up there wouldn't be anything unusual occurring, but only time would tell.

FAYE WOKE UP in very slow stages. It was not a pleasant process. Her entire body felt sore, as if she'd been battered about in a storm and spent the night stretched out on cold ground. Her head ached and was woolly inside all at the same time. Worst was the burning sensation in her hands and feet. They felt as if someone were holding a match against them.

"Oh," she moaned, and brought a prickly hand up to her throbbing forehead. That didn't make her feel any better and she moaned again, louder. "Ohhh!"

Suddenly she heard the sound of footsteps rapidly crossing the wood floor to her bed. "Miss Johnson?"

"Ohhh," was the only thing she could say.

A masculine hand took hers and she was slightly comforted. Then she realized that the strong fingers around her wrist were reading her pulse. A hard palm rested for a moment against her forehead. "Don't worry. You'll be all right in a little while."

Slowly, painfully, she opened her eyes and found herself gazing up into worried gray eyes. For a long fuzzy moment she wondered who this person was and how he had found his way into her bedroom. Strangely, while she speculated she experienced not even a twinge of fear—only mild curiosity. Then she remembered. "Dr. O'Neill," she whispered.

"Yes."

"Oh, I'm so glad!" It was amazingly true. As she gazed up into the rugged masculine face looking down at her with such concern, her wretchedness seemed far less overwhelming.

"Would you like a drink of water?"

She blinked, so caught up in her rapt reaction that she didn't really hear the question.

"Can I get you a drink of water?" he repeated.

"What? Yes. Oh, please." She almost regretted her request when he left the room, and for a moment she felt frightened and anxious again.

But he came back quickly and slipped a reassuring hand behind her shoulder blades. "Just sip a little bit for now," he told her. "Don't overdo it." His palm supported the back of her head and he held the rim of a glass to her lips.

She drank eagerly, spilling a good deal of liquid down her chin and her front. "I'm sorry," she gasped when he took the glass away.

"Nothing to be sorry about."

"I feel so strange."

"Considering the day you've had, you're doing fine."

Faye lay back on the pillow and gazed up at him, once more losing herself in the contemplation of his face. She didn't seem able to think of anything else— only his wonderful, intelligent, strong face.

"Faye?" His voice intruded on her euphoria. "You do remember what happened, don't you?"

"What happened?"

"Yes. Kong holding you prisoner in the ape house."

"Oh...oh yes." She blinked, trying to collect the scattered fragments of her thoughts. "How's Kong?" she heard herself ask.

"He's fine. In fact, I just finished calling about him. He came to a couple of hours before you did with no apparent aftereffects. How about you? How are you feeling?"

Though David asked the question casually, he was far from relaxed about her answer. There was something very strange and disturbing about the fixed way she was staring at him. She was definitely affected by the drug. In what way, he wasn't yet quite sure. But he was beginning to worry. When she didn't respond to his query, he repeated it. "How are you feeling?"

"My fingertips and toes are hot," she murmured.

He nodded. "That's a normal reaction. It will go away after a while."

Her eyes still hadn't left his face. What was that peculiar expression in them? If he hadn't known better, he might almost have described it as mindless adoration.

In a gesture of comfort, he reached down and took her hand. "Don't worry, Faye," he said deeply. "You're going to be fine."

Convulsively, her fingers curled around his and clung. As she gazed adoringly up at him, she believed every word he said. She knew this man would never lie to her. A wave of the same compelling intuitive attraction that had made her trust him back at the ape house swept over her. But now it was so strong that it seemed to carry her with it on a rising forward curl. Strange—she hadn't been truly attracted to a man in a long time. In fact, she'd about sworn off men. Yet what she was feeling toward David O'Neill seemed so natural, so inevitable and utterly right. She couldn't fight it. Why should she fight something so wonderful?

"Are you married?" she asked forthrightly.

"No."

His answer seemed slightly constrained, but she hardly noticed. She was too busy staring at him. Why had she thought before that he wasn't handsome? When she looked at David the term seemed meaningless. Perhaps his straight brown hair wasn't that unusual, but she loved the way it fit his head, the endearing manner in which a lock of it drooped slightly askew over his forehead. What was happening to her, she suddenly wondered on another level. It wasn't normal for her to go gaga over a virtual stranger like this. But in the next instant, she forgot the question. All she could think of was David.

His eyes were wonderful, so honest and intelligent and trustworthy. He had a long, straight nose and a firm mouth. Certainly there was no weakness in that square jaw with its slightly off-center cleft. She'd thought before that he was a nice person. Now she knew that was a monumental understatement. This was a good man, a strong man, someone you could give yourself to with absolute confidence because you knew just by looking at him that he would never let you down.

"You would stick by a woman you loved, wouldn't you, David?" she whispered.

"Uh, yes," he answered, a wary look coming into his eyes. He tried to take his hand from hers, but she held on tight. The thought of his going away now when at last she'd found him was terrifying. Somehow she had to keep him by her.

"I feel so strange," she murmured.

"You've been through a lot. Just rest."

"But I don't want to rest. I want to talk. Won't you sit down next to me so I can talk to you?"

He seemed troubled by her request. Nevertheless, he sat down on the edge of the bed. She hadn't let go of his hand. Her fingers were still curled tightly around his.

"It's the oddest thing," she told him earnestly. "We're strangers and yet I feel as if I know you."

"You can't possibly know me."

"But I do. Let me see if I can prove it to you. I bet I can guess what you were like as a kid. You were very independent, weren't you? You were better with animals than with people. That's why you've specialized in treating them."

"Yes," he admitted slowly. "We lived near a zoo. As a youngster, I spent more time there than I did at home."

She nodded, her wide-open eyes never leaving his. "I didn't live near a zoo. I was raised on a farm. But I was always crazy about animals. It practically killed me when my favorite dog died."

"It does get to you sometimes," he agreed. "I was called in to treat a sick dolphin a while back. But when I arrived it was too late. I felt awful when I realized I couldn't help him."

Faye was completely caught up in the torrent of new emotions sweeping over her. This was like a wonderful dream, and a shining look that reflected her inner state suffused her features. "Oh, I was sure when I first saw you that you were like that."

David was suddenly wary again. "Like what?"

"A man who's capable of taking love and giving it back, a man who can be trusted." With her free hand she reached for him. "Oh, David, I know it sounds crazy, but I feel as if I've been hit by lightning and I think I've fallen in love with you. Would you kiss me?" Faye was almost as startled by what she'd just said as he was. Had she actually just told this man that she was in love with him? But that didn't mean she wanted to take it back. No—not a bit. Suddenly she wanted David to kiss her more than anything in the world.

"Faye," he said, his brow furrowing. "There's something I should explain to you. You're not yourself right now."

"I know I'm not myself. I feel really odd. But that doesn't matter because at this moment I see everything so clearly. You're lonely, aren't you?"

"Yes, sometimes."

"Well, I'm lonely, too, and though I haven't admitted it to anyone before, I need love."

"But you're such a lovely young woman. Surely there must be—"

"No, there's no one, no one important, and hasn't been for a long time. I was in love when I was seventeen, you see, but it didn't work out. He left me when I got pregnant and afterward I lost the baby. Then my folks died and I've been alone ever since. But it doesn't have to be that way now that I've found you, does it? Oh, please tell me it doesn't."

David was beginning to be truly concerned. "Faye, you must stop talking this way...telling me these things. Believe me, you'll regret it when you get well. You probably won't even want to see my face."

"Just kiss me. That's all I ask. Kiss me and you'll see that I'm right." As she spoke, she released his hand and reached up with both her arms. Flinging them around his neck with surprising strength, she drew his head down toward hers.

"Faye!"

"Just kiss me."

"I can't. Faye, you have to stop this! You're under the influence of a powerful drug, and it's having odd side effects."

But for all her delicate build, she was a determined temptress. In the next instant she had pressed her mouth to his in a kiss that expressed such a welter of strong emotions that David was stunned.

CHAPTER THREE

GRASPING EACH of Faye's narrow wrists, David tore her hands from the back of his neck. "You must listen to me!"

"Oh, David, I could listen to you forever!"

How, David asked himself, could the fresh-faced young woman he remembered from the morning have transformed herself into this imperious seductress? That kiss! There had been a hunger and a need—a churning passion that made the sexual stirrings he had felt for her earlier seem paltry.

As he stared down at her, he suddenly realized where he'd seen eyes like hers before. It had been in India, and they hadn't been on a woman but on a tawny tigress he'd glimpsed peering enigmatically at him through tall grass.

Now Faye's expressive eyes looked worshipfully up at him, their emerald depths half-screened by a thick fringe of drooping lashes. Her cheeks were flushed, and between her moistly parted lips her teeth were as even and white as a string of matched pearls. With a sensation he was at a loss to describe, he watched the tip of her tongue graze their edge.

Hastily he continued his speech. "You're not yourself. The feelings you're having—"

"You don't understand my feelings. You can't." She tried to reach for him, but he continued to hold her wrists.

"Oh, but I do. That's just the trouble. The feelings you're having aren't real. They're brought on by that damned banana."

David's words affected Faye not at all. How could the glorious new emotion she had for this man have been created by a piece of fruit? "David!" she cried feverishly.

But he shook his head. "By tomorrow you'll be back to normal, and this will seem like a bad dream."

"There's nothing bad about what I feel. What I feel is beautiful. I'm in love with you, and I want you."

Once again she struggled to reach for him. For such a delicately built young woman, she was surprisingly strong. "You're not in love with me," he tried to explain. "You're having an unusual reaction to a very powerful drug. You just have to ride it out."

Tears gathered at the corners of her eyes and then bathed them until they glistened. "You don't understand."

"I understand enough to know that you're going to regret everything you say to me. Please, Faye, what you need is rest. Forget this nonsense and go to sleep."

He knew from the way she flinched and then went white that he'd hurt her.

"Nonsense," she whimpered. Then she turned her head aside and closed her eyes. Tears caught the light, flashing like precious diamonds as they squeezed out from between her long eyelashes.

All David wanted to do was lower his head and kiss those tears away. Instead, he held himself rigidly above her, his fingers still handcuffing her wrists. She had stopped struggling to clasp him to her. And a good thing, too, he thought as he straightened and slowly relaxed his hold.

"You will take my advice and rest now, won't you?"

After she gave a tiny nod, another tear leaked from beneath her tightly squeezed lashes.

"Faye..." David muttered. Then he stopped himself. Better to leave her while he still could. If she really did drop off, it would be the best thing.

Carefully he levered himself from the bed. Then, casting one last backward glance at her small form, he strode out. Back in the kitchen, he told himself that what he needed was a cup of coffee—hot, black and strong. Unfortunately, Faye was apparently not addicted to caffeine, or food either, for that matter, since all her refrigerator seemed to hold was cranberry and tomato juice and fresh fruits and vegetables. She must be some kind of health nut. *Not my type at all,* he assured himself as he rummaged desperately through her cupboards unearthing a variety of herbal teas, but only one small, unopened jar of coffee crystals.

David heated some water and mixed himself up a mugful of the instant. Then he stood at the window sipping the hot mixture and trying to sort through his thoughts and feelings.

From where he stood a section of the street was just visible. About twenty feet away from the side yard there was a nondescript gray Ford. Through the tinted glass windshield David could see the outline of a man sitting in the driver's seat. He was looking toward the house, which struck David as odd, but he was far too preoccupied to dwell on it. He still felt poleaxed by what had just happened in Faye's bedroom. It was not unheard of for phencyclidine to act on humans as a sexual stimulant. But it was unusual and he certainly hadn't been expecting that complication in Faye. With her blond hair and freckles, she looked so sweet and innocent.

But she wasn't all that innocent, he reflected. By her own admission, she'd lost a baby when she was a teenager. For a moment he tried to imagine Faye as a frightened, pregnant adolescent. But that wasn't the image his imagination conjured up. The picture that floated before his mind's eye was of the way she had looked a few minutes earlier, reaching toward him.

"Damn," he muttered and took too big a gulp of scalding coffee. Coughing, he pressed a palm to his chest. How often was a man alone with a beautiful, desirable woman who was practically begging him to make love to her? "Never," David said aloud. Nothing quite like this had ever happened to him before. He tried to picture Grace reaching for him, her face alight with passion—and failed utterly.

What was he going to do? He couldn't give Faye a sedative. Somehow she would have to ride it out—or rather, they were going to have to ride it out together. Suddenly he turned and tiptoed back toward her bedroom and, cursing himself for a fool, peered through the half-open doorway. Then he let out his breath. She was asleep, one of the orange tabbies he'd seen earlier curled at the foot of the bed.

The things she'd said to him hadn't meant a thing, he reminded himself. Addled as she was, she would probably have made the same passionate declarations to anyone. It was just lucky that he'd been the first man she'd seen when she regained consciousness. *She's perfectly safe with me*, David told himself. *I'm a doctor and an ethical person.* It was true, of course. Sighing, he turned away.

The rest of the afternoon crawled past without incident. Though David knew he should take advantage of this lull to get some rest himself, he hadn't been able to relax. For hours he'd paced around Faye's tiny house. It hadn't taken long to memorize the contents of her comfortable little living room. Her furniture was pretty and homey—overstuffed chairs slipcovered in bright colors, old-fashioned pine pieces that had seen a lot of use, a handmade rag rug.

He'd paused for a long time over the framed photos on the mantel. If they were any indication, she'd had a happy childhood. One picture showed her as a towheaded tyke at the beach wedged between two laughing, fair-haired adults who he supposed were her parents. Next to it sat a snapshot of Faye as a skinny teenager astride a horse and clutching what looked like some sort of trophy. To the right was a photograph of Faye and her mother surrounded by a baker's dozen of squirming puppies. He lifted the picture and stared at it. Then, remembering the golden retriever on the porch, he replaced the frame and went to the door.

The old dog had found herself a shady spot in the yard. "Hello, Missy is it?" he said, crossing over to her.

She was certainly no watchdog. Though her tail thumped, she was too lazy even to lift her head.

"Well, come scratch at the door when you get hungry or thirsty," David told her. Making a mental note to feed Missy and the cats a little later, he returned to the living room where he stood for a moment in front of the old-fashioned lawyer's bookcase next to the fireplace.

Two of its shelves were devoted to books on animal behavior—most of them, unfortunately, somewhat dated. There was also a shelf full of vegetarian cookbooks—so she *was* a health food nut. David wrinkled his nose, but his gaze continued to drift down, and he began reading the titles of books on history and politics as well as an assortment of fiction works—everything from Victorian novels to the latest best-selling murder mystery.

Suddenly he straightened. He was looking for clues to Faye's character, he realized. So what had he found? She was a nice, outdoorsy girl who loved animals and who'd had some bad knocks in her young life but had apparently been gutsy enough to survive them. Nothing so remarkable in that, he told himself as he went for another cup of coffee. These days, who hadn't had to survive bad knocks? And why should he be worrying about it, anyhow? As soon as she was back to normal, he'd be on his way and Faye Johnson would be nothing but a memory.

This was David's third trip to the kitchen and each time as he'd walked to the stove he'd glanced out the window to his right, noticing absentmindedly that the man in the parked car was still there. Could he be watching the house? But why would he be doing that?

Dismissing the idea, David returned to the living room and sat on the edge of the couch. He picked up a *National Geographic* magazine but found himself listening for a sound from Faye's room instead of reading. What would she be like when she finally woke up this time? Would she throw her arms around him again? Or would she be back to normal and have forgotten that whole episode? He should be hoping for the latter. Why wasn't he?

Just then someone knocked at the door. Startled out of his reverie, David dropped the magazine and jumped to his feet. When he threw open the front door, Wallace Gaffey stood there. The old man's round face peered out over the top of an enormous bunch of yellow roses.

"Just stopped by to check on Faye," he said cheerily. "How's she doing?"

"She's asleep." David stepped aside. While he watched Gaffey walk past him into the living room he considered what he should tell Faye's uncle about her condition. Nothing, he decided. She'd be embarrassed enough about all this without letting anyone else in on it. With luck she'd stay asleep through Gaffey's visit and he would leave none the wiser.

"O'Riley, I'm grateful," the old man was saying. "You've been a hero through all this."

"Oh, not really. And it's not O'Riley, it's O'Neill." David shot a surreptitious glance at the hall where Faye's bedroom door was half-open and wished that it were closed. Her uncle's voice bounced off the walls inside the little house like a foghorn in a closet.

"Well, O'Neill, I think you deserve a medal. In fact, would you like to have one?"

"What?"

"I have a collection of medals that I give out to superior employees at the end of every year. We have quite a little ceremony, and the folks around here who work in my crab processing factory love it. I'd be glad to include you."

"No thanks." David struggled to keep from smiling. He could picture Gaffey walking down a row of crab cake cooks all standing at rigid attention. It would be just like him to kiss each on the cheek with all the pomp of a French general handing out the Croix de Guerre. The old guy was probably right about the folks around here loving it. People on the Eastern Shore tended to be clannish. Since Gaffey was their local boy made good, they were most likely proud enough of him to tolerate and even get a kick out of his eccentricities.

"Well, I hope you haven't forgotten your promise."

"My promise?"

"Yes, you said you'd have a look around Wilderness Worlds."

"Oh, that."

"Of course, we're just finishing up construction now. Except for the children's section, there aren't too many animals around, as yet. But we've got some I'd like you to see, and of course I'd appreciate your opinion on everything we're doing."

"Well, if there's time, certainly. As a matter of fact, I have a few recommendations to make already. But not today. I don't think Miss Johnson should be left alone."

"Tomorrow will be time enough. I'll buy your lunch." Gaffey glanced down the hall. "She in there?"

"Yes, but she's asleep."

Ignoring the warning, the old man marched down the short passageway toward the door and threw it open. "How's my brave little heroine?" he boomed. The loud sound wakened the cats on the bed who shot out the door between his feet in a furry orange streak.

David, who'd followed at Gaffey's heels, winced. Neither he nor Faye were going to get off as easily as he'd hoped. Over her uncle's shoulder, he saw her eyes open.

"Wally?"

Striding forward, Gaffey scattered his lavish bouquet of roses on the bed with a flourish. When they'd settled, Faye's face looked as if it were peering out from a floral blanket.

"Golden flowers for a golden girl," he declared. Leaning over, he planted a noisy kiss on her forehead. "How are you doing?"

"Oh, I'm fine." She gazed down at the flowers. "For me?"

"No one else in this world. After what you've been through, you deserve a lot more." Gaffey's jovial expression abruptly sobered and he studied her closely. "How are you, really?"

At that instant Faye's gaze snagged David's. Knowledge of the secret struggle raging between them seemed to flash from her eyes to his like a jolt of electricity, and he held his breath. What would she say to her uncle, he wondered.

"I'm fine, Wally. In fact, I'm wonderful."

"Really?"

"Oh, yes." She gazed adoringly at David. "I've fallen in love."

For a moment Gaffey looked disconcerted. "In love? Who are you in love with?"

"With David, of course."

Interpreting this as a joke, Gaffey beamed across the room at the younger man, who stood frozen in the doorway. Then Gaffey winked. "Does that mean the doctor here is taking good care of you?"

"Oh, yes." Her eyes were still fixed on David's reddening face. The devotion that shone from their depths disconcerted him so much that he turned away. "I'll get a vase for those flowers."

"No need," Gaffey shouted after him. "There's plenty more yellow roses where those came from."

But David had already fled. Once in the kitchen he drew a deep breath and raked a hand through his thick hair. He did not consider himself to be a particularly temperamental man. And in his profession he was certainly no stranger to crises and unexpected turns of events. Why wasn't he handling this one better? He was baffled by his own reactions. In fact, he'd rather face a wounded lion or a hippo with an infected tooth than deal with the emotions churning in his gut at this very moment.

"What a hell of a situation," he muttered to himself. Kneeling, he opened the cupboard doors beneath the sink and began looking for some sort of appropriate flower container. There were several pottery bowls and one large vase made of fluted green glass. As he reached for it, he wondered what Faye and Gaffey were saying to each other now. He hoped to hell she wasn't telling the old man all about her newfound love.

On the other side of the house, Faye said, "Dr. O'Neill has been just absolutely wonderful." She picked up a yellow rose and inhaled its delicate scent. There was a look in her eyes that might have disturbed her visitor if he'd been paying attention to it. But Wally Gaffey was too busy pacing up and down in front of Faye's bed to notice that she wasn't quite herself.

"I was very worried when Kong had you," he told her gruffly. "You're like a daughter to me, you know."

Faye's smile was beatific. "And you're like a father to me."

Gaffey flushed and looked pleased. "What if Kong had hurt you?"

"I'm sure he wouldn't have." She dipped her nose into the heart of the golden bloom she held and inhaled deeply.

"All the same, we have to make certain nothing like that ever happens again," Wally said earnestly. "I'm going to have a talk with O'Connell about it. Maybe it's time I got some professional advice."

"It's O'Neill," Faye said, closing her eyes and sighing dreamily. Twirling the stem of the yellow rose, she touched one of its velvety petals to her lips. If she'd been thinking clearly she would have reminded her uncle that such a professional consultation was long overdue. For months now she'd been urging him to bring in an expert. Wally could be as stubborn as a child when it came to his pet project. He didn't want any strangers telling him what to do. But Faye was not able to think clearly. Since regaining consciousness earlier that afternoon all she'd really been able to concentrate on was David. "Dr. O'Neill is a very, very special man," she mused aloud. "Don't you think so?"

"Well, I suppose he must be. He certainly handled Kong."

"That's not what I meant. I meant..." She paused, searching for the right words.

"Did I hear my name being taken in vain?" David queried with forced cheer. He'd just come back into the room carrying the green vase, which he'd filled with water. As he spoke he cast a worried look at Faye. What had she been babbling? Her expression was guileless, but he knew better than to put any faith in it.

"I was just telling Wally how truly wonderful you are," said Faye.

David fumbled with the vase, very nearly dropping it. "It's nice to be appreciated, but I was only doing my job."

"Above and beyond the call of duty, I'd say." Gaffey glanced at his watch. "Well, I'll have to be getting on."

David heaved an audible sigh of relief.

"Must you?" Faye cried. "I'd love you to stay for dinner."

Who did she think would prepare this dinner, David wondered. Especially since there was nothing but rabbit food in the refrigerator. He didn't relax until he heard Gaffey turn down the invitation.

"Oh, can't do that. Things to do, you know."

She peered at the clock next to her bed. "It's almost seven. What have you got to do so late in the day?"

"Just things," Gaffey replied vaguely. "I'm a busy man." He turned to David. "Take care of this girl. She's pretty special, you know."

"Oh, yes indeed. I'll take very good care of her." David set the vase down on the bedside table.

"He will. He's just the most wonderful man," Faye gushed. As if it were the most natural thing in the world, she reached out to trail her fingers along the outside of his thigh and David jumped back.

"I'll be off then." Gaffey, who'd apparently missed Faye's intimate gesture, spread his gnarled fingers into a V for victory. "See you tomorrow, O'Hara. We'll have a nice long talk."

"Certainly." Hastily David moved to see the older man out. "I'm looking forward to it."

When Gaffey and his chauffeured white stretch limousine were gone, David stood for a moment on the front porch. Suddenly he noticed that the gray Ford with its mysterious occupant was still parked down the street. Staring hard at it, he put his hands on his hips and then walked slowly down the steps. But he was no sooner off the porch when the car's engine roared to life, and the Ford disappeared around the corner. When it was gone, he shrugged his shoulders and reentered the house. His thoughts returned to Faye and he walked back to her room. "How are you feeling?" he asked when he was just inside her bedroom door.

"Beautiful!" She cupped her hands beneath the flowers strewn on her bed and lifted them high enough so that they spilled from her fingers in a golden waterfall. "Oh, David, aren't they the loveliest things? That's how I feel, all soft and beautiful like the flowers."

David refrained from comment. How long was it going to take her to get over this? He wondered why Gaffey hadn't noticed how peculiarly she was behaving. The man was either blind or amazingly self-absorbed. But then the man couldn't even get David's name right. David crossed to the side of Faye's bed and picked up some of the flowers.

"Oh, don't take them away."

"Don't you want me to put them in the vase?"

"No. I like them scattered on my bed this way."

"They won't last long."

She looked surprised. "What do you mean?"

"Faye, they need water."

For a moment she looked confused. Then her brow cleared. "How silly of me. I'd forgotten. Of course they should be put in water right away."

With eyes that were unnaturally bright and wide, Faye watched as David knelt by her bed to gather up the roses. The pinkish glow of the evening sun lit the room. Its last rays touched the top of David's hair so that she could see red highlights flash in the thick brown strands. It lit his skin, bringing out tiny details. He must have to shave twice a day, she mused. A beard already shadowed the lower half of his face, emphasizing the sharp plane of his high cheekbones. There was a fine network of lines around his eyes. But they were the smiley kind, Faye decided. He'd acquired them from living honestly and with humor.

Her own smile widened, and as her eyes grew misty a luminous halo seemed to appear around his lowered head, framing his strongly cut profile. It reminded her of a picture of Prince Charming from a storybook that had been one of the treasures of her childhood. Her gaze dropped to David's hands, so deft and capable as they gathered the roses from her bed.

"Prince Charming," she murmured.

"What?" David's head jerked and he stabbed himself with a thorn from one of the roses.

"Look, you've hurt your thumb," Faye cried. Then she reached down, clasped his hand and raised the injured digit to her lips. There was a tiny spot of blood on his thumb. While David watched in horrified fascination, she tenderly kissed it away.

"Faye, you shouldn't do that."

Her fingers laced themselves through his and tightened. "Why not? Oh, David, do you know how beautiful you are right now?"

"Beautiful?" No one had ever said such a thing to him before in his life. "Men aren't beautiful."

"You are." She leaned forward and framed his face with her hands, smiling intimately into his eyes. "I could look at you all day."

"Faye, you mustn't . . ."

"Do you know what I see when I look at you?"

"An aging veterinarian who's had a long, hard day."

"Why do you say aging?" She waggled a playful finger at his nose and then tenderly kissed its tip. "I bet you're not even forty yet."

He cleared his throat. "I'm thirty-five actually."

"See, you're still a handsome young man."

David blinked. He knew he wasn't exactly ugly—but handsome? It was the drug talking, he reminded himself. He shouldn't even be listening to her.

"When I look at you," she continued in a kind of rhapsodic singsong, "I see someone who's kind and good and strong. Someone who's a truly beautiful person." A thought seemed to strike her and she cocked her head. "Why do you speak with a British accent?"

"I was born and educated in London. I didn't come to this country until about ten years ago."

"I'm so glad you told me. I want to know everything about you. Everything! Now, tell me why you haven't married. How have the women been able to resist you?"

She wasn't joking. It was obvious that she had asked the question in perfect sincerity. David felt his neck get so hot that his collar seemed to be aflame.

"Oh, you're blushing!" Faye cried. She leaned forward and kissed him on the cheek. "You're so sweet—and handsome and smart! Why haven't you been snapped up?''

David tugged at his hand, but she held on tight. "I suppose I'm not married because I'm just not the marrying kind."

"What do you mean? You do like women, don't you?"

"Yes," David quickly assured her. "I do like women. But after a while most women want you to settle down with them and I've never been able to do that."

"Because of your job?"

"In my line of work I have to be free to travel a lot. Marriage just hasn't been in the cards."

"There's got to be more to it than that."

There was, but David saw no reason to tell her his life story. "Maybe I just haven't met the right woman," he finally said.

She smiled like an angel in a Christmas pageant. "But now you have."

"What?"

"Now you've finally met the right woman, and I've met the right man. Oh, David, everything about you is wonderful! We're going to be so happy together."

David's brow began to crease. How had he been drawn into this conversation? Talking to Faye this way was the last thing he should be doing. It was like exchanging confidences with a mental patient who wasn't responsible for her words or actions. It would only make things more awkward when she was herself. Once again he tried to draw back.

She clutched at him. "You aren't going away!"

"I think I'd better. The best thing for you would be more sleep."

"But I don't want to sleep." Abruptly she threw her arms around his neck. "I want you."

Alarmed, David stiffened and reared back. But Faye came right along with him, pushing herself from the bed with surprising agility. Her weight threw him off balance and he toppled backward onto the floor. In the next moment he found himself on the rug with his glasses knocked askew and Faye sprawled on top of his body.

Her arms were still around his shoulders, but her face was buried in his throat. He could smell the fresh scent of her hair, the womanly fragrance of her skin. She was light-bodied and soft. Having her curves molded against him was producing some very unsettling sensations. Through the thin material of his shirt, he could feel her breasts pressed to his chest. It reminded him of the way she'd looked when he'd undressed her—a memory that created an instant physical reaction that made him groan.

Then she lifted her face. Her green eyes were only inches from his and her hair had fallen forward in a gilded halo. "Oh, David," she breathed.

"Faye, you mustn't . . ."

But she didn't seem to hear. Deliberately she removed his glasses completely and lowered her lips to his, kissing him with a tender passion that made him groan again. It was more than flesh could bear, he thought, and he was only human. He kissed her back, abandoning himself to the intense pleasure of his mouth moving against hers. It was indescribably sweet. His arms went up around her waist and then stroked down the elegant length of her back. How perfectly her body fit against his. It was as if they had been made for each other.

"Prince Charming," he heard her murmur against his lips. He shuddered and knew that he must put an end to this madness. He rolled to one side, separating her from him with a wrench. "Faye," he gasped, "you shouldn't kiss me that way."

"But I'm in love with you."

"No, you're not." Suddenly he felt angry with himself and with her, and he glared at her. "You're not in love with me. Tomorrow everything will look entirely different. You won't want anything more to do with me. You'll be embarrassed about this whole episode and you'll want nothing more than to forget it."

CHAPTER FOUR

FAYE'S LIDS OPENED a crack. For several foggy seconds she lay staring at the light flooding her bedroom. It was a beautiful morning, so she should feel good. But for some reason she didn't—not at all. Groaning, she pushed herself up against the headboard and sat blinking in the bright sunshine. Why did she have the feeling that there was something unpleasant she needed to recall? Then, as she began to answer her own question, her eyes widened in horror.

Had she really thrown herself at that man? Had she actually begged him to make love to her?

Faye dropped her hot face into her hands. But that didn't keep memories of yesterday from frolicking before her horrified mind's eye. She recalled every crazy, humiliating thing that she'd said and done. Lord, David O'Neill had actually been forced to hold her at bay!

Faye felt like slinking back under the blankets, but if that man was still in her house, she had to go out and apologize to him. And, to be practical, she wanted a shower and some breakfast.

Sighing, she pushed the covers aside, swung her legs over the edge of the bed, and stood up. "Whoa!" An instant later she was sitting down again and clutching the edge of the mattress while she waited for the dizziness to subside. "That was some banana," she muttered. Then, shakily, she got to her feet again. This time she was able to stay upright, and after an uncertain moment or two she tottered over to the hook on the door where her bathrobe hung.

When she had put it on, she held her breath and listened. Except for the clock ticking on the bedside table and the birds twittering outside the window, she couldn't hear a sound. Maybe her houseguest was gone. *Please be gone,* she silently pleaded as she opened the door and tiptoed out.

After a brief stop in the bathroom, Faye padded softly down the hall and peered around the corner. She let out her breath in a long whoosh of disappointment. Dr. O'Neill hadn't sneaked off in the middle of the night. He was lying dead to the world on the sofa. Except for his shoes he was fully dressed, and the uncomfortable night he'd obviously spent hadn't done his shirt and slacks a bit of good. *Probably afraid to strip down to his undies with a panting nymphomaniac only a few steps away,* Faye thought sourly.

She scanned his rumpled clothing. Sprawled on his back with one long leg resting on the floor and the other draped over the end of the couch, he was a far cry from the spruce individual who'd first sauntered into Kong's compartment.

The thought forced a slight adjustment in Faye's attitude. This man was, after all, her rescuer. She remembered how she'd taken an immediate liking to him. Her gaze shifted to his face. The beginnings of a growth of beard that she'd noticed yesterday were now well established, and his lean cheeks and firm jaw were peppered with stubble. He lay with his head to one side so that she could also take in the outline of his strongly cut profile.

Faye shifted restlessly. Even in his present disarray David O'Neill was a very attractive man. But after the fool she'd made out of herself yesterday it wouldn't matter if he were Robert Redford and Don Johnson shaken up together in a blender. She wished he'd disappear in a puff of magic smoke.

Gingerly Faye stepped forward. Then she paused. Better not touch the man. After her Mata Hari performance she could guess what he might think if he came to consciousness with her bending over him in her bathrobe. No, she'd just go get dressed and then rattle around in the kitchen until he woke up on his own.

DAVID WOKE with a start. Somewhere in his dreams he'd been listening to the sound of pots and pans banging. Now the aroma of something tantalizing but unfamiliar cooking tickled his nostrils. Where the hell was he? He shifted and then groaned as his aching muscles reminded him that he'd spent the night on an unfamiliar couch. Then he recalled the circumstances that went with it and groaned again.

After a day and a night that could only be described as harrowing, he was still in Faye Johnson's house. And the person making all that noise in the kitchen was probably the young siren herself.

David sat up and rubbed his sandpapery chin. Then after a rueful glance at his wrinkled slacks, he felt around for his glasses. Jamming them on his nose, he got to his feet and stretched until his joints cracked. He knew he should go in and talk to his hostess, find out how she was feeling. Instead he decided to put it off for a quarter of an hour and headed for the bathroom and a hot shower. He'd seen a safety razor lying on the edge of the bathtub. Surely after what she'd put him through, she owed him that much.

In the bathroom David turned on the water and then quickly stripped off his clothing. He was about to get under the shower head when he caught a glimpse of his naked torso in the mirror. That made him look thoughtfully at the closed door. If Faye was in the kitchen cooking breakfast, she was probably okay. But after last night he'd better not take any chances. Leaning over, he locked the door before stepping into the shower.

Twenty minutes later David headed toward the kitchen. When he reached the doorway, he paused. Along with the tantalizing odor he'd noticed earlier, the atmosphere was now perfumed by the fragrance of freshly brewed herbal tea. Clad in a cotton-print wrap skirt and blue knit top and looking like a young Doris Day, Faye stood in front of the kitchen counter arranging something on a platter. When she heard his footsteps, she jerked around and then, at the sight of him, flushed until her face matched the peony-pink trim on her skirt.

David had been wondering how she would be this morning. Now he knew. Locking the bathroom door had been quite unnecessary. Faye Johnson was back to normal and as embarrassed as hell.

"Sorry if I startled you."

"That's all right. I don't know why I jumped like that. I heard you taking a shower, so I knew you'd be coming in here pretty soon."

While David listened to her babble, he studied the picture she made. In the morning light her cap of pale hair glowed like sunlit butter, and the brown-sugar freckles stood out against her flushed cheeks. "How are you feeling?" he asked.

She began to fiddle with one of the ties on her skirt. "Much better."

"That tea smells delicious. But I'm a coffee man. Do you mind if I make myself some instant?"

"Not at all. There's hot water in the kettle."

David crossed to the stove, found a mug in the cupboard and took a moment to mix himself up a strong hot drink. Fortified with several sips of it, he turned back to Faye and eyed the platter she was setting down in the center of the table. There were a lot of artistically arranged strawberries on it and something that looked like red pancakes. A moment later Faye pulled out a chair for herself and sat down to stare at him with an odd expression on her face.

She was looking at the beads of water glistening in his freshly combed hair and asking herself why men always look so attractive just after they shower. She was also wondering how to begin the apology she knew she owed him.

"Dr. O'Neill..."

"Please, it's David. You were calling me that yesterday."

Faye felt herself go hot again. She'd been calling him that and a lot of other things like darling, sweetheart and even Prince Charming, for heaven's sake! "I know, that's what I..." She gestured helplessly. "Won't you sit down and have some breakfast?"

David pulled out a chair. When he was settled, he looked frankly across the table at his hostess. "Tell me, how much do you remember about yesterday?"

"Everything," she blurted. "That's why I feel so awkward this morning. I know I acted like an idiot and said a lot of ridiculous things to you. I don't know how to account for it. Really, I'm normally not like that at all. Not at all!'' she repeated emphatically.

"I know you're not."

"I just want to apologize."

"No need for an apology, either." He put down his coffee cup. "Faye, if you remember everything, you must realize that you were forced to swallow a big dose of phencyclidine. You weren't responsible for your behavior."

"Even so—I can't help feeling embarrassed."

David wanted to comfort her. But he knew better than to take her hand or pat her on the shoulder. Treating her with any sort of familiarity would probably only make things worse. *Good grief, some women would come apart at the seams after an experience like that. I should be happy she's back to normal,* he told himself. And, of course, he was. But a part of him couldn't help regretting the loss of the blond temptress. As he searched for a way to lessen her embarrassment, he cleared his throat. "You must keep in mind that I'm a physician. Yesterday I wasn't really seeing you as a woman who was coming on to me," he lied, "but as a patient."

Faye lifted her tantalizing green eyes. "How do you mean?"

"I was viewing the situation clinically. To me your behavior was just a set of symptoms. I wasn't taking any of it personally."

There was a small silence. "You mean as far as you were concerned, I was like an experiment in a laboratory?"

"Yes, that's it." He was lying through his teeth, of course. There had been nothing clinical about the feelings he'd been wrestling with for the past eighteen hours. But he couldn't tell Faye that. Not meeting her gaze, David gingerly lifted one of the red pancakes off the platter and onto his plate. Then he stared down at it curiously. "Is there syrup for these?"

"No. They don't need syrup."

"I see."

"They're fruit pancakes," Faye explained. "There's very little flour in them. They're mostly fresh strawberries from my garden and crushed pineapple and cranberry juice."

"Oh? Are you a vegetarian?"

"Of course. How could anyone love animals and not be? Fruit is the best thing for you in the morning," she continued. "It doesn't clog up the digestive system."

David was hungry and wouldn't have minded clogging up his digestive system with bacon and eggs. But he'd sampled the cuisine of the Masai in a hut built of cow dung and dined with headhunters in New Guinea, so probably he could handle fruit pancakes as well, he told himself as he forked up a piece. It wasn't bad actually. Just not very substantial. He hoped that the lunch he'd be having with Wallace Gaffey later on that day would be more filling.

After a moment Faye, too, began to eat, and there was silence except for the tick of the kitchen clock and the scrape and tinkle of their cutlery.

"Thanks for taking care of my dog and cats," she said at one point.

"Think nothing of it."

"Well, I appreciate it." But the acknowledgment was issued absentmindedly. Actually, she was mulling over what he'd said about viewing the whole episode yesterday dispassionately. In a way it was reassuring. On the other hand, it wasn't exactly flattering to be told that she'd thrown herself at this man and through it all he'd been as interested in her as he might have been in a white rat. What kind of cold fish was he, anyway? Under her lashes she cast him another assessing glance. He looked healthy and masculine, not cold. Sitting there eating his pancakes and drinking his coffee, he looked like the kind of man a woman might like to cook breakfast for more than once.

Which was probably why she'd reacted to him the way she had, she told herself. Faye took a reflective sip of herb tea. If he'd been less attractive, if he'd been Roy Hubbard, for instance, she felt quite certain that she wouldn't have come on to him no matter how many tons of doped bananas Kong had jammed down her throat. She set down her tea and stared at David. "There's something that's been bothering me."

"What's that?"

"When I woke up after eating that banana, I had my nightgown on, but I don't remember putting it on. Did you undress me?"

David cleared his throat. He'd been afraid she might ask him that. "Yes. I wanted to get you comfortable and into bed."

Suddenly Faye didn't know where to look. This man was all but a stranger, yet he knew more intimate things about her than her closest friends.

"Really," David said in an attempt to be reassuring, "there's no reason to get upset. I'm a doctor. I know all about female anatomy. You haven't got anything I haven't seen before."

She threw down her fork and said irritably, "But of course I shouldn't be bothered, should I? Undressing me didn't mean a thing to you. You were just viewing me as a set of symptoms.''

David mopped his brow. Obviously, instead of helping, he'd made the problem worse. ''Look, Faye, I can see that you're still fretting about yesterday. We're two intelligent adults. What happened was an accident and, now that you've recovered, it's over with. Let's just forget it, shall we?''

''All right.'' Faye's voice was icy.

''Let's talk about something else.''

''Certainly. What would you like to discuss?''

Ignoring her frigid tone, David went to the stove to make himself another cup of coffee. ''Well,'' he said when he came back to the table, ''I think Kong and his management bears talking about. Would you mind giving me a bit of his history?''

''All right,'' Faye agreed. ''Actually, Kong is what gave Wally the idea for Wilderness Worlds. Six years ago when he opened his crab cake chain in Africa, he was given Kong as a gift. But Wally didn't know what to do with a baby gorilla, so he handed him over to me. Kong's first year was spent in this house.''

''Where did he live after that?''

''In the children's zoo. That's where I spend most of my time when I'm not doing PR.''

''You do public relations for Wilderness Worlds?''

''Yes, mostly speaking at local service organizations and schools. For a while I took Kong with me.''

''Why did you stop?''

Faye sighed. ''He just got too unmanageable. That's why he had to be moved out of the children's zoo last month. I hated to do it. I know he's not happy in the ape house all by himself.''

"I see." David blew gently on the surface of his hot coffee. "Miss Prior told me about Gaffey's plans for Wilderness Worlds. They're pretty ambitious."

"Wally is that kind of man. He's what you call a go-getter I guess. He makes things happen."

"Admirable when it comes to business, I suppose. But not always the best thing when you're dealing with fragile ecologies."

"What do you mean?" Faye frowned and David directed a sharp look at her.

"Why did your uncle give Kong to you to raise? Did you have any special knowledge about gorillas?"

"No." She hesitated a moment. "I think he just felt sorry for me. I'd been having a rough time of it, and he wanted to do something to help me out—give me a new interest."

David remembered the story she'd blurted about her teenage pregnancy and knew from the way she avoided his gaze now that she was remembering it, too. So Gaffey had given her the infant gorilla to raise for the same reason an indulgent parent might present an un-happy child with a puppy or a kitten. David admired the good-hearted motive but couldn't help being an-gered by the lack of professionalism.

Across the table, Faye was bristling. "All right, so I wasn't an expert on gorillas. I was born on a farm and have been around animals all my life. I've trained horses and dogs, pretty successfully. I read every-thing on the subject of gorillas I could find, and I treated Kong with the same love and care I would have given my own child. You have to admit he's very healthy."

Healthy and spoiled, David thought, and nothing like what nature intended. Aloud, he said, "I'm sure you were a very caring surrogate parent. It's obvious that Kong is extremely attached to you. That's just the problem. Faye, try and understand. The world is losing its wilderness areas. Gorillas, like so many other exotic animals, are threatened with extinction. It won't be long before the only gorillas left are the ones we've preserved in zoos."

"Do you really think so?"

"I know so." David leaned forward. "We've only begun to learn how to keep them alive and well in captivity. One thing we have figured out is that we can't domesticate them, treat them like pets. That way they have no chance of survival." It was a subject about which he felt passionately and some of that strong emotion rang in his voice.

"I don't understand," Faye protested. "Wally's whole idea here at Wilderness Worlds is to preserve endangered species."

"From what I've seen, his whole idea is to build himself a private little playground." For a moment, David let some of the irritation he felt about the lack of forethought he'd seen in the past twenty-four hours show in his expression.

Faye immediately went on the defensive. "You have no right to talk about Wally that way. At least he's trying to do something for the animals. When you get to know him better you'll realize that he's one of the kindest men in the world."

"All right." David held up a conciliatory hand. "I can see that your uncle has good intentions. But good intentions are no substitute for careful planning, and what happened to you with Kong is a case in point. Emotionally, he's become completely dependent on you. Okay, fine, zoo animals should be attached to their keepers. But gorillas are social creatures. In the wild they live in big families. That's how they learn to be gorillas, to mate, reproduce and care for their young. Their survival depends on that socialization.''

''What do you mean?''

''I mean without it they get bored, they can behave pathologically, they lose the ability to produce and rear healthy young, and they die out.''

Faye crumbled the remains of her pancake with her fork. ''I see what you're saying. Kong shouldn't have been raised all by himself in a human environment.''

There were a lot of things David would have liked to add to that oversimplified statement. But he'd already delivered a long lecture. ''What's done is done,'' he told Faye. ''Right now, at the very least, Kong needs a mate.'' He got up and took his plate to the sink. ''When I have lunch with your uncle this afternoon, I'm going to recommend that he acquire a female for Kong just as soon as possible.''

''Do you think that will make Kong happier?''

''I don't know. I hope it's not too late. We'll just have to wait and see.'' As he rinsed his dish, David glanced over his shoulder at her. ''In the meantime, I suggest you stay away from him.''

Faye sighed. ''I suppose you're right.'' She glanced at the clock over the stove and then picked up her own dishes. ''It's almost ten. When was Wally expecting you?''

''Around now, actually. He was planning on showing me Wilderness Worlds before we ate.''

''Then I suppose you'd better be off.''

''Yes.'' David stood drying his hands on a towel and studying her. Was she trying to get rid of him? He supposed he couldn't blame her. Though they'd just managed to have a fairly unremarkable breakfast together, their rational conversation had only formed a thin skin over the disturbing memories of what had gone on between them yesterday—and they both knew it. He turned toward her. "Will you be all right here after I leave?"

Faye lowered her head and busied herself scraping dishes. "Yes, of course. Why shouldn't I?"

"I mean," he said gently, "have you completely recovered from the effects of the drug?"

"Of course I have." Glancing up and seeing his quizzical expression, she added, "You needn't worry. I'm not going to assault the paperboy or the mailman."

"That wasn't what I meant."

"No, of course not." She threw down her sponge. "I'm perfectly fine, really. I just need to get some rest today. By tomorrow I'll be back to work."

"Why don't you give it a little more time than that?"

"I will if I need to. Don't worry." Pointedly she checked the wall clock again. "I don't want to rush you, but Wally is a stickler for punctuality. If he expected you around now, he's probably pacing back and forth in his office."

"Then I'd better be off, hadn't I," David said lightly. She *was* in a hurry to see the last of him, he thought as he walked toward the front door with Faye trailing him. He opened it and, remembering something, turned toward her. "Does one of your neighbors own a gray sedan?"

"Maybe. I'm not sure. Why?"

"Probably nothing. It's just that a car like that with a driver in it was parked out front most of yesterday afternoon.'' Seeing her blank expression, he laughed. ''I did say that it was probably nothing. Well...'' He looked regretfully down at her upturned face, unconsciously memorizing it because he didn't expect to ever see it again and the realization was somehow painful. ''It's been a pleasure meeting you. Take care.''

''I will.'' She held out her hand and gave him a firm, no-nonsense shake. ''And thank you for everything you did. I really appreciate it.''

''All in the line of duty.''

Self-consciously they both laughed and then he was walking away and Faye was standing on the front porch watching him go and feeling very odd. *I'll probably never see him again,* she thought as she went back into the house. After the idiot she'd made of herself with him, it should be a relief. So why did she feel like crying?

Twenty minutes later Wallace Gaffey threw open his office door and drew David inside. ''So here you are at last,'' he said expansively. ''I've been waiting for you. Anxious to get a start on things, you know.'' From behind his round spectacles, he peered up into David's face. ''How's Faye?''

''She seemed fine when I left her.''

''All recovered from that banana?'' Gaffey chortled.

''She'll need a day or so of rest, but then she should be quite all right, yes.''

''Wonderful. Can't tell you what a scare that little fracas in the ape house gave me.''

Erasing the frown that had momentarily puckered his domed forehead, Gaffey offered his guest an open box of cigars. When David refused, the older man lit one for himself and puffed with enjoyment. As David watched, he decided that this was as good a time as any to broach the subject of Kong's management.

"As a matter of fact, I have a few suggestions to offer."

"Good. Good. That's what I wanted you for, and I'm eager as all get out to hear what you have to say. But why are we staying in the office on such a gorgeous day?" Gaffey took his cigar out of his mouth and waved it at the window. "Let's go look the place over, and then you can tell me what you think of my little enterprise."

Beaming, the older man took David familiarly by the arm and ushered him outside onto the gravel pathway system. "It's great to see things really shaping up." He pointed his cigar at newly planted stands of trees and shrubbery.

"It's a very nice piece of property. Did you have any trouble getting the zoning for a zoo?" David asked.

Gaffey laughed at that. "My fishery supports this county. They wouldn't turn me down. Besides, they know I want the best for them and for Wilderness Worlds, the best physical plant, the finest, rarest animals. That's how I like to do business. Everything topnotch." A sly look came into his brown eyes. "This animal park is going to put all the others in the shade and make all the folks who live in my part of the world very proud."

They strolled on, Gaffey frequently pausing to extol the wonders of his pet project and David commenting cautiously. When they came to an exhibit area under construction for North American bears, David cocked his head and studied it with interest. It was a mountain of rock-simulating concrete opening into runs separated from the public by a wide moat.

"I'm looking forward to seeing cubs gamboling about up there," Gaffey remarked. "What do you think? Will the little teddy bears like it?"

David squinted into the sun. "Yes, but if you're considering breeding bears, keep in mind that the maternity den should be arranged so that the expectant mother will be completely undisturbed."

At Gaffey's blank expression, David explained. "Even the scratching of a male on a den door can cause the female to neglect her cubs or even kill them."

"You don't say." The old man ran a hand around his ruffle of gray hair and stubbed out his cigar. "I wasn't aware of that. Don't think anyone else around here is, either. You really know your stuff, don't you?"

David continued to study the naturalistic structure. No doubt about it, expense had not been spared and the facility appeared to be a fine one. "Who was your architect?"

Gaffey looked puzzled for a moment. "Now what was his name, let me see..." He smote his domelike forehead as if that would force the memory to surface. "I have it on the tip of my tongue."

"Actually, that looks like the work of Frederick Lewes."

"Lewes, that's it. That's the man."

David was nonplussed. Frederick Lewes was one of the best known zoological architects in the field and also one of the most expensive. Gaffey's dealings with him must have been extensive, not to mention costly. It seemed odd that he wouldn't remember that name any better than he appeared able to recall David's. It was also strange that the old man would go to so much trouble and expense with his physical plant and yet have inexperienced local people managing the place.

When David brought the subject up, Gaffey brushed it aside. "The last thing I want is to import a bunch of fancy-pants professionals in here. My people would resent that, and I wouldn't blame them. We're all just one big family around Haverton and I intend to keep things that way. Besides, the folks I have working for me are farm people. They've been dealing with animals all their lives."

"But exotics can be quite different from farm animals. Without professional advice, there'll be mistakes, accidents. You're bound to lose animals." And possibly keepers, David thought, remembering with a stab of anger what had happened to Faye.

"Oh, I expect some trial and error. I'm prepared for that. I have confidence in my people. They'll learn."

But what about the animals? Were they prepared to be learned on? All David's professional instincts were outraged by Gaffey's cavalier attitude. "At least you need a full-time vet who's knowledgeable about exotic animals," he urged.

"Yes, maybe you're right about that. Have you got anyone in mind? Could you make a recommendation?"

"I'll give it some thought," David said tightly. "Shall we take a look at the ape house? I should check Kong over before I leave."

"Certainly, certainly. Whatever you say."

David was about to turn to the right, but when Gaffey strolled off in the opposite direction, he followed the older man.

"I could have sworn that the ape house was behind us," he said.

Gaffey squinted up at the sun. "Oh, no, it's off this way." He veered over onto a narrow pathway and David tagged behind. He felt certain they were going in the wrong direction, but his host had built this place, after all. Surely he knew where things were.

After walking for another ten minutes, the old man paused and scratched his head. "Now let me see, I could have sworn..."

"Maybe we should backtrack."

"No, no. It must be off this way."

Looking anxiously from right to left, he hurried down a new stretch of path and once again David reluctantly followed. Suddenly they came upon a large area surrounded by a twelve-foot board fence topped by wicked-looking barbed wire and posted with large Keep Out signs. David stopped and stared curiously. During the rest of his tour that morning he'd seen several other ambitious facilities under construction, but all of them had been proudly and openly displayed. He could hear the sound of hammers and drills behind the fence. What was being built in this spot so secretly?

Gaffey seemed equally struck by the sight of the fence. Abruptly he turned around. He was sweating profusely and a deep frown furrowed the pink skin between his busy eyebrows. "Somehow we got on the wrong side of the park," he muttered. "We'll have to go back."

"What are you building over there?" David asked.

"Just a little surprise. Nothing to interest you, O'Toole. Now come along and tell me where you think this damn ape house is."

After one last brief look over his shoulder, David guided Gaffey back toward the path they'd left. Did the old man often get lost, he wondered. Maybe his years were catching up with him.

Fifteen minutes later, and with Gaffey puffing from the exertion, they approached the rear of the ape house. While the old man sat down on a bench and mopped his brow, David paused to survey the outdoor enclosure that looked as if it would soon be ready for Kong's use. David was pleased to see that it was sufficiently large to provide exercise for a troop of gorillas. On the long walk back he'd talked to Gaffey about finding a mate for Kong and acquiring other female apes so that a family might be developed. At the thought of owning his own tribe of gorillas, Gaffey's eyes had gleamed with the innocent lust of an acquisitive child let loose in a toy department at Christmas.

"Well, what do you think?" he called out after David had walked the perimeter of the enclosure. "Will it do for that family we talked about?"

"It looks very good, actually. How much water do you have in that moat?"

"Oh, I don't know. Six feet, maybe."

David shook his head. "You'll have to drain it down to eighteen inches. Gorillas are notorious nonswimmers. You wouldn't want to lose an animal from drowning."

"Has that ever happened?"

"Yes, as a matter of fact. The zoological park in St. Louis lost a male named Makoko that way."

Gaffey stared speculatively at the younger man. "You really do know your p's and q's. Son, how would you like a job here with me?"

Surprised, David turned around. "I thought it was your policy not to import professionals."

"Well, now, that's right. I want this to be a family-style operation. But you said yourself that we need a full-time vet who knows about exotics. What do you say? I bet I can double what you're making down at that college."

"Maybe, but I'm not interested."

"Why not?" Gaffey's broad face was the picture of innocence, but David wasn't fooled. He'd caught the canny look flickering in the old man's eyes.

"I'm teaching and doing research that interests me and I'm expecting a grant sometime in the near future. If it comes through I'll be going to England for a year."

"But that doesn't mean you couldn't come out here as a consultant, let's say once a week until you get that grant, now does it? You'd be very well paid." Gaffey named a figure that made David's eyebrows shoot up.

Still, he opened his mouth to say no. There were just too many things about Gaffey's operation that he didn't like. At that instant he caught sight of a blond head. Faye Johnson was strolling up the path toward them. Hands on hips and with his emotions suddenly as jumbled as if he'd been set upside down, David turned and watched her approach. With the sun shining down on her head she was as pretty and fresh as the spring. But what was she doing here when she should be home resting?

After she'd greeted her uncle and reassured him that she was okay, she turned to David. "I know what you're thinking. I should be home taking it easy. But you left your wallet in the bathroom when you had your shower. I knew you'd want it."

She held out the leather billfold, and David took it, his fingers inadvertently brushing hers and lingering for just a second. "Thanks."

"You're welcome. Well, I just wanted to give it to you. Now I'll go back home."

"O'Brien and I are going to have lunch. Like to join us?" Gaffey invited.

But after Faye had gently corrected her uncle about David's name, she shook her head. "No. Enjoy yourselves. I'd better get back." Then, as if she were suddenly in a hurry, she turned and walked quickly away.

David stood and watched until she disappeared around a corner. He was thinking that if he were a consultant at Wilderness Worlds he'd be seeing her at least once a week. When she was out of sight, Gaffey said, "I sure hope you'll accept this job I'm offering you. And I know Faye will be pleased, too."

"You think so?"

"I know so. She's been at me to get a specialist in here." Gaffey stood up and slapped David on the back. "Son, there's no need for you to make up your mind this minute. Tell you what, we can go in and take a look at Kong. Meanwhile, you can think it over. Does that sound all right?"

"Yes," David finally muttered. "I guess it won't hurt to think about it."

CHAPTER FIVE

"YOU'RE SURE YOU'RE READY to go back to work? It's only been a day."

"Of course I'm ready. I've never felt better." Faye smiled across the office at her uncle, who was sitting with his feet propped up on his desk, puffing away on one of his cigars. "And thanks again for the roses. They're just beautiful."

Wally beamed. "Glad I picked them up. I was a little worried about you being all alone with that O'Connor character, but when I dropped by with the posies the two of you seemed to be getting along like a house afire."

Faye felt the back of her neck go warm. How much had Wally noticed the other day? "Dr. O'Neill was very kind," she said a little uncertainly.

"Sorry to see him go, were you?"

"Well..." Faye's feelings on that had been mixed—and still were. Finally she said, "He seemed very competent. I'm sorry we don't have someone like him here at Wilderness Worlds."

Rubbing his hands together and chuckling with satisfaction, Wally pushed his swivel chair away from his desk and surged to his feet. "Well, I have a little surprise for you. We're going to have O'Neill here weekends as a consultant. What do you say to that?"

Faye's jaw sagged. "We are?"

"I want him to get started right away on this gorilla family idea. He discussed that with you, didn't he?"

"Yes, well, it wasn't exactly a discussion. I mean it was just—"

"I've already made some calls about a mate for Kong," Wally rushed on, starting to pace back and forth behind his desk.

Faye took a deep breath. "And Dr. O'Neill has agreed to help out with all this?"

Wally chuckled. "Have to admit it wasn't easy to sell that young man on the idea of working here. He said something about England and a grant. I had to do a lot of fast talking. But he finally came around. So, what do you think?" He ambled across the room and draped a fatherly arm around Faye's shoulder.

Thoughts awhirl, she looked down at her feet. "I think," she said at length, "that it's a good idea. Now that the exhibit areas are nearly complete and you're beginning to buy animals, we're really going to need expert guidance."

"Good, then it's all taken care of. O'Dell will be coming around again next Saturday."

"O'Neill," Faye muttered absently as she counted to herself. This was Tuesday, so she'd be seeing him again in only four days. A little shiver ran down her spine and Wally, noting it, looked at her with concern.

"You aren't cold, are you?"

"No, of course not."

"You sure you're okay?"

"I'm fine. Uncle Wally, I really want to get back to work."

"That's my girl." The old man gave Faye's shoulder a squeeze. "Never let anything get you down and always keep smiling."

Affectionately Faye grinned back at her uncle. "I'll remember that."

"See that you do, my girl. See that you do. Now shooo! This old man has a lot of paperwork to attend to and important phone calls to make. There are some very big plans afoot right now, very, very big."

Muttering distractedly, Wally headed back toward his desk and Faye pushed open the door and left him alone with his "big" projects. In the outer office, she glanced over at Miss Prior, who sat at the electric typewriter methodically clicking out a letter.

Since Faye had greeted the aging secretary earlier, she saw no need to disturb her now and started to walk quietly past. But when Miss Prior caught sight of her she stopped typing. "Pssst." After glancing at Gaffey's closed office door, she motioned to Faye. "I suppose you've heard he's hired that O'Neill man?"

"Yes, he told me. Don't you think it's a good thing?"

Miss Prior pursed her lips. "Oh, I suppose. He seemed very nice and clean. And quite good looking, too," she added with a sharp glance at Faye, who kept her face carefully blank. "It's just that I can never tell what your uncle's going to do next," Miss Prior continued. "It hasn't been easy working for him all these years, let me tell you."

"Oh, I'm sure it hasn't," Faye soothed, suppressing an amused smile. Despite Ruby Prior's frequent complaints, it was obvious to everyone that she thought the world of her unconventional employer. Indeed, Faye sometimes wondered if Miss Prior's feelings for Wallace Gaffey didn't run deeper than answering his phones and making sure he kept his appointments.

"Just keeping track of his correspondence would take a baker's dozen of secretaries. He's become so careless." Her brow puckered in a worried little frown. "Leaves things all over the place, forgets things."

"When it comes to practical matters, he's always been a bit absentminded," Faye agreed.

"More than a bit." Miss Prior shook her head like an adoring mother fretting over her much-indulged five-year-old. "Do you know that he sometimes comes in here with his shirts half-buttoned and his socks mismatched?"

"Really?"

"Yes, and he constantly forgets his wallet. It's lucky he gave up driving. You remember how he started off for Baltimore a few months ago and wound up on the Pennsylvania Turnpike?"

"I remember," Faye admitted.

"I'm perpetually having to look for his glasses, which he leaves in the most unlikely places."

"Well, he wouldn't admit it, but he's getting on and he needs someone to take care of him," Faye said. "I think he's awfully lucky to have you."

Blushing, Miss Prior patted her stiff curls. "Oh, I don't know..."

"Don't deny it. Everyone knows he couldn't get along without you." Faye wasn't just being diplomatic. It was hard to imagine Uncle Wally without Ruby Prior somewhere in the background clucking over him like an affectionate hen. And it was true that lately he'd become outrageously forgetful. In all the things that counted, he was as sharp as ever, Faye reassured herself. Ever since she could remember, her eccentric but brilliant relative had been a benevolent force in her life. To the people who worked for him he was like some sort of crazy wonderful magician, making wild schemes materialize out of what seemed like smoke. It was impossible to think of him in any other way.

"Well, I'm off," Faye told Miss Prior with a wave and a grin. "Don't let Wally's shenanigans get you down. He always means well. And everything he does usually comes out all right in the end."

With a grimace, the older woman returned to her typing and Faye strode outside into the bright morning light. As she walked along with the sunshine warming her back, she smiled and hummed a little tune to herself. All yesterday she'd been feeling glum, but the visit with her uncle had lifted her spirits. Could it have anything to do with David O'Neill's part-time job at Wilderness Worlds?

She knew that it did. The minute he'd walked out her door she'd realized that she didn't want to let him go. She'd been delighted to find that wallet and have an excuse to see him again. But the brief glimpse she'd had of him behind the ape house had only made things worse. Hearing Wally say that David would be coming back had been better than winning the lottery.

"Careful, Faye, old girl," she muttered under her breath. "Don't go off the deep end over this." So she'd be seeing him again—what did that mean, exactly? After what had happened, she couldn't flirt or ask him to dinner or do any of the things a woman did to let a man know she's attracted. It would make him think she was still affected by the phencyclidine. *I'll have to treat him very, very correctly,* she warned herself. Still, she kept on smiling.

It was a lovely day. The sky was a cloudless blue and buds were beginning to appear on the trees. Crocuses had sprung up on either side of the path, their leaves glowing in the sun like spikes of pure emerald. By contrast the interior of the ape house was dim and cool. Though Faye was eager to see for herself that Kong was really all right, she found her steps slowing as she neared his compartment. Maybe she really wasn't quite recovered from the experience on Sunday, she reflected.

Disconsolately, the young gorilla rested in the corner picking at his toes. A three-quart container of his breakfast drink—a mixture of powdered milk, corn syrup, baby food, cod liver oil and vitamins—sat near his door. Usually Kong slurped it down first thing. This morning it was untouched.

"Oh, dear," Faye exclaimed.

At the sound of her voice the ape looked up. His expression brightening, he shambled across the room and pressed his flat nose against the Plexiglas.

"How are you doing today? Not so good?"

He tilted his massive head.

"You'll never grow up to be a big strong gorilla if you don't eat your breakfast," she admonished.

Kong looked hopefully at the door, and Faye knew that he expected her to come in and play the way she'd always done in the past.

Sadly she shook her head. "Sorry, but I'm afraid I can't."

When he waddled over to the door and pounded on it, Faye's heart was torn. She felt as if she were shutting out her adopted child. "Oh, Kong, you know what you need? You need a nice little girl gorilla like yourself to play with.'' As Faye stood watching him, she remembered what David had said on the subject. Now she could see that he was right. It had been shortsighted to bring Kong up with nothing but human companionship. He needed to associate with his own kind.

He gazed at her accusingly, clearly insulted because she wasn't coming in to resume their old relationship.

''Wally's promised to find you a mate just as soon as possible,'' she told him. ''You won't be lonely much longer.''

But Kong wasn't reassured. In a sudden fit of temper, he kicked over his breakfast concoction and jumped up and down pounding his chest.

Sighing, Faye backed away. Now she'd have to let Roy know there was a mess to clean up. Far less cheerful than when she'd entered the ape house, she plodded back outside and down the path to the trailer where the maintenance chief usually hung out. The trailer was empty, however, and Roy was nowhere in sight. Faye tacked a note about the spilled food on his bulletin board and headed for the children's zoo.

When Wally had first opened the children's section, Kong had been the only exotic animal in it. The others had been what you'd find on a farm or in a pet shop: guinea pigs, snakes, squirrels, goats, sheep and birds. Now that Wally planned to open Wilderness Worlds to the public in July, he'd begun to acquire exotic youngsters who could be moved to the larger facility as they grew. These, mostly orphans who had been sold to him by other zoos that didn't want them, now included two llamas and a tapir, baby lions and cheetahs and several monkeys.

Faye loved them all, but her favorite was Pollyanna—a sweet creature with impossibly long eyelashes that she had fallen in love with on sight. The little elephant seemed to return the feeling. The first time Faye had walked into her enclosure, she'd thrust the moist tip of her trunk into her face and lovingly stroked her cheek. Since then the relationship had developed into a close one. Faye was Pollyanna's trainer and had already taught her a number of tricks.

"Hello, you silly ol' thing," she said as she let herself into the enclosure and the baby elephant lumbered up and lowered her broad head for a pat. Faye scratched the leathery skin with her bull hook, a rounded wooden cane she used for control. "Ready to practice some of those tricks you've learned?" Faye proffered a carrot, which Pollyanna rolled her trunk around and delicately maneuvered into her mouth. When she'd chewed and swallowed, Faye gave Pollyanna another pat. "Okay," she said, "let's begin our workout. Then afterward I'll give you a wash-down and a massage. How does that sound?"

Judging from the way Pollyanna nuzzled Faye with her trunk, it seemed to sound fine and they set to work. Pollyanna had learned to walk forward and back up on command, to stay in one position, to pick up a foot so that a leg chain could be put on and taken off for night security. Relying on her background with horses and dogs, Faye was now trying to teach her to sit and pick up objects. Since it was such a lovely March day, the children's zoo had an unusual number of visitors—mostly young mothers with preschoolers. While they crowded around the outside of the elephant enclosure shouting questions and encouragement, Faye put on a little show.

The morning flew past and Pollyanna made good progress. After hosing her down with warm water and massaging her skin with a stiff broom, which the visitors seemed to find even more entertaining than the tricks, Faye rewarded her with more apples and carrots, several loaves of bread and finally a head of cabbage. Then, her own stomach rumbling with hunger, Faye left the enclosure to get her lunch.

Usually she packed herself a sandwich and a piece of fruit. Today, however, she decided to visit a coffee shop half a mile down the road from Wilderness Worlds. As Faye headed out onto the highway, she glanced up into her rearview mirror. Her car was an old Chevy that she'd inherited from her parents. It was like a dinosaur on the road, much too big and guzzling gas like an alcoholic on a spree. But she didn't owe any money on it, and it got her where she wanted to go.

Suddenly Faye found herself speculating about David O'Neill. What kind of car did he drive? She hadn't noticed, but she could make a few good guesses. Nothing flashy, for one thing. If it was a match for his personality, it would be solid and subdued on the outside, but built for quiet comfort. And it would be equipped with a powerful, no-nonsense engine that you could rely on to respond to your slightest need. Faye glanced back up into the rearview mirror and made a little face at herself. She should stop thinking about the man. If she kept this up she'd be a nervous wreck by Saturday. And who was in that gray sedan that had followed her all the way from Wilderness Worlds and was now pulling into the coffee shop's parking lot right behind her?

As she got out of her car, she remembered David's parting question—something about a gray sedan that had been in front of her house all afternoon. At the time it hadn't made much sense. She shot a glance at the automobile that had followed hers. Behind its tinted glass windows, she couldn't see the driver clearly.

Frowning slightly, Faye walked into the coffee shop and, after greeting Sally the counter girl, who was an old friend from high school, ordered a chef salad. A moment later a man wearing rumpled slacks and a windbreaker walked in and took the stool next to hers.

"Whew, warm enough out there. Makes you think summer is just around the corner," he said to Faye.

"Certainly does," she agreed, eyeing him sideways. He was the man in that car; she was sure of it.

Her food came and she concentrated on eating it. However, when the stranger had ordered a hamburger and coffee, he turned back to Faye. "Name's Bob, Bob Selden. I think I was behind you on the highway coming here. Didn't I see a Wilderness Worlds sticker on the back of your car?"

"You could have. There's one on it." Faye took a bite of her salad and decided not to tell him her name. Normally she wouldn't have thought twice about striking up a friendly conversation with a stranger. But something about this situation was hitting her wrong.

"You work there or something?"

She nodded. Her mouth was full of raw broccoli, so there was no way she could respond verbally.

"I've been hearing a lot about that place," the man continued. "The old guy who owns it is quite an eccentric, isn't he?"

Faye managed to swallow. "I suppose you might say that, but everyone who works for him loves him. Wallace Gaffey has done a lot for the people around this part of the Eastern Shore."

"He can afford it. From what I hear, he's a multi-millionaire. Owns a string of crab cake shanties all the way to the Pacific, right?"

"Yes." Wally had franchises all over Europe, Japan, and now two in Africa, but she saw no reason to mention that.

"And a boatload of hotel and condominium properties on the beach at Ocean City. And who knows what else? The guy's a real wheeler-dealer."

"He's a smart businessman and his investments have paid off," Faye responded curtly. She took a large bite of tomato and used the time it took chewing it to study her interrogator. He was very forgettable—thin brown hair, light brown eyes, a round face with indistinctive features. Just why was he asking her all these questions? And why was he so interested in Wally?

"If I were his age and had his kind of money, I'd be taking it easy on my own private island in the sun, not opening up an animal park. What's the deal, anyway? What's in it for him?" Selden's hamburger arrived. Without taking his eyes off Faye's face, he lifted the top half of the bun and reached for the ketchup and mustard.

"There's no deal," she told him. "He just likes animals."

Selden laughed disbelievingly. "You mean, the way he likes crabs?"

Faye was beginning to feel quite irritated. "Well, no."

"Oh, I betcha he's not opening this park just for laughs. It's too big an investment. He's got some angle." Selden scrutinized Faye. "You work there, so you have the inside track. Mind telling me what your guess is about the whole operation?"

"Not at all," she retorted as she began digging in her purse to pay her bill. "My best guess is that Wallace Gaffey isn't getting any younger. There are a lot of interests he's never had time to pursue. Providing a home for exotic animals and endangered species is one of them."

"You're serious, aren't you?"

"Very." Abruptly Faye stood, grabbed her jacket and, after paying her bill, slung her purse over her shoulder. "He's a man who's worked hard all his life," she continued. "Maybe now he wants to just enjoy himself. I think we're all very lucky that he's doing it in a way that's going to benefit a lot of people, not to mention the animals themselves." And with that, she stalked out of the coffee shop and into the cool March breeze that had sprung up.

On the drive back to Wilderness Worlds, Faye mulled over the odd conversation. It was still on her mind when she stopped by Roy's trailer to make sure Kong's spilled breakfast drink had been cleaned up.

"Yeah, I got your note," Roy drawled as he downed the last of a can of beer and then snapped open the tab on another. His sneakered feet were propped up on a battered, paper-strewn desk and he wore his baseball cap sideways. On the floor beside him empty sandwich wrappings spilled from a grease-stained paper bag. "Kong's floor is now a heck of a lot cleaner than the one in my apartment."

Faye could easily believe that. "Did he do any better with his lunch?" Kong would get sick if he stopped eating properly.

Roy yawned. "Not to worry. The stupid ape ate the whole thing. Gave me a lot of evil looks while I watched, but he polished off the entire fruit salad."

"You didn't forget the Jell-O, celery and lettuce?"

"I didn't forget nothin'. He got everything on the menu." Roy looked Faye up and down. "You okay?"

"I'm just fine."

"You and the doc get along all right?"

"Of course."

"Sure looked cozy last I saw."

Faye's eyes narrowed. "What are you getting at?"

Roy grinned at her over his beer can. "Last I saw you were knocked out and practically naked and O'Neill was carrying you off like a battle prize. Have to admit I was a little jealous. That guy got closer to you in ten minutes than I have in ten years."

Faye had known Roy since grade school, but except for one unpleasant experience at a Junior Achievement dance in ninth grade, she'd never dated him. She never would either—no matter how persistent he got. "Well, let's keep it that way, shall we."

"That was mighty snappish. You sure you're feeling all right?"

Faye was getting tired of being asked that question. "Of course, I am!"

"Something's bugging you. You got ants in your pants or what?"

Faye rolled her eyes. "I just didn't have a very pleasant lunch." Briefly she described the interrogation to which she'd been subjected in the coffee shop.

Halfway through her account, Roy went pale and yanked his feet off the desk so sharply that he almost fell over backward. "You say O'Neill saw this guy in front of your house?"

"He saw a gray sedan, not necessarily the same one."

Scowling, Roy twirled the bill of his cap around to the front of his head and hopped to his feet. "And this jerk was trying to pump you about Wilderness Worlds?"

Faye stared up at Roy's angry face. "Sort of. He seemed to think there was some secret reason why Wally was building the place."

"What did you tell him?"

"What is there to tell? We both know the reason behind Wilderness Worlds." She gestured out the trailer's tiny window. "Now that Wally's reached retirement age, he wants to enjoy himself. And this is his way of doing that."

Roy frowned at her. "You sure that's the story you gave this Selden?"

"Of course. What do you mean 'story'? What else was there to tell the man?"

"Nothing." Roy stepped so close that Faye could see the tiny red veins in the whites of his eyes. "But promise me you won't talk to him again, or any other stranger who starts asking you a bunch of questions that aren't anybody's business but ours."

Disturbed, Faye took a step backward. "All right, but I don't understand. What's the big secret?"

"Never mind, just don't let anyone talk to you like that." Roy leaned closer, his voice suddenly hushed and conspiratorial. "Listen, I can't talk about it yet, but this much I'll say. Something big *is* about to happen."

"Like what?"

"Something very special. A surprise for the opening day here."

Faye's mind raced. "Wally's not in any trouble, is he?"

"'Course not. But you know how he is, always pulling off deals that no one else would have the guts to even imagine. Well, he's about to yank another rabbit out of his top hat—a big one. So, mum's the word. Okay?"

"How can I keep a secret when I don't know what it is? You'd better tell me what's going on."

"Can't do that, little Faye. Promised the boss I'd keep my mouth shut."

While Faye stared at Roy uncertainly, he dropped back down into his chair, rubbed his bony hands together and reached for his beer. Obviously he was delighted to be in on some secret operation of Wally's. She just hoped it wasn't anything foolish. Suddenly a shiver snaked down her back and she didn't want to know. As long as it didn't harm anyone, let the two of them have their fun.

ABSENTMINDEDLY DAVID O'NEILL pushed open the door to his apartment. Most of the mail he'd fished out of his box downstairs was of the junk variety, but along with the phone bill there'd been a letter from Grace. Dumping the other envelopes and brochures, he opened it and began to read.

David, you clever old thing. I should never have doubted your judgment. You know how the rumors fly around here. Well, the other night at a party I heard some very fine gossip, indeed. Sounds as if our grant may be coming through in the next few weeks and we'll both be off to 'Merrie olde England.' Tallyho.

Frowning, David reread the brief note and then consulted his watch. It would be early now in California, but not too early. Grace would probably be in her office. He went into the kitchen, picked up the phone and began to dial.

She answered on the fourth ring and at the sound of her familiar warm contralto, David leaned against the counter and smiled. He could just picture her face with its intelligent brown eyes behind oversize horn-rim frames. Her dark hair would be caught up untidily on top of her head and she would probably be chain-smoking her way through her second pack of the day—a habit he'd been unable to persuade her to break. Grace was no saint, and no beauty either, but she had character and a kind of encompassing motherly warmth. He always felt comfortable around her.

Suddenly David found himself comparing Grace with the pixielike Faye Johnson. Did Faye have character and warmth? In some ways he knew a lot about her, and in other ways nothing at all. What's more, he certainly hadn't felt comfortable around her—anything but. David frowned. Somehow it didn't seem right to be thinking about Faye when he was talking to Grace. "Well, hello stranger," he said a little too emphatically.

"Hello yourself. And what do you mean with that stranger crack?"

"Only that I've stayed up late the past couple of nights to call you at home. But you're never there. Where've you been spending your evenings?"

There was a pause and then Grace cleared her throat. "It's been a busy week. I've been working with a new colleague. We're collaborating on a paper."

"Oh? Who is she?"

"His name is Benson, Mark Benson. He's quite brilliant—has a wonderful sense of humor. I think if you met him you'd really get on together."

"If you like him, I'm sure I would."

"Actually, I have been doing a certain amount of partying lately. Did you get my note?"

David glanced down at the counter. "Yes, it's right beside me. I dialed your office the moment I read it."

"So what do you think?" she queried brightly.

"About the grant?"

"Of course, silly!"

"I don't know. I guess I wouldn't advise you to pack your bags on the strength of a rumor."

"Oh, but Mark says—"

David lifted an eyebrow. "Mark? What has he got to do with our grant?"

"Well, I told him about it, naturally. He has some very highly placed friends. He says the source of this particular rumor is very reliable."

"I see."

Grace chuckled. "David, for heaven's sake, you sound jealous. You aren't, are you?"

"Of course not."

"We did agree that while you were gone we wouldn't make hermits of ourselves. You are doing that, aren't you?"

"Doing what? Making a hermit of myself?"

"Socializing. You know what I mean."

"Certainly. Every night I barhop until dawn and then spend the rest of the day fighting off gorgeous sex-crazed women." Suddenly David grinned, realizing that his words held a grain of truth. Fighting off a gorgeous woman was exactly how he had spent the day before yesterday.

Grace laughed indulgently. "All right, all right, I just hope you aren't sitting home alone every night working. I want you to get out and enjoy yourself."

"I will, don't worry."

"Well, see that you do. Now I have to hang up. I have a meeting to attend. Write and tell me everything that's going on in your life, and keep your fingers crossed about that grant."

"It's hard to handle a microscope and slides with your fingers crossed," David objected dryly.

Grace trilled another laugh and a moment later the phone clicked on the other end of the line. David slowly hung up the receiver, lost in thought. Almost from the first he and Grace had agreed that what they both wanted was something casual—no commitments, no restraints. Yet since leaving her in California he hadn't really tried to meet other women. In fact, except for a few casual dates, he'd avoided the ones who made overtures to him. It hadn't exactly been a conscious decision, just a feeling that he owed Grace some loyalty combined with a distaste for one-night stands and meaningless physical encounters where not even friendship was involved.

Maybe it was time to revise that policy. After all, hadn't Grace just encouraged him to see other females—which was new. Did her attitude have something to do with this Mark Benson? David was surprised and a little disturbed to find himself not feeling nearly as jealous as he thought he should. Crossing to the refrigerator, he took out a can of beer.

Satisfying as David found his profession, there was a price he paid for his maverick life-style. Early on he'd learned that it wasn't fair to love a woman and encourage her to love you back if you couldn't really commit yourself to her. But even in this era of liberated females an honest relationship wasn't an easy thing for a rolling stone like him to find.

When he'd met Grace, she'd seemed like the perfect solution—a mature, independent woman who wasn't looking for marriage and who could say goodbye as easily as she said hello. But maybe that was growing stale, for both of them, he suddenly thought. Maybe they either had to move on from there with each other, or each move on to someone else.

Once again an image of Faye Johnson rose before David's mind's eye. He knew he'd allowed himself to be talked into consulting at Wilderness Worlds because of Faye—which was stupid. The woman was so mortified by what had happened between them that she was bound to avoid him. Besides, they had nothing in common and she was too young for him. It would be better all around if he just didn't see her again. Suddenly he felt like a fool for having agreed to get involved with Wallace Gaffey's private playground. Popping the tab on his beer, he stalked into the shabby living room of his sublet apartment, put on a favorite recording of a Beethoven symphony and turned the sound up loud.

THE NEXT AFTERNOON David told Bill Abbott about his new job. Bill, a big, untidy teddy bear of a man, was a colleague at Hopkins. In addition to their professional concerns, he and David shared a fondness for swimming and Chinese food. The two of them had gotten into the habit of having lunch once a week at a little Szechuan place near campus after working out at the pool.

"Well, consulting can be a very handy way to pick up a few extra shekels," Bill commented as he eyed his Kung Pao chicken appreciatively and picked up his fork. "And being a bachelor, you lucky dog, you have your weekends free. The wife would skin me if I tried to go off on my own on one of my free days."

As David watched Bill dig into his food, he experienced a twinge of jealousy at Bill's settled home life. *What's wrong with me,* he wondered. He'd always enjoyed his freedom. In his line of work, being tied to a woman who got touchy if you had to go away for a weekend, or a month, or a year would be an impossible situation. That was part of the reason that he and Grace got along so well. On the other hand, what would it be like to have someone really care about you—someone who was more than a pal and an agreeable bed partner?

"And what you'll be doing on the Eastern Shore is in a good cause," Bill was saying. "I know how you feel about preserving endangered species."

Toying glumly with his food, David nodded. "Did you know that between 1900 and 1950 we've lost one species every eight months? By the end of the century we could be losing some species every hour of the day."

Bill wiped his mouth and full beard with a napkin and belched appreciatively. "Of course, there are the wildlife preserves."

"Yes, but even inside those the endangered creatures aren't safe.''

"Poachers?''

David grimaced. "That's the trouble. When an animal is rare, it's also valuable. A giraffe taken from its natural habitat sells for $25,000 and a female gorilla will bring $100,000. A white tiger is worth at least $75,000 and the price tag on an Asian one-horned rhinoceros is $125,000.''

"Not to mention the giant panda,'' Bill interjected. "I hear a pair of those would cost a million.''

"Easily.''

"Hmm.'' Bill looked reflectively at the tiny tea cup balanced in his large palm. "I've heard some very sad stories about poachers trapping protected animals and selling them on the black market.''

David pushed his plate away, his gray eyes narrowing. "I can tell you one myself. Ever hear of a guy named Morton Baker?''

"I don't know. Name is vaguely familiar. Who is he?''

"In my line of work, he's almost a legend. Baker is a renegade white hunter who's the brains behind much of the poaching in the African preserves. I'd give anything to see that guy behind bars.''

"Sounds as if you have more than a professional interest. Is that a personal grudge I hear talking?''

"You might say so. A few years back I was consulting on the elephant population in Zaire. You know how all the big herds are being decimated by ivory poachers. Well, I caught a gang of cutthroats redhanded. But when I stumbled on their dirty work, one of the thugs hit me on the back of the head with his rifle butt and left me for dead.''

Bill raised his bushy eyebrows. "You know, David, I envy you. Not only are you at the top of your field professionally with a shelf full of critically acclaimed books, you've led a hell of an adventurous life. No wonder you never married. You've been too damn busy having a good time. Now, how did you survive that little mishap in Zaire?"

David laughed. "Luck. I was discovered and treated in time, and I guess I'm not easy to kill. I don't know if Morton Baker had anything to do with it, but I'd sure like the chance to find out."

Bill shook his head. "All of a sudden, I'm glad I'm not Baker. Mild-mannered professor that you pretend to be, O'Neill, I have a feeling that you could be a very dangerous enemy. For one thing, you have a highly developed sense of right and wrong. Speaking of which . . ."

"Yes?"

"I suppose I should warn you that there have been some strange rumors recently about this place of Wallace Gaffey's."

David sat up straighter. "What kind of rumors?"

"Oh, that it might be a front for a smuggling operation. Nothing concrete, really." Bill gestured vaguely. "Just loose talk that it's not exactly what it seems. I suppose that's inevitable because of Gaffey's history as a businessman. In his heyday he was involved in some pretty bizarre deals. Anyhow, I thought you should know."

"Thanks, I think," David responded. Bill had just given him something else to worry about. Was it possible that Wallace Gaffey was using Wilderness Worlds as a front for something illegal? David remembered the closely guarded fenced enclosure he'd stumbled upon. What was Gaffey building behind that fence and why was he so secretive about it? Did Faye know? Faye and the old man were so close, like father and daughter almost. If there were something shady going on at Wilderness Worlds, could she be in on it, too? David shook his head. No, surely not. He simply couldn't believe anything like that of her.

Two fortune cookies arrived with the check and Bill broke his. "'Tomorrow will be a brighter day,'" he intoned as he scrutinized the tiny slip of paper inside.

"Sounds hopeful."

"Can't miss since it's been raining all of today. What does yours predict?"

Smiling, David broke the thin pastry, withdrew a strip of paper from its interior and studied it.

"Well?" Bill prompted.

David cleared his throat. "It says, 'Be alert. Adventure, romance and danger await you.'"

CHAPTER SIX

"THE PROBLEM WITH PENGUINS," David began, "is that they're very susceptible to a disease carried by sea gulls."

Wallace Gaffey scowled. "What are you getting at?"

"Here on the Eastern Shore you've got the ocean on one side and Chesapeake Bay on the other. How are you going to keep the gulls away?"

Gaffey's round face went a shade of burgundy. With his heavy jowls aquiver, he looked more than ever like an angry old bulldog. "Are you trying to tell me that I can't have penguins?"

"The disease is fatal and wipes out whole rookeries. Unless you can figure out a way to keep the gulls away, you'd be wise to forget the penguins."

"Damned if I will!" Gaffey thrust out his lower jaw. "O'Grady, the word 'quit' is not in my vocabulary. It's time you learned that. We'll just have to figure a way."

By now David knew it was useless to argue. In the three weekends he'd spent at Wilderness Worlds it had been the same story over and over. Gaffey had made elaborate plans and launched costly building projects without really knowing much about the animals upon which he intended to heap his largesse. When David tried to explain that for breeding purposes it would be better to have fewer species and more individuals from each separate species, Gaffey refused to retrench. Oh, he listened and took David's advice when it didn't interfere with some private fantasy. But he refused to give up gracefully on any of his half-baked schemes.

As they strolled down the path toward the old man's office, David debated offering his resignation. Then, through the screen of budding trees that separated Wilderness Worlds from the children's zoo, now dubbed "Wee Wilderness Worlds," he caught sight of Faye Johnson. She was working with Pollyanna in the elephant enclosure. As she gently urged the massive creature to put her forelegs up onto a stool, David's eyes lingered on Faye's slim figure. Next to Pollyanna's gray bulk, she made quite a picture. "Beauty and the beast," he muttered under his breath.

"What?" Gaffey shot him an inquisitive stare. "What did you say?"

"Oh, nothing. I was just noticing Miss Johnson over there. She seems to be getting on very well with your young elephant."

The old man paused and shaded his eyes. "Faye gets on like a house afire with all the animals. Something about her they like, you know."

David nodded. "Yes, it's a gift some people have, a kind of empathy."

"Empathy, that's it." Gaffey swatted away one of the first flies of the season from his forearm. "Whenever I get a new animal, I always bring Faye over to talk to it. Calms it down right away."

David had already seen for himself that Faye had a way with animals. Unfortunately, all his observations had had to be made long distance. He'd guessed right about what her attitude toward him would be. She slipped off whenever she saw him coming, and on the few occasions when she'd been forced to endure his company for several minutes, she'd treated him with wooden formality.

"Did I tell you that I have two new female gorillas coming in today?"

David was startled. "No, you didn't. That was fast work. How did you manage it?"

"Oh, I had some luck." Gaffey winked mysteriously. "Found a private collector who wanted to get rid of them. And money talks."

"What about the paperwork? Permits for the sale of endangered species could take three months to a year to obtain."

"Oh, that's still going on. Until it's settled, they're officially on loan for breeding purposes."

"I see." David took a moment to digest this. Gaffey couldn't remember his telephone number half the time, but obviously he hadn't lost his flair for wheeling and dealing. "Does Faye know?"

Eyes twinkling, the old man shook his head. "No, and don't tell her. I want it to be a surprise. She's been fretting about Kong being lonely. This ought to cheer her up. Let's go back to the office." He pulled out a large gold pocket watch. "The new gorillas might even be here by now."

FIFTY YARDS OFF, Faye rubbed the tender spot behind Pollyanna's ears and crooned words of praise. Faye was pretending that she didn't know David O'Neill stood on the path with Wally and that he was watching her. Nevertheless, every cell of her body seemed to feel the weight of his regard. Several times during the past few weeks she'd noticed him staring at her. What did he think about when he saw her, she wondered.

Well, she certainly knew what she thought about. At this very moment her face and neck were hot—a reaction she suffered every time she caught sight of the man. Faye sneaked a peek through the trees—David and Wally were gone. Half relieved, half let-down, she turned back to Pollyanna and pointed at the big up-side-down tub in front of her. "There's an apple in my pocket. If you'll get all four feet up on the pedestal, I'll give it to you," she wheedled.

To Faye's delight and amazement, Pollyanna jumped right up onto the tub and stood swaying on the tiny surface.

"Pollyanna, that's wonderful!" Faye stood back to admire the effect. "You look like a real circus performer. You're going to be the star of the whole zoo!" She gave the little elephant her apple and watched happily while she crunched it up.

But a moment later Faye's smile was replaced by a worried frown. When she told Pollyanna to get off the tub, she couldn't. Gingerly the young elephant reached down with her front leg, but it didn't quite reach the ground. She would have to let her weight drop forward to successfully get off the tub, and she wouldn't do that. While Faye tried to coach her, she kept reaching down and stretching, first with one foot and then with the other. But even though she came within a couple inches of touching the ground, she couldn't quite make it.

As soon as Pollyanna realized her predicament, she began to shake and trumpet with terror. People all over the children's zoo heard and came running. Soon the elephant enclosure was surrounded by excited visitors and several other attendants. They shouted advice and encouragement, but nothing helped and Faye was beginning to feel frantic.

"You look as if you're having a problem," a calm male voice said in her ear.

"What?" Faye's head snapped around and she met David O'Neill's amused gray eyes. He'd let himself into the enclosure and was standing just behind her. "Mind if I make a suggestion?"

"Oh, please, anything!"

"What she needs is a step stool. I think I spotted a sawed-off stump over by the office. Why don't you see if you can calm her down while I get it?"

Faye did her best to comply, but by the time David returned with the stump in a wheelbarrow, she was close to hysteria and Pollyanna had already gotten there.

"Maybe this will shut her up," David shouted over the elephant's earsplitting shrieks. He maneuvered the stump into place next to the tub.

It worked like a charm. The moment Pollyanna realized she had an escape route, she stepped down onto it and from there to the ground. The people surrounding the enclosure gave a cheer and David grinned.

"Oh, thank God," Faye cried out, wringing her hands while she watched the elephant lumber off to the back of the enclosure. "I was so worried. This is all my fault!"

David put a comforting hand on her shoulder. "Looks to me as if Pollyanna is okay. Don't get yourself all worked up over nothing."

"Nothing!" Faye exclaimed. But he was right. When she looked over at Pollyanna, the baby elephant was standing next to her pool spraying herself with water as if nothing had happened. Faye started to laugh. "Just look at her. I think she enjoys being the center of attention."

"Obviously. You've got yourself a real prima donna there." David stood with one loafer-clad foot on a bale of hay, and despite her overwrought state Faye found herself noticing how that posture made his snug-fitting black jeans mold his muscular, clean-limbed body. "Sorry if I startled you, by the way," he added. "But with all the noise and commotion you would never have heard me from outside the enclosure, so I thought I'd better just come in and offer my assistance."

"I'm very glad that you did." Now that the crisis was over, Faye cursed her luck for a new reason. This was the second time David had needed to come to her rescue. Faye was proud of her work with the animals, but he probably considered her an incompetent bungler. "I should have thought of the stump myself," she said a little stiffly. "I don't know why I didn't."

"You were upset."

"That's no excuse. I should have realized that she'd have trouble getting off that tub. If she'd been hurt it would have been my fault."

David regarded her quizzically. "Don't be so hard on yourself. You handle that elephant very well. Are you about done working with her for a while?"

Faye gave a little laugh. "Oh, I don't think I should teach her any more tricks today."

"Better give her a rest." David's face relaxed into an engaging smile. "I was wondering if I could persuade you to come up to the ape house with me. Your uncle has arranged a surprise for us. And believe me, it's quite a surprise."

"Oh? What is it?"

"You'll see."

She shrugged. "Sure. Lead the way."

The crowd around the elephant enclosure had thinned, but when Faye and David let themselves out they had to stop and talk with several visitors who'd seen what had happened and wanted to ask questions and make comments. At last they managed to extricate themselves and start up the path.

"Is Kong okay?" Faye queried anxiously.

"He seems in pretty good health physically."

"Just physically?" Her face clouded. "Oh, you don't have to tell me. I know he's been upset these past few weeks."

"And so have you been." When she shot him a questioning look, he quickly added, "I mean about Kong's being unhappy."

"Well, he is sort of like my own child. I hate to see him moping around."

"Of course."

"I know Wally's trying to find him a mate, but who knows how long that will take."

David changed the subject. "You know I meant it when I said you handle Pollyanna well. Where did you learn to train elephants?"

Faye's ego was a little bruised, so the compliment was gratifying. "I talked to a trainer at a circus. But basically I haven't found teaching Pollyanna much different from handling horses and dogs. It's just a matter of reward and discipline."

They were now close enough to the ape house to see and hear the activity underway there. A large truck was pulled up to one side. Roy and several other of the men who did heavy work hovered around the entrance.

Faye turned to David. "What's going on?"

He smiled down at her. "Come on in with me and see."

When they walked past the little knot of workers, Faye looked inquiringly at Roy. But he was too busy joking and shooting the breeze with his cohorts to pay attention, so she got no enlightenment there. Inside the dim building, she blinked for a moment while her eyes adjusted. Then they stretched wide. The compartments adjoining Kong's were both occupied by gorillas.

"They're females," David told her, enjoying the astonished expression on her face. "And the amazing thing is that the larger of the two is pregnant."

"Pregnant?" Faye ran forward to peer through the Plexiglas wall. Sure enough, the large furry creature on the right had a distinctly protruding belly.

"Name's Violet," Wally's voice declared from behind her. "The other one's called Daisy Mae." Faye turned to find her uncle puffing on a cigar and grinning like a benevolent Santa Claus.

"Oh, Wally, this is wonderful. How did you manage to do it so fast?"

"That's for me to know. What's important is that we now have the makings of that family David here has been talking up."

"Yes." Faye turned back to the window. "When does Violet expect her baby?"

"Beats me. O'Guin, what do you think?"

David came up alongside Faye. "My guess is that if we're lucky, the happy event will take place around the end of the month."

"But that's only four weeks away." She shot him a glance. "And what do you mean, 'if we're lucky'?"

"Well, look at her. I just hope she's not too upset to carry this baby to term."

Faye turned back to the window and pressed her hands together. She had to admit that Violet appeared even shier than her name implied. She was huddled against the far wall, her arms wrapped protectively around her swollen body while her dark eyes darted fearfully from one unfamiliar face to the next.

"Poor thing. She's terrified. And so is her friend," Faye added, glancing over to the other compartment where Violet's companion huddled in equal misery.

David restrained himself from once again dropping a comforting arm around Faye's shoulder. "Consider what they've been through. Yanked from their home, trucked and flown cross-country, subjected to all kinds of upsetting experiences. And now this. They don't know what's going to happen to them here. And they're not exactly getting a warm welcome from their new lord and master, either."

"No," Faye agreed. She turned to look at the middle compartment where Kong was making a terrible ruckus, racing back and forth, hollering and beating the walls with his fists. "He's behaving like a maniac."

"What's wrong with that crazy ape?" Gaffey demanded. "I thought he'd be happy to get a new pair of girlfriends. Look at him running around screaming bloody murder. He acts as if he'd like to throttle both of them."

David eyed the half-grown male gorilla, who appeared almost beside himself with rage and anxiety. David was certainly glad that Faye wasn't in there with Kong now. The animal really did look dangerous. "Keep in mind that this is a new experience for him."

"Oh, of course that's true," Faye exclaimed. "He's never seen another gorilla. Does he even realize that Violet and Daisy Mae are like him?"

David's eyes remained fixed on the excited animal. "Kong's instincts are telling him a lot of things. That's why he's putting on such a show. My guess is that it's actually part of an extended mating ritual. The male has to establish his dominance over the females in his harem."

"By scaring them to death?" Faye questioned.

The beginnings of a smile twitched at David's mouth. "'Fraid so. There's not much women's liberation in the animal world."

Wallace Gaffey guffawed. "Sounds like they know how to handle their females better than we do."

Faye hid her irritation, telling herself that her uncle was part of another generation and couldn't be blamed for his chauvinist attitudes. She turned to David. "They all seem so upset. Do you think they'll ever get along with one another?"

"They'll need time to adjust. Violet is going to require peace and quiet. I think for now she should be separated from Kong."

"Now?" Gaffey queried. "Roy won't like that. He said that trucking them here was worse than driving a school bus full of rowdy fifth-graders."

"Okay, not right this minute. Violet's exhausted, anyway. Let her get some rest before she's moved again."

Gaffey looked skeptical. "How could anyone rest with Kong making all that racket?" He tapped his niece on the shoulder. "Think you could calm him down?"

Faye had once again pinned her anxious green gaze on the three gorillas. "I don't know, but I'd like to try. Could you leave me here alone with them for a while?"

When David raised his eyebrows, Gaffey whispered, "Wait and see. This girl is magic with animals. I bet if we do what she says and come back in a couple of hours, she'll have them all settled in and peaceful as babies."

"Babies aren't all that peaceful," David pointed out. But, after exacting another promise from Faye that she wouldn't enter any of the compartments, he agreed to do what she and Gaffey suggested. Faye was already sitting cross-legged in front of Daisy Mae's compartment, crooning softly, when he and the old man walked out of the building.

An hour later, David stopped back in. He paused just inside the door. Faye was now sitting in front of Violet's window. "Just think how beautiful your baby will be, and how good it will feel to hold him in your arms," she was murmuring in a gentle singsong. He came farther into the room and stood there for several moments, gazing down at her blond head. But when she kept on talking and didn't look up, he tiptoed back out again.

After another hour he returned carrying two cups of tea. "I thought you might appreciate this," he said in a low voice as he handed her one of the Styrofoam containers.

"Thanks." Faye got to her feet and accepted the hot beverage. Sipping his own tea, David peered in at Violet and then Kong. They were both dozing. "Maybe you are a miracle worker."

Faye laughed self-consciously. "Eventually Kong just wore himself out, and poor little Violet was exhausted."

"Sleep is the best thing for her right now. Daisy Mae seems better, too." The younger female gorilla was awake and still huddled in a corner, but she appeared much more relaxed. David turned toward Faye. "You look as if you could do with a nap yourself."

"I am a little weary. But I'm more hungry than sleepy. Somehow I never got around to eating lunch today."

David glanced at his watch. "I have an idea. It's not that long until dinnertime and this calls for a celebration. How about letting me take you out for a meal?"

The suggestion flustered Faye. "Really, I wasn't hinting...."

"I know you weren't. I'd like to take you out."

"But..." She hooked a thumb at the trio of gorillas. "They shouldn't be left alone, should they?"

"Someone else can keep an eye on them tonight. I'll arrange it. Besides, we do have some things to talk about."

"We do?"

He nodded. "Apparently your uncle is serious about trying to get a gorilla community established, and he wants you to be their keeper. I'd like to discuss strategy with you. And why not do so over a decent meal in a restaurant?"

Faye had run out of objections. "Certainly, but I'll have to change. I'm not dressed to go out."

David opened his hands and looked down at himself, calling attention to his own casual attire. "It'll be some place informal. I'll pick you up at your house in an hour. How's that?"

"Fine." Though Faye made herself sound nonchalant, the thought of spending an evening in David O'Neill's company made her distinctly nervous. Of course, that didn't make much sense. For the past three weeks she'd been hoping for something like this, and she'd long ago acknowledged that she wanted to get to know him better. *It's a business meeting,* she told herself as she drove home. *And we're not going anywhere fancy. It's not really a date.*

All the same, she took the time to shower and wash her hair, spent more than her usual two minutes on her makeup, and carefully chose what she would wear. It should seem casual, like something she'd just reached in and grabbed out of the closet. But it should also be especially flattering. Five minutes before David pulled up in front of her house in his Volvo, she settled on white pleated slacks, teamed with a red-and-white-striped knit top. She was just stepping into high-heeled sandals when she heard his car.

Did she look too young, too unsophisticated? What sort of woman would a man like David O'Neill normally date? After a last flurried glance in the mirror, she grabbed her purse and jacket and hurried to the front door where she met David outside as he was strolling up the walk. "All ready," she told him brightly.

"So I see. You look very nice."

"Thanks."

He was smiling as they both walked toward his maroon Volvo, but she couldn't help wondering if he was offended that she hadn't invited him in for a drink. Maybe it was stupid, but she didn't want him revisiting her living room, where he was bound to be reminded of the bizarre day they'd spent together.

"I thought I'd drive to Oxford," he said as he opened the door on the passenger side. "I hear there are a couple of nice seafood places there."

Faye nodded. "Yes. There's a good one in a marina where we can sit out on a glassed-in deck and look at the boats."

"Sounds just the ticket."

As he started up the car's engine, Faye sank back into the cushiony depths of its leather seat. If her nerves hadn't been wound so tight, she would have smiled. His automobile was exactly what she'd imagined: solid, comfortable, top-quality. Was she right in thinking that it matched the man? Faye stole a glance at David's profile. She liked what she saw. But what did she really know about him? Not a lot. There were a million questions she'd like to ask.

Instead, they drove along through the April evening in virtual silence, with only the scented spring air and the throb of the Volvo's powerful engine between them. Briefly Faye considered mentioning the man in the gray sedan. But then she reconsidered. She hadn't seen him since that day at the coffee shop, and her nebulous suspicions seemed too silly to even bring up. Roy had just been dramatizing when he'd made such a fuss over the incident. Besides, David already had a bad enough impression of Wilderness Worlds.

"Can you direct me to this restaurant?" he asked when they rolled into the outskirts of the little town.

"Yes. Just stay on this road until you come to the water and then turn right."

"It looks almost like an English village," he commented a few minutes later.

Faye glanced to the right and left, admiring the neat little cottages, smooth green lawns and brick walks. "In a way it is. The English were the original settlers here, you know. And since the Eastern Shore was relatively hard to get to for so long, not many other people came here. There are isolated places around this area where the dialect is still almost Elizabethan."

David nodded. "I've heard that."

"Do you miss England?" Faye asked.

He kept his eyes on the road. They were now driving along the water's edge toward an area lined with marinas. "Sometimes."

She remembered that he'd said something about having lived near a zoo as a boy. "You were always interested in animals, weren't you?"

"Yes." He laughed. "As a matter of fact, I was interested in almost nothing else. From a very young age, I was driving the other members of my family mad, catching or buying and then bringing home every conceivable sort of creature from snails to baby owls."

Faye smiled. She could easily imagine David as a youngster. Though his gray eyes could be so cool and intelligent, they still had something enthusiastic and boyish in them as well. "I was like that, too," she admitted. "I was always filling the house with pets—millions of dogs and cats, squirrels, guinea pigs, even a skunk once."

"I noticed you have a dog and three cats now."

"Yes, and I stable a horse at a farm near my house. But that's nothing compared to the menagerie I used to keep. When I started working at the children's zoo, I decided to donate most of my pets. I was spending so

much time there, it didn't seem fair to keep animals
stuck in the house alone. Did you ever work at the zoo
near where you lived?''

David cast Faye a quick glance. So she did remember the details of their conversation in her bedroom.
He'd wondered. Aloud he said, ''I applied for work
there when I was a teenager, but instead I was offered
a position at Whipsnade, the London Zoological So-
ciety's country zoo. It was wonderful luck to get that
job and a chance to leave home along with it. After I'd
worked at Whipsnade for two years I knew what I
wanted to do with my life.''

''You wanted to help animals?''

''It was a little more complicated than that. I wanted
to learn all about them and to help preserve the species threatened with extinction—that's almost all of
the exotic ones, you know.'' He shook his head ruefully. ''Actually, what I ultimately wanted was my own
zoological park.''

Faye laughed. ''So you and Wally have a lot in
common.''

''I suppose we do,'' David answered thoughtfully.
''Actually, maybe I'm a bit jealous. He's a wealthy
man. On a whim, he can do what I've wanted to do all
my life but won't ever be able to afford.''

''Turn right at the next corner and we'll be there.''

David did as she instructed and a moment later
pulled into the parking lot of a restaurant surrounded
on three sides by water and the bobbing masts of
docked sailboats.

''I hope we'll get a table. It's the weekend,'' Faye
said.

As David followed her through the door, his gaze
lingered on her shining hair and then drifted down to

the round contours of her derriere just visible beneath the hem of her jacket. "I'm sure we will," he murmured. But his mind was on other things. He was remembering how that delightful little bottom of hers had felt when he'd had to lift her into her nightdress. Did she ever think about him undressing her when she'd been unconscious, he wondered. Unfortunately for his peace of mind, he thought about it quite a lot.

They were lucky and got a table outside on the deck. "This will really be nice when it gets a little darker and we can see the lights on the water," Faye commented.

"Yes. Would you like to order a drink?"

Faye hesitated.

"I'm going to have a martini."

"All right, then I'll join you."

While they waited for their drinks to arrive, David looked out over the smooth water and Faye, under cover of studying the menu, looked at him. In his jeans, white knit shirt and casual jacket he could have stepped off one of the boats moored below them. He looked muscular and fit enough to be an America's Cup racer. His glasses didn't detract from his appearance, either, she thought. Why was such an appealing man unmarried? Maybe he had a serious girlfriend back in Baltimore. Again she tried to picture the type of woman David would take out. Someone older? Someone sophisticated and well-educated like himself? Not someone who'd had to drop out of high school because of a teenage pregnancy. The thought made her scowl down at the list of entrées.

After the waiter came with their drinks and took their dinner orders, Faye toyed with the olive in her cocktail and studied David more openly. "You said you spent two years at Whipsnade. What did you do there?''

"I was the keeper for various animals."

"Which ones?"

He ticked off the names on his fingers. "Lions, tigers, bears, wombats, zebras, gnus, camels, giraffes."

"Sounds like Noah's ark."

He looked amused. "It was a bit like that."

"Which were your favorites?" For Faye this was tantamount to asking his philosophy of life. She was sure that David's answer would tell her a lot about him.

"Let me see." He put his hands behind his head, leaned back and looked up at the darkening sky where stars along with a sharp white sliver of moon were just beginning to pierce the azure gloom. "That's an easy question to answer, actually. My favorite animal has always been the giraffe."

"The giraffe?"

He nodded. "I remember the first time I saw one walk." His expression softened. "It was as if a tree started to drift across the landscape. They are the tallest mammal on earth and yet they move as gracefully as deer and as silently as clouds." His mouth curved in a reflective smile. "The beauty of their enormous dark eyes has to be seen to be believed. And they are such delicate, polite, gentle creatures. In my opinion, they and not the lions are the true aristocrats of the animal kingdom." He sat up and took a self-conscious sip of his martini. "I must sound like a fool, going on that way."

"No," Faye said, "no, you sound..." Wonderful was the word she wanted to use, but she choked it back. How could she tell David O'Neill that she thought he was wonderful when she'd already told him something like that under the influence of phencyclidine? He would think she was having some sort of relapse. She toyed with her fork. "I've been thinking about Violet. Will she need any special care?"

"I'd like to suggest some adjustments in her diet and she'll need to be treated very gently." David gave Faye a thoughtful look. "Keep in mind that this is a traumatic situation for her. She'll have to be monitored very carefully. In fact, I'm going to suggest a camera be set up in her compartment so that she can be watched around the clock. That's one of the things I wanted to talk to you about tonight."

Faye didn't answer because just then the food arrived.

"I see your vegetarianism doesn't extend to seafood," he commented, glancing over at her plate.

"No. You can't grow up around here and not eat crabs and clams and oysters." She dipped a clam in sauce and returned the conversation to Violet's problems. "I think a camera is a good idea. What were the other things you wanted to talk to me about?"

"The baby's postnatal care, for one."

Faye waited expectantly, but when David concentrated on his crab cake rather than elaborate, she leaned forward and asked, "What do you mean? Violet will take care of her baby herself, won't she?"

"Probably not. I've had a look at her records and this is her second pregnancy. Her first infant died because she refused to nurse it. Chances are this baby will have to be taken away from her and raised in a nursery, which means it will have a one-in-three chance of survival." When Faye frowned, David put down his fork and added, "That's one of the problems with gorillas in captivity. They often abandon their young."

"Really? But why? Why would they do such a dreadful thing?"

"It's not out of any evil intent," he reassured her, a little startled by the strength of her reaction. "In nature they learn how to take care of their offspring by growing up in a family, being fed and groomed by their mothers and seeing other mothers care for their babies. Apes raised in zoos abandon their young because they simply don't know what to do with them. They're too much like us. They need to learn how to behave, and I'm afraid mothering isn't really all that instinctive."

"Oh, I disagree," Faye declared. "Mothering *is* instinctive!"

David wanted to explain that he'd meant the mechanics of mothering, but Faye didn't give him the chance.

"Next to survival, it's got to be the strongest instinct there is. From the moment you feel your baby move inside you, you love and want it. It doesn't matter how difficult your circumstances are. I would never have abandoned..." She stopped, and tears sprang to her eyes as she realized what she was about to say.

Staring across the table at her, David was torn by a myriad of emotions. He reached for her hand. "Faye, I know that you lost a child when you were very young. Would you like to tell me about it?"

She looked down at her plate. "I already told you."

"Not really. You weren't yourself then."

"I never talk about it to anyone."

"Maybe you should. Maybe you should talk to me. Think of me as your doctor. As your therapist, if you like."

That wasn't how she thought of him. Nevertheless, a torrent of pent-up words and feelings rushed past her guard. "All right," she heard herself say. "It happened when I was only seventeen."

CHAPTER SEVEN

"He was the local football hero, and I had worshiped him from afar ever since ninth grade." Faye pushed a slice of tomato around with her fork.

"Were you going steady with this young man?" David asked. Already it was beginning to sound like a story he'd heard a million times.

"Not until that summer when he came home from college to shuck oysters at Wally's plant. Jim had never noticed me before. I was always such a skinny tomboy. But by that time I had blossomed out a bit and he made a big play for me."

David tried to imagine Faye at seventeen. She looked so young and fresh now. At that age she must have been spring incarnate, as tender and fragile as a tightly furled rosebud and just as vulnerable.

"When Jim started asking me out, I practically swooned at his feet." That wasn't an overstatement, Faye thought. She'd been so blind with adoration for him that she'd actually been walking into things.

"And then you got pregnant."

"Yes." She stared out at the water. It was dark now. Only the stars and the gently bobbing lights of the moored sailboats streaked the river. "It shouldn't have happened. I mean, I had been raised around dogs and horses and farm animals all my life. I knew the facts of life. But somehow I didn't connect them with . . ."

"With love?"

"Yes. I should have known better."

"You were very young."

"That's my only excuse. I thought I was in love. I thought he was, too. That's certainly what he told me. But Jim was horrified when he found out about the baby. He wanted me to get an abortion, and he was really angry when I refused."

"What happened?"

Faye laughed humorlessly and pushed her plate away. Though she'd eaten only half her clams, she knew she wasn't going to finish the rest of her meal. "It was an incredible mess. His parents were local people. They didn't like me or my family much, but they thought he should marry me—you know, do the honorable thing. A wedding was arranged. Then, at the last moment, Jim just disappeared."

"Disappeared?"

"He just ran off. I guess anything was better than having to marry me." Restlessly her fingers smoothed the material of her slacks over her crossed knee.

"Did you ever hear from him again?"

"No, never. His folks moved away not long after that."

David hesitated. "And the baby?"

"I miscarried when I was around five months gone. It . . . she didn't survive."

David stared at Faye's pale face. Sitting there gazing blankly out into the night and reliving what should have been the happy, carefree years of her youth, she looked utterly forlorn and his heart went out to her. "You've had a rough time of it."

She nodded, her thoughts still enmeshed in the past. "Yes, but losing the baby and getting jilted was just the beginning. At first I was so depressed that nothing seemed to matter. Then I wanted to run away. It wasn't easy living here where everyone knew about me. But my parents wouldn't allow that and after a few months I tried to pull myself together." She shook her head. "I really tried. I even passed my high school equivalency, enrolled in college and started taking classes."

"What was your major?"

"Animal husbandry. I thought I'd like to help my father run our farm."

"Sounds reasonable."

"Yes, but that didn't work out, either. My mother was killed in a car accident. Six months later I lost my father in a hotel fire. Well..." She made a sound in her throat. "After that I just fell apart. If it hadn't been for Wally, I don't know what would have happened to me."

David ran his thumb along the edge of his plate. "Is that when he gave you Kong to raise?"

"Yes." She turned toward him. "I couldn't run my folks' farm all by myself, so I sold it and moved into my grandmother's little house in Haverton. But I really didn't know what I wanted to do. My life didn't seem worth much. By giving me Kong, Wally changed all that," she said earnestly. "David, I know you're upset because he didn't get professional advice soon enough and made some mistakes with the animals at the park."

"Some serious mistakes. And about certain things he still won't listen to reason."

"I can see your point of view. He's always been stubborn and seems to get more so with every passing year."

David remained silent. In his opinion, Wallace Gaffey suffered from more than mere stubbornness.

"But," Faye continued, "I could never be angry with my uncle. He's been wonderful to me, and I just owe him too much. Kong and my work at the children's zoo gave me a new lease. Then when Wally started making plans for Wilderness Worlds... Well, it was a whole new world opening up for me, too. I'll always be grateful to him." A random breeze lifted a strand of her fine straight hair and blew it across her forehead. As David studied the silken pattern of it against her skin, he pushed away his own plate and signaled the waiter.

When their plates had been cleared and they each had a cup of something hot to drink, David added cream to his coffee and stirred it thoughtfully. What Faye had told him explained a lot, he mused—her devotion to her uncle, her commitment to the zoo and its animals. But he still had unanswered questions. Her social life, for instance. She was so pretty and appealing, yet under the influence of the phencyclidine she'd said she was lonely and claimed not to have any lovers. Could that possibly be true?

As David looked speculatively across at her, Faye sat once again locked in her own thoughts. Although she hadn't intended telling him her story, she didn't regret it now that she had. What a peculiar relationship was developing between her and this man. In so many respects they were strangers, yet in other ways he knew her more intimately than almost anyone else. The reverse wasn't true, however. She still knew next to nothing about him. Was that because he didn't want her to get too close to him? Or, perhaps, because he, too, had something to hide?

"You must think I'm some sort of dimwit," she said aloud. "Every time we're together I do something weird—first what happened with the banana. Now I roll out all the skeletons in my closet."

"Faye, I think you're a very bright and lovely young woman. I'm honored that you've told me about yourself." He gazed at her a moment and then continued. "I realize that you're not altogether comfortable around me, and I don't blame you. It was just fate that we got off on the wrong foot. And I'm sorry, really sorry."

He sounded sincere and Faye's curiosity was aroused. "Why?"

"Because we're going to be working together, and I wish we could be friends." He wished they could be more, but that was quite impossible, he told himself. She was too young and too vulnerable.

Shaking off a faint twinge of disappointment, Faye smiled. "I don't see any reason why we can't be friends."

"Good."

"In fact," she added with growing enthusiasm, "I'm looking forward to having your help with the gorillas. It's wonderful to be able to ask questions and get the answers from someone who really knows what he's talking about."

"Thanks for the vote of confidence." Smiling, David called for the check.

"There are a million things I'd like to ask."

"Then why don't you fire away on the drive home? We can stop in and see how Kong, Daisy Mae and Violet are doing, if you want."

"I'd like that."

"Great. Sure you don't want dessert?"

"Absolutely."

"Then let's get started."

The drive back from Oxford was very different from the trip up. Comfortably ensconced in the Volvo's soft leather passenger seat, Faye pinned her gaze on David's shadowy profile and began to pick his brains. "What happens when a gorilla refuses to nurse her newborn?"

"Sometimes she just carries it around with her while it gets weaker and weaker. Other times she treats it too roughly or ignores it. It's a very sad thing to watch. You sense that she's very disturbed because she'd like to do the right thing. Trouble is she doesn't know how because she hasn't been taught by one of her kind."

Faye was silent a moment, reflecting on this. "Is there any way that a human could teach Violet how to be a mother?"

In the dark interior of the car, David slanted Faye a brief look. "As a matter of fact, it has been done."

"Really?"

"Yes. It was a research project at San Diego's Wild Animal Park. The mother was Dolly, a Western lowland gorilla captured in Africa at the age of nine months. Like Violet, she'd never seen a baby gorilla until she gave birth. She resisted her baby's attempt to cling to her and he had to be taken away."

"How terrible." Faye imagined the tiny little creature trying to hold on to a mother who didn't know what to do with it and felt her throat constrict. "What happened then?"

"When Dolly became pregnant for the second time, a student at San Diego State University began to train her." David shot Faye another glance. She was listening intently. "At first he showed her movies of apes caring for their young," he explained.

"Really? Did she pay attention?"

"Unfortunately, no. So then he tried training her with a handmade canvas doll."

"A doll? What an interesting idea. Did it work?"

David chuckled. "Yes, as a matter of fact. He spent hours working with her through the bars of her cage, rewarding her when she performed correctly."

"What did he teach her?"

"Let me see if I remember." David took his foot off the gas pedal, downshifted and turned into Wilderness Worlds. After his vehicle had been waved through by the guard, he parked and he and Faye got out. As they strolled toward the ape house, he recounted what he remembered of Dolly's training. "As I recall, there were four commands. Something like, 'Pick up the baby'; 'Show me the baby'; 'Be nice to the baby'— meaning Dolly should hold the doll to her breast and pat it—and 'Turn the baby'—in case Dolly was holding the doll upside down or with its face away from her."

Once again he glanced over at Faye. He sensed that she was taut with excitement.

"What happened when Dolly's child was born?"

"She began caring for it right away. The student stayed around to prompt her when she became confused by the baby's crying. But after a while she didn't need him."

"Oh, that's wonderful!"

"Yes, it confirmed what we'd suspected about primates. A lot of their behavior is learned, not instinctive."

Faye was too caught up in her own thoughts to listen closely. At the entry to the ape house, she stopped and faced him. "Why couldn't I do the same thing for Violet?"

Instead of answering, David held the door open. Once they were inside, he said, "You could, but it wouldn't be easy. You'd have to conduct training sessions every day. Apes have short attention spans. They're not easy to teach."

Faye lowered her voice. "But I could try, couldn't I?"

"I suppose. We'll have to talk about it."

Inside the ape house all was quiet. Betty, a local college student who worked part-time at the children's zoo had been assigned to watch the three apes. Obviously she'd dozed off, and when Faye and David walked in, she jerked awake and looked around at them guiltily.

"How are they doing?" Faye whispered.

"Doing fine as far as I can tell. You can see for yourself." She pointed to the right. "They're all asleep."

Faye tiptoed over to the enclosures with David just behind her. She paused to look at all the gorillas, but finally concentrated her attention on Violet. The pregnant animal was sleeping with her knees drawn up and her long hairy arms curled protectively over her rounded belly. "Poor creature. This must all be so hard on her."

"Yes," David agreed. "She's doing pretty well, considering."

"I want to help her."

"It won't be easy."

"I know, but I want to try."

Speculatively David looked down at Faye. Maybe he'd misjudged her. Maybe she was tougher than she looked—and had sounded earlier at the restaurant. He'd heard the determination in her voice just now, and he respected her more for it. Actually, he'd been hoping for a development like this. It would be fascinating to conduct the Dolly experiment. "All right," he said. "I'll give you all the help I can. But I'm afraid, since I can only be around on weekends, you're going to be pretty much on your own with her."

"I don't mind."

"Remember, don't go into the compartment. Violet probably wouldn't hurt you deliberately, but like most apes, she doesn't know her own strength."

"I understand, and I won't do anything foolish." She looked up at him and laughed. "Believe me, I've learned my lesson."

A few minutes later they left the ape house and walked out into the moonlit night.

"Where to now?" David asked.

Faye shot him a surprised look. "Home, I guess."

"All right."

He guided her back to the car and headed it out onto the road toward Haverton. As he drove silently, Faye began to feel nervous again. Did David regard this as a date or a business meeting? What would happen when they arrived at her house? Would he want to come in? Should she invite him? He was without a doubt the most appealing man she'd met in a long time, and she wanted to get to know him better. But it would be embarrassing to entertain him in the place where she'd made such an idiot of herself. Faye glanced at the clock on the car's dashboard. It was almost ten. "Are you driving back to Baltimore tonight?"

"I suppose so."

"It's going to be very late when you get there."

"True. And I could use another cup of coffee to keep me awake," he said as he pulled up in front of her house. He killed the engine and turned to her. "Would you mind?"

Like a deer caught in a headlight Faye stared back and blurted, "I don't have any coffee. You drank it all up."

"Oh? Sorry. Tea will do."

Since he hadn't left her any choice, she said, "Of course. Won't you come in and let me fix you a cup?"

"Thanks. Don't mind if I do." David slid out from behind the wheel, but by the time he'd strolled around to the passenger side of the car, she was already out and on her way up the walk.

As he followed at a leisurely pace, David wondered why he had forced Faye to invite him in. He hadn't intended to do that, and it was all too obvious that she'd agreed only under duress. He didn't have any designs on her, did he? No, he told himself. He didn't need to complicate his life right now, and it wouldn't be fair to her. What this pretty young woman needed was some nice local farmboy who would give her a home and a half dozen kids, not a dead-end affair with the likes of him.

Inside the house, Faye stood still for a moment, staring around the living room as if she'd never seen it before. David searched for a way to put her at ease, but truthfully he was feeling far from comfortable himself. He and Faye had experienced something uniquely intimate in this setting and now it all came back in a rush.

"I'll just go into the kitchen and put the kettle on," Faye said a little breathlessly.

"Mind if I come along with you?"

"Of course not. Make yourself at home."

Once again he followed behind, his gaze lingering on the gracefully rounded lines of her body. So far there'd been plenty of chemistry between them but not much biology. If he wanted to keep things that way it had been really stupid to invite himself in, he realized. Now, looking at her and remembering the way she'd once begged him to make love to her, he was beginning to feel warm below the belt. *Watch it, O'Neill,* he warned himself. Just as soon as he decently could, he'd leave.

While Faye busied herself in front of the stove, David pulled out a pressed-oak chair and straddled it. "How long have you lived here?"

"Almost five years." She paused to reach for a pretty blue and white china teapot that sat on a high shelf. David's gaze went to her lifted breasts.

"Couldn't you have gone back to school after your parents died?"

"I could have. Somehow, it seemed pointless. I felt out of place on a college campus. It wasn't that I was any older than the other students. It was just ... after everything that had happened I felt worlds apart."

"How old are you?"

"Twenty-five."

"You look younger."

She grimaced. "Yes, I know. Everyone tells me that." Faye turned and under cover of wiping off a painted tray studied David. Sitting there, he appeared so cool and self-possessed. How did she appear to him? Did he see her as some sort of childish hick? Suddenly she wished she *had* gone back to school. Perhaps if she'd completed her formal education she wouldn't feel quite so at a loss around him. He was like no one she'd ever met before. What was it that set him apart? His confidence? His worldliness? Though he didn't put on airs to impress her, she sensed that he knew things, had done things of which she couldn't even dream. That was true of some of the other men she'd met, of course. But none of them affected her the way he did. None of them could make her skin go hot just by looking at her.

"Did you ever consider leaving the Eastern Shore?" he questioned.

"Yes. I would have liked to start fresh. But..." Faye shrugged. "I didn't know where I could go. I'm a country girl, and this is my home," she added a bit defiantly. "I couldn't imagine being happy living in a city with strangers all around me. So I stayed and made the best of things."

The kettle started to whistle, and she turned away to make the tea.

"Can I help?"

Faye gave a little start, realizing that he'd come up behind her and was standing very close. His compact, muscled body fairly radiated a compelling virility, and try as she might, she couldn't turn off her sensitivity to that animal magnetism. His low voice so close to her ear set her nerve endings vibrating like tuning forks. "You can carry the tray into the living room," she told him huskily.

"Certainly." Deftly he reached out and lifted the tray without rattling a single cup. Then he walked to-

ward the entry in that smoothly controlled gait of his.
Everything about him was quiet and controlled, Faye
thought. Yet somehow, that only seemed to underline
his masculinity—as if behind that leashed manner
there were a jungle cat on the prowl.

As she followed David out she allowed herself the
pleasure of admiring the view from the rear. Maybe he
wasn't tall, but he was tall enough—and so well put
together. It didn't seem fair that he'd undressed her
but she would never see him. As he preceded her into
the living room, she couldn't stop herself from trying
to picture him naked.

"Where would you like me to put this?" David had
pivoted to shoot her an inquiring look. The split second her eyes met his, she felt blood swarm to her face.
For a long moment she stood before him, speechless
and glowing like a bug light.

"Something wrong?" he asked as he observed her
flushed cheeks.

"No, it's just that . . ."

"Just that you're embarrassed to have me in your
house." His lips twisted and he set the tray down on
the coffee table. "Look, let's be honest with each
other. Would you like me to leave?"

"No, no, I wouldn't." She hurried over to him and
touched his arm. "Really, I've enjoyed your company tonight. Won't you sit down and let me pour you
some tea?" She gestured at the couch behind them and
then dropped down on it so that he would have to stay.

After a moment, he sat next to her. "I was hoping
that we could forget about that whole banana thing,"
he muttered. "But it's impossible, isn't it?"

"No. Really. It's just me—for me it's especially...difficult." Keeping her face averted from his, she started to pour tea into both their cups.

"Why 'especially'?"

Conscious that her skin was still very pink, she raised her eyes. "David, you have to understand how it's been for me, living here." She set down the teapot and began to twist her fingers together. "It's not easy to be an unwed mother in a small town. Everybody for miles around knows it. And afterward, they talk about everything you do. It's like—" She hesitated. "It's as if you have an audience just sitting there waiting for you to make another mistake."

David was silent while he digested this. "Was dating a problem for you?"

"A big problem. For the longest time I didn't date at all." She folded her hands tightly. "For one thing, all the young men in this area knew about me, which meant I had a certain reputation. It was a reputation I felt I had to live down, so I didn't really want to go out with any of them. And then, to be honest—" Her green eyes seemed to go a shade deeper. "After the way Jim treated me, I wasn't really much interested in the opposite sex."

"But that was a long time ago. Surely...I mean, it's been seven years . . . surely you're past all that."

Faye shook her head. "Not really. Maybe if I were in some big, anonymous city I'd be past it. But living here, with these people, with reminders everywhere, I don't think I'll ever be able to put it entirely behind me. Oh," she added quickly, "I do date." Last year there had been occasional evenings out with the high school basketball coach. And Don, a salesman with a wacky sense of humor, looked her up when he was in town. "But nothing serious, nothing..." She paused again, searching for the right way of putting what she wanted to say. Finally abandoning the attempt, she gave David a quick look and then lowered her gaze to the cups on the tray. "I've been thinking about why I reacted the way I did to the phencyclidine. It's unusual, isn't it?"

"Yes," David replied. "A reaction like that isn't unheard of, but it's uncommon." Suddenly he knew what she was thinking. Faye was a healthy young woman who, if she was telling the truth, had spent most of her adult life walking on eggshells around the opposite sex. No wonder her suddenly unshackled libido had gone into overdrive.

"I behaved that way because..." She hesitated, not quite able to say the words.

David finished the sentence for her. "Because you were sexually frustrated."

Faye straightened and for a long moment she and David sat on the couch with their knees slanted toward each other like opposing sides of a triangle. "But I'm certain," she finally said in a low, husky voice, "that I wouldn't have behaved that way with a man who wasn't...who wasn't physically attractive to me."

David's blood began to drum. "Am I physically attractive to you?" he asked.

"Yes."

Finally she lifted her eyes to his so that their gazes met and fused. Her features seemed to burn themselves into his consciousness—her hair, her cheeks, her lips. Attractive didn't begin to describe the effect she was having on him. But instead of trying to put it into words, he could only mutter thickly, "Same here," and reach for her.

From the first time he'd walked into this house David had wanted her. Before, knowing she wasn't in control of herself, he'd had to resist her encouraging words. Now as her admission made the fire already glowing in his loins flare out of control, he didn't stop to debate the situation. An instant later they were kissing feverishly.

David's hand stroked up and down Faye's back. As their kiss went on and grew more intense, his restless fingertips memorized the contours of her rib cage, measured the span of her narrow waist, absorbed the silken vitality of her skin as if they could not only touch but taste and smell and see all at the same time.

Faye's hands were busy as well. At first they locked around his neck. Then they inched up to his hair and began sifting through the short, crisp strands, unconsciously tugging now and then as if to assure herself that he was really there and that he was hers. All the while little gasps, moans and sighs punctuated the room's sudden dense silence.

"Faye...my God..." David muttered. Drawing back the merest fraction, he lowered his lips to her cheeks, her forehead, the smooth skin below her hairline. Just kissing her like this felt unbelievably good to him—as if he had thrown himself into the heart of an open rose and was drowning in the most delicious nectar imaginable. The fragrance of her just-washed hair seduced his senses, and her warm breath on his throat made his heart race. Her body felt so delicious and eager! Suddenly he was on fire to lose himself completely in her incredible sweetness.

There could be no doubt that she was willing, he told himself. Kiss for kiss, touch for touch, she'd met his overtures without retreating. Now, eyes tightly closed, she clung to him as if afraid he might suddenly vanish. But he wasn't going anywhere—not when he had this lovely bundle of yielding femininity in his arms. On that thought his hands slipped around to caress her soft breasts. Against his fingertips her nipples thrust imperiously, and he could feel her heart racing with the same delirium that fueled his.

Balanced on the knife edge between pain and pleasure, David groaned and pressed his palm to the small of Faye's back, lowering her flat on the couch. In the next instant their bodies were meshed, her slight movements beneath him keenly erotic. He rubbed his leg tantalizingly against the slim length of hers. In return she pressed her knee to the outside of his thigh in an unconscious provocation that made him want to tear her clothes off then and there.

He didn't normally attack a woman in this frenzied manner. In about another minute he'd be losing control of himself completely. The realization made David struggle to regain some small measure of sanity. Before things went any further there was something he had to get settled.

"Faye," he said, fighting hard for the restraint to draw back from her. "Faye, I want to make love to you. Is that what you want, too?"

Dazedly she stared up at him. She'd been so carried away by his kisses and his caressing hands that it was a full minute before she could even understand what he was saying. As she tried to make sense of his words, she saw the flush along his cheekbones and felt the masculine thrust of him against her stomach. His arousal didn't offend her. How could it when she was as aroused as he was? Her breasts and thighs glowed and she wished he hadn't asked her any questions because she didn't want to have to think. Right now she only wanted to feel.

When she finally managed to reply, her words were slurred. Even to her own ears she sounded half-drunk. "I . . . I don't know."

But that didn't settle the matter. David continued to hold himself away from her while his eyes demanded a better response.

Faye struggled to gather her wits. "I guess I don't want just a one-night stand, if that's what you're asking."

"What do you expect of me, Faye? What kind of lover do you want?"

Her tongue felt as if it were tied in knots. Why was he posing these questions? Jim had never asked her such things. He'd been solely concerned with his own needs and desires. But of course her surrender to Jim had ended in disaster. The memory jolted her enough so that at last she was able to give David an answer. "I want someone who won't go away." She knew that sounded childish. But, God help her, she also knew that it was true.

"Someone who won't go away?"

"Someone who'll be here." Her hands tightened around his neck as she willed him to say the right thing.

Above her, David was almost frantic with frustration. But tempted as he was to ignore Faye's words and kiss her into submission, he couldn't lie. "I'll be here until Violet has her baby. Maybe a couple of months after that, but I can't promise anything more."

"A couple of months?" She stared up at him. "But I thought—"

"Faye, the job here is just temporary. I've applied for a grant and it looks as if it's going to come through. If it does I'll be going to England."

With a sinking sensation, David watched the desire slowly drain out of Faye's face. Her body went limp beneath his and her hands fell away.

"I see."

She averted her eyes, and he knew it wasn't going to be any good. Carefully he levered himself away and sat up. Then, as matter-of-factly as he could, he helped her upright, too. She began to straighten her clothes, tugging down her top and brushing her hair out of her eyes with jerky little motions.

"I'm sorry," she said. "This was really dumb of me."

"It's my fault. I'm the one who should be apologizing," David replied grittily. He leaned his head against the back of the couch and looked up at the ceiling. His body hadn't calmed down yet, and he silently cursed himself. Wasn't he old enough to know better than this?

"I suppose this grant is really important to you," Faye muttered.

"Yes, it's important." He hesitated. "And there's something else you should know. I'm not exactly sure what you meant by 'someone who won't go away,' but I'm not the marrying kind, Faye. Any relationship we had would just be—"

"Just be fun and games?"

He didn't like putting it that way, but maybe brutal honesty was best. "Yes."

Faye's heart felt like a ball of lead suspended by a dangerously stretched cord in her chest, and she couldn't think of anything else to do but look down at her hands.

"Faye, I'm really sorry. This shouldn't have happened and, honestly, I didn't mean it to."

From the corner of her eye she saw him spreading his own hands, indicating the couch—which only made her feel worse. In a brief spurt of resentment she wished he hadn't asked for her consent. If he'd kept his mouth shut they would probably have gone ahead and made love. At least that way she might have gotten it out of her system, though she knew there would have been regrets later. Aloud she said, "Why? I wasn't exactly uncooperative. I wanted you." If she were really going to be honest, she'd admit that ever since the last time he'd been in her house she'd been fantasizing about being in bed with him.

"I'm not sure that's really true."

She slanted him a look. "You think I'm still reacting to that drug?"

"I think we both had an experience that distorted things between us. Besides, by now I know enough about you to be sure that a dead-end affair with someone like me is the last thing you need."

"Oh?" At that she raised her head. "What is it that you think I need?"

Now that David's body had at last cooled off, he was beginning to feel ridiculous. It was absurd to sit here lecturing Faye. He should just get up and leave. But he felt he had to answer her questions. "You're a sweet, vulnerable girl. You need a man who'll be able to appreciate that—one who can settle down with you in a big old house where there's plenty of room for half a dozen kids and a full complement of dogs and cats. That lucky guy, unfortunately, isn't me."

As she continued to stare at him, her eyes seemed to take him apart and put him back together all over again. Suddenly he was uncomfortably reminded of that tigress he'd once spotted peering at him through the grass.

Faye cleared her throat and said very distinctly, "You're wrong. I'm not a sweet, vulnerable girl. I'm a woman. And one more thing, Dr. O'Neill—I wasn't really a laboratory rat, was I?"

"What?"

"When I fixed breakfast for you that morning, you told me that you viewed the whole thing between us clinically. That wasn't true, was it?"

If he hadn't been feeling so damn foolish, David would have laughed. He'd look pretty ridiculous trying to stick to that little fairy story now. "No," he admitted. Then, quickly, he rose to his feet. "I think I'd better go."

Faye continued to look at him in that same unnerving fashion. "Yes," she said. "I'll see you to the door."

CHAPTER EIGHT

SEVERAL WEEKS LATER David and Bill Abbott walked into the pool area of the Johns Hopkins Athletic Center. As was their custom, they planned to get in a swim before their weekly lunch together at Uncle Lee's.

"Listen, Dave, we're throwing a little dinner party Friday night." Bill padded to the edge of the water and dipped a cautious toe. Then he looked back over his shoulder. "An old college friend of Donna's is in town interviewing for a job with the Psych department. Real attractive gal, divorced but no children." Bill winked. "On campus the other day Donna pointed you out to her, and she indicated that she wouldn't be averse to meeting you. How about coming over and satisfying my old lady's matchmaking instincts?"

"Thanks, but I think I'll pass." David dropped his towel on a bench. He knew Bill meant well, but right now a blind date was the last thing he wanted.

Bill was in the process of sliding his bulk into the chlorined water. When his feet hit bottom, he glanced up, his eyes sparkling with interest. "Have you got another lady friend hidden away somewhere, or what?"

"No."

"Come on, what about this job of yours on the Eastern Shore? Is there a beautiful water-ski instructor over there that you're rendezvousing with on the sly?"

"Sorry to disappoint you." David began a few preliminary stretches to loosen up before he hit the water.

"But there's a female somewhere on the other side of the Chesapeake Bay Bridge who interests you, isn't there? I can tell from the gleam in your eye."

David had to laugh. "There's a pregnant gorilla named Violet," he admitted.

Bill rolled his eyes. "A guy with a body like yours can't be that desperate. How do you keep so damn trim, anyhow? You're all muscle."

Lithely David bent from the waist and touched his outstretched palms to the tile floor. "When I go home at night there's no nice little wife waiting there with a martini and a fattening meal. I'm lucky if I can scratch up a beer and a frozen hamburger pattie."

"Maybe, but I bet you don't have any trouble scratching up interested females. Come on, who is it?"

David straightened. "Well, Violet does have a very attractive keeper."

"Aha! So that's why you're taking such an interest in this cockamamy zoo of Wallace Gaffey's. What's the old boy really like, by the way?"

"You chose the right word. 'Cockamamy' about says it. You know, when I checked in the first weekend he didn't remember hiring me. His secretary had to remind me."

Bill laughed. "Not playing with a full deck, huh?"

"That's my theory. Though all the people who work for him think he walks on water." David's eyes darkened as he thought of Faye and how blind she was to her uncle's failings.

"You're thinking about this mystery woman of yours, aren't you?" Grinning from ear to ear, Bill began to tread water. "Come on, what's she like? Tall? Brunette? Built?"

"Small, blond, and very nicely put together. But," David added quickly, "she's young, for one thing. And—"

"And you go for the mature, sophisticated type. This lady on the West Coast that you're planning to spend the year in England with—what's her name?"

"Grace."

"Yes, well she's older than you, isn't she? Just how serious is it between the two of you?"

"Grace and I are friends and colleagues, and we don't crowd each other."

"I get it." Bill winked again. "It's not the love match of the century, but it's convenient. Well, more power to you." He kicked off from the edge of the pool and began a lazy backstroke.

Hands on hips, David stood watching him for a moment. Then he walked to the pool's rim and dived in. When he surfaced about fifteen feet from the edge he began a smooth Australian crawl. As his body sliced through the water, he thought about Bill's comment on Grace. Was that all their relationship really was—convenient? He had to admit that he really hadn't missed her much lately. And judging from her brief notes, she wasn't exactly pining away for him. When she wrote, her letters were breezy reports on her work and their mutual friends—and one that wasn't so mutual. Mark Benson's name came up a lot, with Grace constantly singing his praises.

So far there'd been no further word on the grant, so until it came through they'd agreed not to make any more plans for their year together abroad. "Keep your fingers crossed," she'd written.

When David swam his final lap and grasped the tile rim to take a breather before hauling himself out of the water, he found Bill watching for him. "I get short of breath just watching you. How many laps did you swim, O'Neill. Twenty? Thirty?"

"Thirty-six."

"I've got to admit, you look damn smooth and fast. Were you on the swim team in college?"

David pushed wet hair out of his eyes. "I was a scholarship boy, so I made it my business to qualify for just about every team. To get the kind of education I wanted, I needed more than top grades. I needed to be good in athletics, too."

"You came from a poor family?"

"Poor and numerous." David pulled himself out and sat down next to Bill with his legs dangling over the edge. He didn't care to talk about his family. Perhaps Bill sensed that, because with his next question he referred back to their earlier conversation.

"Tell me about this pregnant gorilla."

"It's an interesting case." Briefly David outlined the experiment he and Faye were conducting.

"You mean this little blond keeper of yours is actually going in there every day and spending hours mothering a cloth doll in front of a gorilla? Holy moly!"

David chuckled. "Put that way, it does sound a little odd. But yes, she's really doing it. I have to hand it to her, she's no shirker. She's putting everything she's got into this project."

Actually, during the past few weeks David had been amazed by Faye's patience and dedication. Not only had she followed his instructions to the letter, but she'd been faithful—spending hours alone with Violet in the ape house. And it was paying off. The last time David had been up to Wilderness Worlds, Faye had shown him the fruits of her labor. When she'd passed the cloth doll through Violet's bars, the pregnant gorilla had picked it up and unhesitatingly followed all of Faye's commands.

"Hey, congratulations," he'd told her. "You've done a great job."

She'd given a little shrug. "Maybe you shouldn't congratulate me yet. We don't really know whether it will work or not."

"No," he'd admitted. "But you still deserve a lot of credit. There aren't many people who have the care and concern to do a job like this."

For a moment they'd just looked at each other. Since that night when he'd walked out of her house, they'd kept things between them strictly professional. Faye had been reserved, her manner cool and distant. And he'd taken his cues from her. It was best, he'd told himself. She was looking for a soul mate and that couldn't be him. Still, his work with the gorillas had meant that he spent a lot of hours conferring with Faye. Each time they met there were unspoken questions between them and a palpably mounting tension—at least, that was how it was for him. He couldn't fool himself that he wouldn't still like to go to bed with her. The sooner he finished his stint at Wilderness Worlds and moved on, the better for his peace of mind, he thought.

After David's lunch with Bill, the rest of the day flowed along in its customary routine. Around three o'clock he left the lab to get himself a cup of coffee from the machine down the hall. He was carrying it back when he passed a student lounge and heard a familiar feminine voice. Stopping so abruptly that the hot coffee sloshed over the edge of the cup, he turned and looked into the open doorway. Several students were sitting around watching a local talk show on a beat-up television set at the far end of the room. It had been Faye's voice that David heard and to his amazement hers was the face dominating the seventeen-inch screen.

Slowly he walked into the room and stood staring. Why was she on television? Then he remembered her saying something about doing PR for Wilderness Worlds. That must be the explanation. His coffee forgotten, he cocked his head. She had a wolf cub in her lap and was stroking its ears with one hand. The other held a bone-shaped biscuit for the animal to gnaw on while she talked to the suave curly-haired host. The man was leaning toward her and smiling as if she and not the cub were what he found interesting.

"The wolf is a beautiful and fascinating American predator that we intend to feature when Wilderness Worlds opens to the public this summer," she was saying. "Don, your audience might be interested to know that the timber wolf could be found all over North America at one time, but now it's extremely rare."

Don's oily response was drowned out by one of the male students in front of the TV set, who chose that moment to do a very good imitation of a wolf call. "Not around here, baby," he commented loudly. "What a dish! Wish I were that wolf she's got on her lap. I'd have her for my supper."

Unaware that David was standing behind them, the other young men in the room laughed and shouted their agreement. Eyes narrowing, David almost snapped a reprimand. Then he thought better of it and focused his attention back to the screen. They were right. Faye *was* a dish. Around Wilderness Worlds she always wore jeans and a keeper's jacket. But for the TV interview she'd dressed in a stylish green linen suit and silky blouse. The outfit made her look quite different from the way he was used to seeing her. The camera panned back to show her curvy crossed legs and small, elegant feet shod in sexy-looking green sling-back heels.

Then the camera closed in on her lap and David found himself staring at the V where her skirt had settled into the juncture between her hips and crossed legs. Unconsciously lifting his coffee to his lips, David forced himself to concentrate on the way she was dealing with the rambunctious wolf cub. She was handling it and herself very well, he thought. Though she was on television, she didn't seem flustered. Her answers to the smooth-talking host's rather silly questions were direct and to the point. Don was obviously charmed. And suddenly, so was David.

For the first time since that night on her couch, he admitted to himself that what she'd said was true. Faye Johnson might have freckles and an unlined face and the ability to look as if she were about sixteen, but she was not a girl. She was a woman. What's more, she was a very capable woman. He knew that from watching her run things at the children's zoo. It was she who kept the operation working smoothly, and all the other employees there had nothing but respect for her, even Roy Hubbard.

When the interview ended David went back to his lab. But though he spent the rest of the afternoon working with medical students, he had trouble concentrating. He kept thinking about Faye. She must have come to Baltimore for that television show. Of course, she was probably on her way back to the Eastern Shore by now. But what if they'd been on better terms and she'd called or stopped by to see him? What if she'd stayed to have dinner with him and perhaps even gone back to his apartment to make love? That could have happened if he'd told her what she wanted to hear that night on the couch. But he knew he couldn't lie to her.

Still, he couldn't keep Faye out of his mind. It was even worse the next day. David's thoughts kept drifting to Faye at Wilderness Worlds. What was she doing? Was she making any more progress with Violet? The ape's baby was due any day now.

These questions continued nagging him even after he left the office and pulled up in front of the brick building that he now called home. As he sat in his car looking up at the rather grimy windows of his apartment, he made a sudden decision. He didn't feel like spending the evening alone, and tomorrow was a free day. If he left now he could drive over to Haverton before dark. David told himself that it was because he wanted to check on Violet, but he'd never been very good at self-deception. It was really because he wanted to see Faye.

IT WAS LATE—time to go home and fix dinner. But instead of getting up to leave, Faye sat staring through the bars at Violet. "You all right, girl?" she questioned softly.

Violet stood on her hind feet, rubbed her distended belly and moaned. Then she squatted down and gazed unhappily at her keeper.

"You're about to have that baby any minute, aren't you? Think you'll be ready for it when it comes?" Faye looked down at the doll cradled in her own arms and wished she knew the answer. Sure, on command Violet would now pick up a cloth imitation of a baby and hold it gently. But there was more to being a successful mother than that. Since they'd started working together, David had lent Faye several books on the subject. She knew from her reading that the major reason why infant gorillas had to be reared by humans was the refusal of their natural mothers to keep them on the breast where they could grow strong on the mothers' milk.

"Just doesn't seem like the thing to do unless you've seen someone else do it before you, I guess," Faye muttered as she eyed Violet. Had the pregnant ape learned enough about holding an infant against her breast to allow it to suckle?

At that moment the door opened and Betty came in. "Well, your relief is here," she sang out.

Faye turned her head, a thoughtful expression still sobering her face. "Hi. How are you doing?"

Betty shook her dark curls. "I'd be doing great if I didn't have to work tonight. After a day explaining the chick-hatching display to bus loads of school kids, I'm beat."

"I know you're here to keep an eye on Violet. How long is your shift?"

"Two hours now and then another two hours around midnight. Since Roy went with Mr. Gaffey to Alaska, we're short on gorilla watchers."

"I know," Faye said. She had learned of the Alaskan trip only the day before, and it worried her. When Wally had called her into his office to tell her that he and Roy were taking his Lear jet north to make arrangements to buy a bear, he'd seemed almost beside himself with excitement. He'd rubbed his hands together and danced about the office like a six-year-old on Christmas morning. That same afternoon she'd caught sight of the man in the gray sedan driving out of Wilderness Worlds. Though the two events were unrelated, Faye was unsettled.

Betty had started to open a folding chair. "You know, the kids weren't the only ones bugging me. There's a guy who's been hanging around lately asking all sorts of funny questions."

Faye's head jerked up. "What kind of questions?"

"Oh, I don't know. About Wally and the zoo and why he went to Alaska. I'm just a peon. How should I know why he went to Alaska?" Betty grinned. "Another thing I don't know is how you can sit cross-legged on the floor so long."

"Yoga. What did you tell this man?"

The girl shrugged. "Nothing. What's to tell?"

She was right, Faye reflected. There was nothing to tell. It just didn't make sense. Aloud, she said, "Listen, Betty, why don't you go on home and get some rest? I'll take the first shift for you."

The girl's friendly brown eyes widened. "But you've already been here most of the afternoon. You must be exhausted yourself. And it's after dinnertime. Aren't you hungry?"

"Well, now that you mention it..." Faye cocked her head. "What's in that paper bag you've got?"

"A peanut butter sandwich and an apple. Not exactly the gourmet fare you fixed when you invited me for lunch last week."

"Sounds okay to me." Faye shifted her weight. "Tell you what, leave the bag and I'll do your time for you. Is that a fair exchange?"

"Not hardly. Are you really sure?"

"Really."

Betty made a tentative little face. "Well..."

"C'mon. Give me that delicious peanut butter sandwich and scoot." After several more assurances from Faye, Betty finally agreed, deposited the brown bag on the floor and left. When she was gone, Faye waited five minutes and then glanced around. Kong and Daisy Mae had been put in compartments that were out of sight so as not to disturb Violet. From where Faye sat, the building appeared empty, and she knew that at this late time of day it would stay deserted. She would be alone with the expectant gorilla for the next two hours. "Which should be more than enough," she said aloud as she began to unbutton her shirt.

When it lay on the floor next to her, she reached around to unhook her bra. "Violet," she said, glancing up at the ape who'd been watching this unprecedented disrobing curiously, "pay attention. This could mean life or death to the little one you're carrying."

The motions Faye proceeded to go through were no different from what she'd already tried to teach Violet. Only instead of holding the cloth doll up against a blouse or her keeper's jacket, she pressed the imitation baby firmly against her naked breast, making sure that its painted mouth touched her nipple.

Violet seemed fascinated by this display. She looked from Faye's breasts to her own enlarged mammary glands and touched them curiously.

"That's right," Faye encouraged. "We're built pretty much the same, you and I. Only you're a little hairier. And maybe," she added with a chuckle, "a cup size smaller."

After about an hour's work, with frequent interruptions while Violet lost interest and wandered off, the pregnant gorilla began to imitate Faye and hold her own doll close against her breast.

"Good girl!" Faye exclaimed when she saw that the simulated baby's mouth was in the right position. She'd run out of rewards and, still naked from the waist up, turned to fish in Betty's bag for the apple she'd mentioned. Violet was very fond of apples. Faye had just taken it out and was polishing it with her elbow when her skin began to prickle. Instinctively she knew someone was looking at her. Jerking her head around, she gasped and froze. David was standing about fifty feet away, staring.

A split second later, Faye had dropped the apple and was scrambling for her shirt. Seizing it, she rocked back on her heels and held the garment against her breasts.

All the while David stood as if the sight of her had turned him to stone.

"How long have you been there?" she croaked, looking up at him.

"A minute or two." David's voice was husky and as he spoke he started to walk forward.

Faye shivered, though whether it was from the cold or from the start he'd given her, she couldn't guess. "I didn't hear you come in."

"No, you were pretty absorbed in what you were doing." His gray gaze drifted over her bare arms and shoulders and the place where she still clutched the crumpled blouse to her front. "What *were* you doing, by the way?"

Faye's cheeks flamed. "I was trying to teach Violet how to nurse her baby."

"I see. Well, you're certainly much better equipped for the job than that male graduate student at the San Diego zoo ever was." Suddenly David's eyes, which were still fixed on her, gleamed in amusement.

Faye, on the other hand, struggled with annoyance. Was she doomed to perpetually embarrass herself in front of this man? It hadn't been easy keeping her cool while she worked with him these past few weeks. But until this moment she thought she'd been doing a pretty good job.

"Would you mind turning your back?"

"Of course not."

"I know you're a doctor," she added tartly as he swiveled around, "and breasts are about as interesting to you as a head of lettuce would be to a greengrocer." Irritably Faye shook out her blouse and slipped her arms into it.

David set down his medical bag and put his hands on his lean hips. "On the contrary. I've always had a keen interest and admiration for breasts. It's true that in my line of work I've seen quite a few matched pairs. So I can really appreciate yours, which are particularly lovely."

Faye's fingers fumbled as, torn between laughter and anger, she tried to slip a button through its hole. "What do you know about my breasts?"

"Not nearly enough—even though this is the second time I've had the pleasure of seeing them."

Faye's gaze ran over his back, taking in the white short-sleeved shirt and narrow-waisted gray slacks he wore. "Are you flirting with me?"

When he didn't answer, she added, "Why would you bother? You've already made it very clear that you're not interested."

"Can I turn around?"

"No, I'm not finished yet."

"Having trouble with the buttons? Let me see what I can do."

While Faye clutched the edges of her half-open shirt together, David swiveled and walked purposefully toward her. When his feet were inches from hers he hunkered down and took the cloth out of her nerveless fingers. Deftly he slipped the button just beneath her bosom into its closure.

Faye felt as if her skin had suddenly taken on a thrilling new life of its own. She knew that her stiffened nipples must be clearly visible beneath her cotton blouse. It was getting cool in the ape house. Might she claim that for her excuse?

"You button up ladies' blouses very well," she mumbled.

His lids were lowered so that she couldn't make out the expression in his eyes. "It isn't that I've had endless practice." He slid the last button into place. "My lab work involves a lot of surgical procedures. Nimble fingers are a requirement." Balancing on his heels, he waggled his fingers in front of her face and smiled. Then his smile faded and for a long moment they regarded each other. "Faye," he said, "God knows it isn't that I'm not interested. You've been hurt once by a careless man, and I don't want to be the one who does it to you again.''

Resentment surged through her. How dare he treat her as if she were still a naive teenager. She was a woman—a frustrated woman, dammit! "I'm a big girl now. Maybe I should be allowed to decide whether or not I need protection.''

He stared at her, his eyes full of questions. Before he could put any of them into words, Faye cleared her throat and asked, "What are you doing here, anyway? You never came in the middle of the week before.''

Once again his attractive mouth curled up. "Believe me, if I'd known about your topless act, I would have been on the road a long time ago.''

"This is the first time I've done it." Faye would have laughed only David's gaze was fixed on her in a way that made her hold her breath.

"Perfect timing," he said. Then, all at once, his hands went to her shoulders. He leaned forward and their lips touched.

Hardly believing that this was really happening, Faye closed her eyes. But the kiss had barely started when it was abruptly terminated by a yelp from directly behind them. They pulled apart and turned toward Violet's compartment. She was lying on her side moaning and clutching her stomach.

"What is it? What's wrong with her?" Faye exclaimed.

David shook his head. "Looks like my timing really was perfect." He got to his feet and stood studying the unhappy gorilla. "It's likely to be a long night. Violet is going into labor.''

DAVID WAS RIGHT about Violet's condition, but wrong about the timing. Violet delivered what looked like a normal, healthy baby gorilla in less than two hours. Faye, torn by so many different emotions that she couldn't begin to sort them out, observed every minute of the brief labor. As she sat concentrating on Violet's struggle and, with soothing, encouraging words, trying to offer what help she could, she twisted and untwisted her fingers. The drama unfolding before her made her feel frightened, sad and hopeful all at the same time. These emotions were pushed aside by a rush of joy when the baby's tiny dark head appeared. That elation was trebled and quadrupled as his crumpled body finally slipped away from his mother's.

"Way to go!" shouted Peter, the young man who'd arrived to relieve Betty and then stayed to watch the birth. When David laughed and began to cheer with him, Faye tried to join in. But even as she grinned and applauded, tears rolled down her cheeks.

When David turned and saw her face, he knelt and dropped a comforting arm around her shoulder. "I believe this was harder on you than it was on Violet."

"Oh, no!"

"Oh, yes, you look exhausted. But I'm afraid the ordeal has just begun."

Faye gazed at him through her tears. "What do you mean?"

"I mean now we'll have to watch every move Violet makes to see whether the baby will need to be taken away from her."

"Oh."

They both turned back to the window. The new mother lay on her side, obviously amazed by the tiny struggling creature she'd just produced. It was still attached to the afterbirth.

Keeping her eyes fixed on the scene, Faye asked, "Will she know enough to bite off the umbilical cord?"

"Probably not. That's instinctive with most animals, but not with apes. Eventually if she doesn't remove it herself, it will just wither and fall away. The important thing right now is for her to pick him up and put him to her breast."

Once again Faye began to twist her hands together. Now was the time to see if all the hours she'd spent with Violet would pay off. "Pick up the baby," she told Violet and then heaved a sigh of relief when at last the novice mother did exactly that.

But a moment later Faye frowned. "Why is she thumping and jiggling it that way?"

David studied the manner in which Violet poked and patted her baby's small body. All the while she manipulated it she held it close to her face and eyed it curiously, cocking her head first one way and then the other. "That's normal," he told Faye. "She's just making sure it's alive."

"But she might hurt it."

David didn't try to minimize the problem. "She might. That's why this stage of the birth is so tricky, and why we have to keep an eye on her. How about trying out another one of your commands."

"Be nice to the baby," Faye ordered. The words should have inspired Violet to hold the infant to her breast and pat it more gently. But she seemed too distracted to react properly. Faye had to repeat the instruction several times before the ape finally began handling the child more gently and clasped it to her in the general vicinity of her breast. Yet though the contact made the little creature's hungry lips seek her nipple, he didn't find it.

"Not holding it in exactly the right position, is she?" Peter commented. The tall, blond young man was pacing back and forth just behind Faye and David.

"No," David agreed, "but give her time. This is just her first try."

Faye picked up the cloth doll, held it close to her own breast and urgently issued the command again. But somehow Violet didn't seem to quite have the idea. Though she was gentle with her baby, holding it and continuously patting it, she refused to put it to the nipple.

Again and again Faye tried to get Violet to nurse her child. After two agonizing hours of hovering in front of the compartment and praying for a successful feeding that never happened, Faye was ready to bury her face in her hands.

"The baby looks weaker," David commented in a worried voice. "If he doesn't get nursed soon, we'll have to take him away from her."

"Is that really necessary?" asked Betty who'd shown up to check on Violet.

Regretfully David nodded his head. "I'm afraid so. It's great that she's being gentle and motherly with it, but if it doesn't get fed none of that counts for anything."

While Faye listened to David's discouraging words, her gaze remained pinned on Violet. "I don't think she's unwilling. She just doesn't understand."

"Comes to the same thing, though. That baby needs milk and isn't getting it."

Faye fingered the top button on her blouse. "There is something else I could try," she said.

"What's that?"

She looked up at David. "Have you forgotten what I was doing when you found me in here?"

He lifted an eyebrow, his gray eyes warming as he recalled walking into the ape house and coming upon her naked to the waist. At that moment she had looked like a fair-skinned island beauty from some artist's erotic fantasy. Or had it been his own erotic fantasy? "I remember," he said dryly. "All you needed was a waterfall, a grass skirt and a flower in your hair."

"What?"

"Nothing. Are you thinking Violet might be helped by—" his gaze lightly skimmed Faye's blouse "—a somewhat more graphic demonstration?"

She was too worried to respond to his gentle teasing. "Well, anything's worth a try at this point, isn't it?"

David cleared his throat. "It can't hurt." He glanced over his shoulder. "Would you like Peter and me to clear out?"

"Yes, please. And Betty, too. I think it stands a better chance of working if Violet and I are alone."

David nodded, and a few minutes later he and the young people stood outside in the cool night air.

"This has really been an experience," Peter declared.

"I just hope we don't have to take the baby away from Violet," chimed in Betty. "Though," she added, "it would be fun to raise a little gorilla."

Faye had once felt the same way, David thought ruefully. Aloud he said, "Look at the adjustment problems Kong is having."

"Yeah," Betty agreed. "He and Daisy Mae aren't exactly the lovebirds of the century. He's mean to her."

"He's not mean, exactly," Peter countered. "When she's around he acts as if he resents her. But when we take her away, he hollers and screams to get her back."

"A typical male," Betty commented.

Peter hooted at that and David laughed, too. There was, he had to admit, a certain amount of truth in it.

"Kong's problem," Peter joked, "is that he's still in love with Faye. Can't say I blame him. If she came into my cage, I probably wouldn't want to let her out, either."

Betty looked distinctly unamused and David guessed that her interest in Peter was more than merely friendly. He couldn't say that he was particularly entertained by Peter's remark, either. It had conjured up a picture of Faye in the lanky youth's arms, and though David had no reason to think that had ever happened, or ever would, even the thought of it disturbed him.

"We shouldn't be joking around," Betty said. "I feel really sorry for poor Violet. What's Faye doing in there, anyway?"

"Oh, just trying out a little experiment," David replied. In his mind's eye he saw her slowly unbutton her blouse and slip it from her shoulders. Only in his imagination she wasn't doing it for Violet's benefit, but for his.

"Well, I hope it works."

"Me, too," David said. He checked his watch and then began to pace up and down.

Inside the ape house, Faye once again held the cloth doll to her naked breast. "See, Violet, this is the way to do it. Be nice to the baby."

On the other side of the bars, Violet eyed her anxious teacher curiously. So far that was the only response Faye had been able to elicit, and she was beginning to lose hope. But just at that moment, Violet shifted the infant in her arms. Whether or not it was deliberate or purely accidental, Faye would never know. But suddenly the struggling newborn found what it had been instinctively seeking and latched on to its mother's nipple. When this happened, Violet gave a startled grunt and pulled it away.

"Oh, no," Faye cried. "Be nice to the baby. Be nice to the baby." Desperately she pressed the doll's mouth to her own breast. "See, be nice to the baby! Oh, Violet, please be nice to the baby!"

Violet couldn't have understood the words, but she did seem to respond to the urgency in her keeper's voice and Faye's body language. Once again she clasped the child to her body, and this time when the tiny creature began to suckle, she didn't jerk him away.

"Oh, Violet, that's right, that's good—you're doing exactly right." Unaware that tears of relief were streaming down her face, Faye sat gazing at mother and child, assuring herself that what she saw happening, really was occurring. Then, murmuring words of approval and encouragement, she very carefully set down her doll and reached for her clothing. When she was decent, she tiptoed to the door and opened it a crack. David and the others were just outside. "You can come in now," she whispered.

"Any luck?" David queried, trying to make out her expression in the uncertain light.

"Come in and see for yourself."

He came closer and stood looking down at her. "You've done it, haven't you?" he said softly.

Faye's wide smile was misty. "Yes, I think I have. I really think I have."

CHAPTER NINE

DAVID PULLED UP in front of Faye's house and killed the Volvo's engine. Then he looked at her. She was leaning back against the headrest with her eyes closed and her mouth curved up in a beatific smile.

"Oh, I wish Wally had been here to see Violet's baby," she murmured.

"Yes, I heard he and Hubbard were off to Alaska to buy a bear." It sounded crazy to David. Why go so far to purchase what you could get much closer to home? But he didn't voice his opinion to Faye. Gaffey's antics were already enough of a sore point between them, and he didn't want to spoil the pleasant mood that had been established.

For just an instant a tiny frown marred her smooth forehead. "Thanks for the lift," she said. "I suppose I should have driven my own car."

"You're in no shape to navigate through two stoplights and a thirty-five-mile-an-hour zone. You're too high on Violet's success to even stay on the right-hand side of the road."

She giggled. "Maybe you're right, but now I have no way of getting to work in the morning."

"I'll take you." He checked the glowing numerals on the dashboard clock. "Anyhow, it's already morning. It's after two a.m."

"Really? I don't feel sleepy at all." She cocked her head at him. "If you're going to be here in the morning, that must mean you won't be driving back to Baltimore tonight."

He shrugged his shoulders. "I'm not really fit for a long drive. Besides, after I've had a bit of rest I want to check on that baby again."

"Where are you going to sleep?"

"There's a motel a few miles down the road."

Faye glanced toward the darkened front of her cottage. The thought his words inspired made her heart speed up. Did she have the nerve to gamble on her instincts about David and her feelings for him? "Tell me, Dr. O'Neill, are you brave enough to come into my house one more time?"

There was a moment of silence. "Sounds intriguing. Are you inviting me in for a cup of coffee?"

"You drink far too much coffee. Don't you find that it makes you jittery?"

"No, and I hope you're not going to offer me herbal tea. Somehow it just doesn't hit the spot."

Faye chuckled. "All right, then what would you say to a bottle of Chardonnay? I have one I've been saving for a special occasion."

"This is certainly a special occasion."

"Yes, it is." She waited, her chin high and her fingers curled around the edge of the leather seat.

David took his keys out of the ignition. "Lead the way."

It was almost eighteen hours since Faye had had any sleep, but as David followed her up the path to her house adrenaline fizzed through her system. She'd never felt more alert in her life, and when she switched on the light in her living room, she looked back at him brightly. "You must have dangerous associations with just about every room in my house. In the bedroom I attacked you. In the kitchen I fed you fruit pancakes. And now the couch in the living room probably gives you the shivers. Where do you think we should go to drink our wine?"

David's eyes glinted. "We could try the bathtub."

"Too small."

"My associations with that couch are not unpleasant. Let's chance it."

She grinned. "Okay. Make yourself comfortable. I'll be right back."

Ten minutes later Faye returned with the uncorked Chardonnay and two of the prettily etched stemmed glasses that she'd inherited from her grandmother. David was leaning back against the couch cushions, his legs stretched out before him and his arms resting behind his head. He gave her a lazy smile and when she poured and handed him his wine, he raised it ceremoniously. "A toast is in order, wouldn't you say?"

"Yes." The edges of their two crystal goblets clinked. "To motherhood."

"To motherhood," David repeated as he watched Faye sit down beside him.

"And to a big, happy family for Kong, Violet and Daisy Mae. May this new little one have many brothers and sisters."

"I'll drink to that, too."

Smiling at each other, they both sipped their wine. "Big families are wonderful, don't you think?" Faye remarked.

"Some are, I guess."

Faye noted that David's smile had been replaced by a cynical expression. "You don't sound too sure. What kind of a family do you come from?"

"Big and poor," he told her. "There were eight of us, five boys and three girls. I was the eldest."

"Sounds wonderful to me. I'm an only child, so I was jealous of all my friends with brothers and sisters."

"People don't always want what's best for them." David drained his glass. "Unless I miss my guess, you had a happy childhood in part because you had the undivided love and attention of your parents."

"My parents had enough love for more than one." She regarded him curiously, remembering what he'd said about the kind of man she needed. Something about him being one who would commit his life to her in a big old house full of children and dogs and cats. "Didn't you have a happy childhood?"

"Not particularly." He reached for the wine bottle to top up her glass and refill his own. "The O'Neills were shanty Irish. We lived in a tiny house that smelled of diapers, poverty and unrealized dreams. By the time my mother was forty she looked, and I think felt, twenty years older. My brothers and sisters were always squabbling among themselves and whining after things we couldn't afford. That's probably one of the reasons why my dad worked and then drank himself into an early grave."

Faye blinked. "I gather you don't exactly miss your family much."

"I go back for visits now and then." He sipped his wine reflectively. "But you're right. I don't miss them. We're related by blood, but in all the ways that count we're strangers who really haven't much to say to one another.''

"How sad. Where are they now?"

"Back in England. Doing rather well for themselves. My sisters are married and my mother lives with Kathleen, the oldest girl. My brothers all have professions." David didn't go on to explain that after he'd gotten through medical school on scholarships, he'd paid for their education himself and that he still sent checks to Kathleen for his mother's support. "Actually," he pointed out, "you and I are opposites in that respect."

"How do you mean?"

"You love the Eastern Shore so much that you won't consider leaving it. After sixteen years in the place where I grew up, I couldn't wait to get out. And I've been a traveling man ever since."

Faye studied him. "Don't you ever get lonely? Don't you ever want a family and a home of your own?"

"Sometimes. But then I remember what mine was like and I realize I made the right choice." He gave her a level look. "I've always been a loner, Faye. I said it before, and I'll say it again. I just wasn't cut out for the marriage and family bit."

Over the top of her glass, Faye met his gaze with equal directness. He was wrong, she thought. And it was a pity, because all her instincts told her that this man would make a wonderful husband and father. So many times over the past few weeks she'd watched him treat animals and seen his gentleness and concern. Surely if he ever showed that capacity for love with people, it would flower into something strong and beautiful.

"Is there..." She hesitated. "Is there someone in Baltimore that you care for?"

"A woman, you mean? No." It didn't even occur to David to mention Grace. He didn't connect her with Baltimore and, in truth, over the past few months he'd stopped thinking of her as his lover. At this moment, Faye was the only female he could focus on.

She was silent, but the question in her green eyes said it all. "It wasn't easy for me to walk away from you," he admitted. "I wanted you from the first, so you're not the only one who's been feeling frustrated lately. For that matter, it's not going to be easy for me to walk out of here tonight."

She sat very still. "Then why go? Why not stay?"

Neither of them moved a muscle and, like two wary creatures of the jungle unsure about what the next move would or should be, they regarded each other tensely.

When David spoke, his voice sounded tight and dry, as if his throat were constricted. "Faye, before when we were on this couch you said you needed someone who would always be there for you. God help me, I'm not that man. I don't want to hurt you."

Faye's heart was pounding so hard and fast that she was afraid it might jump out of her chest. "I've had time to think about that." She set her glass down and then very carefully reached for his. "Part of growing up is accepting that this is not a perfect world. Since you can't always have what you want, sometimes you just have to take what you can get." *And sometimes,* she thought, *you just have to take a chance and hope for the best.* "I'm a big girl now, David. I can take care of myself."

Both their fingers were wrapped around the stem of his wineglass. Together they set it down on the table beside them. Then David took Faye in his arms. He looked down at her open, accepting expression, and when he was convinced that she'd really meant what she said, he covered her mouth with his. There was an awkward moment when their noses brushed, but that was soon over and their lips melded.

Faye closed her eyes and gave herself up to sensation. For weeks now she'd been thinking about David's kiss. When he had taken her in his arms that last time, she'd thought to find warmth and strength—and she had. But she'd been unprepared for the bolt of wide and shimmering excitement that had shot through her. Now it hit her again. Her bones turned to jelly, and like vines creeping toward sunlight, her hands slipped under his arms and up to his shoulders where they clung. Beneath his mouth hers softened into mindless receptivity. And her skin, which an instant before had been cold with nerves, began to glow.

Still holding her tightly, David drew back a fraction of an inch and whispered in her ear, "Your heart is going like a jackhammer."

"I guess I'm nervous." She turned her face into his neck and inhaled his scent. Nothing fancy—no lemon after-shaves or musky colognes. He smelled of soap and healthy skin and honest work. He smelled like a man, and she wanted him—wanted him so much that even her teeth seemed to ache with desire. "I've never offered myself like this before. At least," she added with a watery chuckle, "not when I was in my right mind."

"Are you sure you're in your right mind now?" he asked huskily.

"As certain as I can be." Her expression turned serious. "You're not going to walk out on me again, are you?"

"No." He reached over and turned off the light next to the couch. "I know the way to your bedroom. As a matter of fact, it's a path I've taken in my imagination quite a few times lately. Let's go there now."

Shakily she agreed and let him help her to her feet. With their arms around each other's waists, they walked out of the shadowy living room and down the short dark hall that led to Faye's wide brass bed. Once in the bedroom, Faye asked, "Do you want me to put on the light?"

"What do you want?" David could feel her body trembling. Was she getting cold feet, he wondered. God, he hoped not, but if she were, he preferred to be told now rather than later.

"I like it the way it is," Faye said, "with just the moonlight."

He stroked the back of her neck and then turned her toward him. "I want to undress you."

"Yes."

"But before I do, Faye, I must tell you that I haven't brought any protection with me. Is there something you need to do?"

"Yes." Shyly she dipped her head. She wasn't on the pill, but she wasn't stupid, either. She'd thought to provide herself with protection should the need ever arise. "Wait for me. I'll be right back."

He watched as she went into the hall and closed the bathroom door behind her. Then he walked over to the window and took several deep breaths. Control was not usually something he had trouble with. He was not, he reflected, a young boy coping with hot, irrepressible urges that were dangerously new.

Yet tonight young was exactly how he felt. With Faye in his arms he'd been as eager as a teenager on a lonely country road kissing his first willing girl. But she deserved better than that, he reminded himself. How many days, months, years since she'd been made love to? Not since this Jim who'd gotten her pregnant and then abandoned her? If that were so, then she deserved a night that would wipe him out of her memory forever. And suddenly that was exactly what David was determined to give her. Still breathing deeply, he went to the bed, sat down on it and began to remove his shoes and socks.

When Faye came back into the room, he had pulled down the quilt and was lying on the sheets, his ankles crossed and his hands behind his head on the pillow. He wore only his slacks, and on his bare chest the moonlight gleamed.

Just inside the door she paused. "I've never seen you without your shirt before. You have more hair than I thought."

"I hope you don't mind."

"No, I don't mind at all." She gazed at the mat tufting the area between his small nipples and then plunging in a narrowing line to his waistband. His pants rode low on his hips so that she could see for the first time how really flat his belly was. The muscles there were so well articulated that even in his relaxed posture there was a washboard effect. She walked toward the bed and then, gingerly, sat on its edge beside him and lightly touched his bare stomach. "Talk about an iron hand in a velvet glove, your skin is soft but underneath you feel like solid oak. Do you work out twice a day or what?''

Bemusedly David gazed up at her. Did she realize what she was doing, touching him that way, he wondered. ''When I was young I learned to be very disciplined about my body. I had to since a lot of my education money depended on athletic scholarships. But the habit stuck. I'm still careful about exercise.'' In one effortless motion he sat up and grasped Faye by the shoulders. ''I don't want to talk about my fitness regimen.''

''Me, neither.''

''Then why are we doing this?''

She licked her lips. ''I don't know. I'm still nervous, I guess. I'm no sophisticate, and it's been a long time.''

In the darkness their faces were very close, their lips and eyes only a breath apart. ''Don't be nervous. I won't rush you.'' Very gently, he kissed her forehead, then each temple, and then, as her lids fluttered down, the corners of her closed eyes. ''Let me unbutton your blouse.''

''Yes.'' Keeping her lashes sealed, she waited, hardly breathing, while he undid the front of the garment and then softly pushed it from her shoulders. A moment later he reached around and unhooked her bra. When that, too, fell away, she sighed as she felt his hands brush lightly down the swelling sides of her naked breasts.

''Faye, you're like springtime.'' His head lowered so that he could touch his lips to the peak of each full breast. Then he took her in his arms and guided her down on the bed beside him.

Wonderingly Faye pressed her cheek against his. She was surprised and a bit taken aback by his patience. Before, he'd been urgent to the point of roughness. And that was what she remembered about her brief couplings with Jim all those years ago—his hoarse groans, his legs pressing hers apart, his groping hands that wouldn't be denied.

David's hands on her body were as light as feathers, as silken as rose petals. "Let's talk," he said as he stroked the hair back from her eyes and then began to drop soft kisses on her cheeks and throat.

"Talk about what?" Faye gasped.

He lifted his head and smiled down at her, his fingers all the while lightly caressing her breasts. "When I first saw you I was fascinated by your eyes. People think of tiger eyes as being golden. But the tiger that sticks in my mind had eyes exactly the same color as yours."

"Really?"

"Oh, yes." The pad of one thumb began to slowly circle her nipple. "Have you ever seen tigers mate?"

"No. Have you?"

"Yes."

Her own hands had started to busy themselves, touching his back and shoulders. "What's it like when tigers mate?"

"Beautiful." He kissed the corners of her mouth and then chuckled deep in his throat. "Will it make you angry if I tell you that normally a tigress is timid with a male of her own kind?"

"No. I knew that." Faye was only partly conscious of her reply. The warmth of David's body entwined with hers, the sound of his deep, calm voice, his stroking hands and subtle erotic kisses—all of these had banished her nervousness. In its place a thin wire of excitement coiled within her.

"Maybe, but a tigress isn't timid during court-ship," David continued. "When it's time to mate, the sun glints off her golden flanks and she becomes a slinking, dangerous animal." He kissed Faye deeply and for several minutes they silently tasted the heady flavor of wine lingering on each other's tongues.

When their mouths finally parted, she pressed her lips against the side of David's neck and questioned breathily, "What's the male tiger like?"

It was a moment before David finally answered, and when he did his voice was low and husky. "The poor beast is confused by his beautiful, ferocious lady, ab-ject in his desire for her, so heavy with passion that he can barely move." As David spoke, his fingers slipped down to the closure on Faye's jeans and unsnapped it. Then, in a slow erotic slide, he began to pull the zip-per open. All the while he whispered hypnotically into her ear. "Once in India I hid in the trees and watched a mating pair. The male was like a tawny shadow, fol-lowing his tigress through the bushes, but not getting too close because he knew that in her dangerous mood, if she wasn't ready for him she would scratch."

With excruciating finesse David stroked the super-sensitive flesh beneath Faye's undone zipper. At the same time his lips once more tasted her breasts.

"Oh, David!" As she felt his tongue sensuously flicking her aroused nipples, Faye arched and locked her hands around his shoulders. Clasping him, she shuddered with pleasure. Then, blindly, she reached to try to undo his waistband.

"Careful," he warned with a low chuckle. "It's rather a tight fit down there at the moment." Alternately teasing her mouth and kissing her throat and breasts, he guided her fumbling fingers to help him slide free of his pants. When he was naked he knelt on the bed and peeled hers off as well. As the moon from the window gilded them with pale light, Faye thought not of tigers but of ancient gods and goddesses. Certainly what she could see of David's silvered body seemed as perfect and as potent.

When he lay down beside her again, he began once more to murmur in her ear. As his hands roamed over her feverish flesh with ever-increasing intimacy, he told her more about what he knew of tigers.

"All day, burdened with his desire, the male paces," he whispered. "But when his love overwhelms him, he approaches his lady with a purring moan."

"What does she do?"

"She shows her teeth and holds him at bay."

Faye stroked David's muscled flank and nipped at his ear. "She's cruel."

"Yes, she seems to enjoy this mastery over her mate, but it only makes him want her more." He shifted his position and with a low laugh, kissed her thighs and then her belly and the warm undersides of her breasts. Then he slid his hard body up her length and framed her face with his palms. "But finally she picks her moment."

Faye's throat was so constricted that she could barely speak. "What does she do?"

Through the moon-streaked darkness surrounding them, she caught the flash of David's white teeth. "At last her walk slows and her back curves. She sways from side to side and the expression in her emerald eyes becomes dreamy and mysterious." Sensuously David's leg rubbed along Faye's and beneath him she shivered with anticipation. But when she tried to move, he held her still. Unlike the tigress teasing her frustrated suitor, it was he who now held her at bay.

David's deep voice whispered on hypnotically. "Languidly she seems to drift to a place where the grass is long and thick. While her mate watches eagerly, she begins to purr and then she lies down."

"What happens then?" Against her belly, Faye could feel the imprint of his fully aroused masculinity. But so was she fully aroused. Between her thighs she ached to receive him, and once again she struggled to free her legs from his so that she could wrap them around his lean waist. But still David held her fast, and the part of her mind that could still think wondered how he could be so restrained.

"Her mate moves swiftly toward her, rumbling eagerly in his throat. And finally she answers with her first invitation."

As Faye wriggled beneath him and pulled his head down to hers, she felt a sweet, blurred vibration in her own throat. "David!"

"Yes!" he growled. Abruptly his control seemed to desert him. Kissing her fiercely, he freed her legs and when they were parted, his sinewy body blended with hers. As he thrust deep inside her, Faye closed her eyes and seemed to see the mating tigers. And just as David had said, they were beautiful. With fierce tenderness the tawny male imposed his strength upon his lady love. Drowned in waves of simmering passion, their bodies melted down together until she was hidden in the grass. Faye could almost smell the rich earth and the pungent jungle greenery surrounding them. She could almost feel the heat of the sun, which struck sparks from their pulsing burnished hides.

As Faye clenched David's waist and matched his rhythmic assault with her own, it seemed to her that they became one with the tigers. Her mind's eye was dazzled, and like those untamed jungle lovers, she and David beat their way upward to a golden conflagration. At last, when the fiery shower of sparks had settled around them and slowly winked out, their bodies were still entwined. For a long time after that, except for soft sighs and faint moans, the room was quiet.

"DAVID?" THOUGH IT WAS just past dawn and Faye couldn't have had more than three or four hours of rest, she was wide awake. For the past fifteen minutes she'd been propped up on her elbow, staring at the naked man sleeping next to her.

"David," she said again, and reached out to touch his shoulder. Though she'd intended only the lightest of nudges, her fingers lingered. His skin was like velvet. When he opened his eyes and looked at her, she apologized. "I'm sorry to wake you up so early, but I thought you might want to check on Violet and her baby."

"Why? Is anything wrong?"

"No."

He turned his head to glance at the clock on the bedside table before rolling back toward her. "Then I think I can stay here for a while longer, if that's all right with you."

It was more than all right and Faye snuggled against him, pressing her face to his chest. But the affectionate gesture aroused something more than affection in David. Soon nature took its course and she was beneath his taut length, gasping and then sighing with release when once again they both found the ultimate satisfaction. After that, while the morning light gathered strength outside the bedroom window, they lay dozing in each other's arms—or, rather, David did. Faye was too stirred by the experience they'd just shared to really sleep.

"David," she finally whispered.

"Ummm."

"What do tigers do after they make love?"

"They lie down next to each other and take a snooze in the sun." The corners of his mouth twitched.

"I can't sleep. I'm too excited."

"What are you excited about?"

"About you. About us. About everything." Her fingers toyed with the hair on his chest. "I feel so...so..."

"Relaxed?"

"No-o-o. I feel so alive—like that tigress of yours."

He ruffled her hair. "My tigress was sleepy. But you do look a lot like her with that yellow hair and those bright green eyes." His gaze drifted down over her slim body, taking in the high, full breasts, the nipped-in waist, the delicately rounded hips and smooth legs. "Making love to you was easy. You're very lovely, Faye."

"Did I...did I please you last night and just now?"

"Very much."

Her long lashes screened her eyes. "You did more than please me. It was very different from what I experienced before."

"You mean with Jim?"

"Yes. I didn't know that men could be so different." Coloring slightly, she looked past his shoulder toward the window. "With him it all happened so quickly. Now I realize that he really wasn't taking my pleasure into consideration.''

"He was very young. You were both young."

"Yes." Thoughtfully Faye returned her gaze to David and studied him, seeing in the clear morning light the beginnings of his beard, the faint lines around his eyes, the grooves that ran from nose to mouth and gave his strong face added character. Suddenly she felt less confident about her gamble than she had last night. Sexually, Faye knew she was inexperienced for her age, but she had no reason to think David was and he had ten years on her. Undoubtedly he'd made love to a lot of women—women who'd been unable to hold him.

Was she any different from those women? she wondered. Certainly David was the opposite of the only other lover she'd known. Jim had encouraged her to think that what they shared was a grand passion that would last forever. Yet at the first hint of trouble he'd run away. David insisted he wasn't interested in commitments. Was there any reason to hope he might, when put to the test, prove Jim's opposite in that, too?

She cleared her throat and asked as casually as she could, "Have you heard anything yet about your grant?"

"Not yet."

Immediately a guarded look came into David's eyes, and Faye knew she should change the subject. But her tongue seemed to have a will of its own. She pulled the sheet up around her breasts and began to pleat the flowered material between her fingers. "What sort of a grant is it?"

"It's complicated."

"But I'd like to understand your work. Will it involve animals?"

He sighed and lay back on the pillow. "The grant involves behavioral studies with primates."

"Primates? But you can study primate behavior right here at Wilderness Worlds."

"Faye, I know what you're saying, but I'm afraid it's more complicated than that."

"In what way?"

"In lots of ways. I applied for the grant along with someone else, a research biologist. Even if I wanted to turn it down now, I couldn't. That wouldn't be fair to my colleague."

There was a brief silence while she mulled this over. "Who is your colleague?"

This was the last subject David wished to discuss while lying in bed with Faye. But he wasn't going to lie to her, either. *Might as well come clean,* he thought with a sigh. "She teaches at Berkeley in California, and her name is Dr. Grace Palmer."

"A woman?" Faye's brows began to lift. "How long have you known her?"

"A couple of years."

"A long time, then. Is she your age?"

"She's a little older, actually. We're very good friends."

"Are you friends with her husband, too?"

David's gaze stayed pinned to the ceiling. "She's not married."

"I see." Faye clutched the sheet even more tightly. "I suppose I shouldn't ask this, but I need to know. Are you such good friends with this woman that you share her bed?"

A dark flush appeared on David's neck. Frowning, he sat up. "Faye, Grace has nothing to do with us."

"You haven't answered my question."

"All right, Grace has been more to me than a friend."

"Oh." Faye was suddenly hurt and coldly angry. It didn't help that she also felt like an idiot. When he'd said there was no one in Baltimore, she'd assumed that meant he was free and that she at least had a fighting chance with him. She should have guessed that he would be involved with another woman, a woman with a Ph.D. who was as sophisticated and well educated as he. "You deceived me," she said stiffly. "You let me think you were unattached."

"I am unattached. Grace and I have no claims on each other."

"How can you say that when you make love to her?"

"I say it because it's true. I haven't slept with her or anybody, for that matter, in months."

"But you'll be sharing her bed when you accept this grant and go off to England with her, won't you?"

David swung his feet over the bed, grabbed his pants and stepped into them. "Try to understand, Faye. Sex doesn't necessarily include the happily-ever-after in the fairy tales. Grace and I have an adult relationship based on respect, mutual liking and common interests."

"David, marriage is an adult relationship. What you really mean is that you use her for sexual gratification, but don't really care much about her. Is that your attitude toward me, too?" Something cold and sharp twisted in Faye's gut. Jerkily she dragged the sheet free of the mattress and began wrapping it around her like a sari.

His face set, David yanked his shirt from a chair. "You know, last night you almost had me convinced that you were a big, grown-up girl. Now I see that you were putting on an act."

"When I told you I could take care of myself, it was no act," Faye shot back. "And now I think it's time I started doing just that." Abruptly she stood, picked up David's shoes off the floor and, with all the cool dignity she could muster, thrust them at him.

CHAPTER TEN

"WALLACE WILL BE SO PLEASED when he hears about Violet's baby." Over the top of her typewriter, Miss Prior beamed at David.

"Yes, well, we're all pleased. She and the baby are doing fine, too. I just looked in on them. It's a boy, by the way."

"A boy." The aging secretary clapped her hands. "We'll have to start thinking of names, won't we?"

"I suppose so." David wished he could match Miss Prior's enthusiasm. But that wasn't likely, not after Faye had regally wrapped herself in a sheet, handed him his shoes and shown him the door. Even his visit to Violet and her newborn hadn't put him in a good mood. In fact, he was still feeling about as cheerful as a bear with a thorn in its paw. And it didn't help that he'd had to stop at a diner to get his breakfast, that his pants were rumpled from their night on Faye's bedroom floor, and that he needed a shower and a shave. "Miss Prior," he said, setting down his case and rubbing his hand along his sandpapery jaw, "before I leave, there are some forms I need to fill out and mail. Do you have an envelope with the Wilderness Worlds letterhead?"

"Oh, I just ran out of those." She frowned down at the typewriter. "But, let me see, I believe Wallace has

some in his right-hand desk drawer. He's not here, you
know."

"I know. I heard he and Roy went to Alaska."

"Yes, Wallace was so excited." Her smile was suddenly conspiratorial. "To be honest, that man was so
beside himself that I had to go over to his house and
pack his suitcase for him. If I hadn't, he would have
flown off with nothing but a pair of pants, his bathrobe and one sock."

Knowing Gaffey, David could easily believe it.
"Miss Prior, about that envelope..."

"Oh, yes. Do you mind finding it yourself? If I get
up in the middle of typing a letter, I always make a
mistake when I sit back down. And then I have to start
all over again. It's so annoying."

"Of course I don't mind. Just stay right where you
are."

She should get herself a word processor, David
thought as he pushed open Gaffey's door and crossed
to the massive mahogany desk. But like everything else
at Wilderness Worlds, the office was a paradox. No
expense had been spared on costly furnishings, yet its
equipment was outdated and its management anti-
quated. Miss Prior, who was close to being an anach-
ronism herself, had probably refused to have anything
to do with a computer.

Irritably David opened the right-hand drawer and
reached in for one of the elegantly engraved cream
envelopes piled toward the back. Then his hand froze.
On top of a rat's nest of pens, paper clips and rubber
bands, a telegram lay open. David could hardly avoid
reading its terse message. "If you want to go for the
payload, I need to see more of that million. You know
where to call."

The telegram had been sent from Pakistan and left unsigned. Apparently the sender expected Gaffey to know what was meant by those two cryptic sentences and how to contact him about them.

"Good God," David muttered as he picked up the telegram and stared. A million? What was the old man involved in? What sort of "payload" would require that kind of money? Of course it could all be perfectly innocent, but something about the thing made the hair on the back of David's neck stand on end. From the beginning he'd been nagged by vague suspicions about Wilderness Worlds. Suddenly he thought of the fenced enclosure he and Gaffey had stumbled upon that first day. From time to time he'd wondered about it. Yet, because it was in a section of the park as yet undeveloped and that he didn't have occasion to visit, he hadn't gone back. Maybe it was time to take a walk that way and have another look.

"Did you find the envelope?" Miss Prior called.

"Yes." David shut the drawer and strolled back out into the office. "It's right here," he said, holding up the cream-colored rectangle.

"Is that all you'll be needing?"

"That's all."

David reached for his case, but Miss Prior wasn't yet ready to let him go. "I do hope Kong is being nicer to Daisy Mae."

"They're having a pretty rocky courtship, but I think eventually they'll settle down."

The gray-haired secretary nodded sagely. "Faye spoiled that animal."

"Yes, I'm afraid she did." David didn't want to discuss Faye or even think about her. The subject was too painful. And now there was this thing with her uncle. David remembered Bill's warning. At the time he'd dismissed it, but maybe he shouldn't have. Could Gaffey have become involved in something illegal? And was it possible that Faye knew about it? Oh, surely not!

With a brief goodbye for Miss Prior, David strode out of the office. Frowning, he glanced around and then headed down the path. Now that everyone was working double time getting Wilderness Worlds ready for its July opening, the walkways were busy. But as David wended his way past the most popular exhibits activity gradually died down. The area in which he remembered finding the fenced enclosure was virtually deserted.

After going down several blind alleys, he began to hear the sound of hammering and drilling in the distance and knew that he was finally on the right track. The last fifty feet before the fence came into view he walked rather cautiously. When he emerged from the trees, it was just as he had remembered—a tall board barrier topped by barbed wire. Whatever was being constructed beyond it was beginning to take shape. Over the top of the dangerously spiked wire David could make out some sort of low building.

Curiously he began to circle around looking for an entrance. A few yards to the right he spotted the place where workmen were taking supplies in and headed for it. As he approached, a guard wearing a firearm on his hip focused on him.

"Hey, where's your badge? Only authorized personnel are allowed near here."

David observed the green plastic badge the guard was wearing and saw something similar on one of the workmen passing near the gate. Still, what could be so secret that they'd try to keep even him out?

"I think I must be authorized," David said pleasantly. "I'm the consulting vet here. What's going on in there, anyway?"

The guard, a fierce young man who didn't look overly bright, squinted at him suspiciously. "You don't have a badge."

"What difference does that make? I can prove that I work here, and I just want to have a look."

David started to walk through the gate when to his amazement, the bristling young man whipped out his gun. "Better not take another step, mister."

Torn between laughter and amazement, David stared. It was like a scene from an old cowboy melodrama. Surely this character couldn't be serious. To test the issue, David ignored the warning and took another step. The guard immediately assumed a defensive stance and leveled his weapon. David heard an ominous click.

"Don't try it," the man snapped. David knew a thing or two about the fight-or-flight reaction, and the manner in which the guard had clenched his teeth and suddenly gone pale convinced him that he was capable of actually pulling the trigger.

As David stood contemplating the barrel of the gun, his Irish temper was close to the flash point. Keeping it from exploding wasn't easy. Only the realization that getting himself killed or injured in such a stupid fashion as this would be ridiculous restrained him from flinging himself at the guard's throat. Instead, with one last glance at the mysterious fence, he turned and stalked off.

But he was angry, so angry that he felt like hitting someone. He would have been delighted to vent his spleen on Wallace Gaffey—only the man was out of reach, up to God knows what in Alaska! Fuming, David headed for the parking lot. But once in his car he didn't aim the vehicle toward Baltimore as he'd originally intended. Instead, he pulled out onto the highway and turned south in the direction of Haverton.

AN HOUR LATER Faye climbed into her Chevy, slumped over the wheel for a moment, and then wearily turned on the ignition and headed the big old car north toward her home. As she drove, it was all she could do to keep the unshed tears still burning at the backs of her eyes from obscuring her vision. Last night she'd been in a beautiful dream. Now it looked as if that dream had been the second landmark mistake in her jinxed love life. She supposed she couldn't blame David for not living up to her fantasies. After all, he'd tried to warn her that he was no starry-eyed, true-blue lover. He'd told her straight out that he had no interest in commitment—yet she'd gone right ahead and insisted on inviting him into her bed.

What a fool I am, she thought miserably. *I just couldn't believe that he really meant what he said.* Her desperate attraction to the man had made her blind, of course. Because she'd been so overwhelmingly drawn to David, her feminine instincts had urged her to forget caution and take a shot at the moon. Well, hearing that he had another woman had brought her back to earth in a hurry.

After calling in sick and hiding under the covers for an hour, Faye had been unable to stay in the house a minute longer. Hitching a ride from a neighbor, she'd retrieved her car from the parking lot at Wilderness Worlds and headed to the farm where she kept her horse, Sunspot. There she'd spent what remained of the morning riding him until his sides were lathered with sweat and then apologetically rubbing him down and mucking out his stall.

When Faye got back to Haverton it was long after lunchtime, and she was pretty hot and sweaty herself, not to mention dirty and tired and emotionally bruised. She was totally unprepared to find David's maroon Volvo parked in front of her house, and as she pulled her old Chevy up behind it she felt her stomach lurch. Turning her head, she caught sight of him sitting in a rocking chair on the porch with Missy sleeping at his side. Faye's breathing accelerated and her heart seemed to skitter in her chest like a loose pinball. With fingers that trembled, she took her key out of the ignition and got out. Forcing a deep breath, she shaded her eyes against the glaring sun and headed slowly up the walk.

"What are you doing here?" she questioned when she reached the foot of the steps.

"Waiting for you. Where have you been?"

"Riding."

"So I see. You have straw in your hair."

David watched as Faye lifted a small, tanned hand to pluck out a length of dried grass. Since he'd been cooling his heels on her shady little porch more than an hour, he'd had some time to calm down. Yet he was still far from composed, and as his burning gaze played over her he rehearsed what he wanted to say.

Resting one booted foot on the bottom stair, she looked as if she'd given herself quite a workout. Her pants were dusty and there was still more than one wisp of straw left in her short yellow locks. Perspiration sheened her face and her damp blouse clung fetchingly to her high breasts—breasts he had a vivid memory of caressing only a few hours earlier. Suddenly David ached to take her into the bedroom and make love to her all over again—feel her underneath and around him and hear her gasping in ecstasy against his ear. But she was angry with him about Grace, so it wasn't likely she'd go willingly. And he had a thing or two to be angry about himself, dammit!

"Faye," he began, "there's something I need to discuss with you."

"Is it about us?"

David opened his mouth to tell her that it wasn't, but she hurried on before he could.

"Because if it is, I've already made up my mind. David, none of this is your fault. You were really very honest with me. You never tried to fool me into thinking that you were looking for true love. But I know now that last night was a mistake—a mistake I don't intend to repeat." Her gaze flittered away from his. "You were right all along. I'm not like you or your friend, Grace. I wasn't cut out for a casual affair that leads nowhere."

David cleared his throat. "That's not what I came here to talk about."

"It isn't?"

"No, it isn't." He stood up and walked to the edge of the porch. "There's something going on at Wilderness Worlds that I don't like."

Faye stiffened. "What do you mean?"

Briefly he told her about his encounter with the guard at the fence. When he described how he'd been threatened with a gun, Faye's green eyes widened.

"There must be a mistake. I'm sure that man wasn't following any instructions he received from Wally."

"Could he have gotten his orders from Roy Hubbard."

Faye opened her mouth to deny that. Then she hesitated. Roy was not the smartest guy in the world. It was just possible that he might be responsible for something this ridiculous. "If Roy told someone to use a gun on trespassers, he did it without Wally's authority."

"But he's your uncle's right-hand man, isn't he?"

"Yes," Faye reluctantly admitted. It was certainly a relationship she found extremely puzzling. Roy was the last person she would rely on. Yet Wally seemed blind to the younger man's faults, and over the past couple of years had delegated more and more authority to him. "But I'm sure—"

With an abrupt wave of his hand, David cut her off. "Faye, what's being built behind that fence?"

"I don't know."

"You've seen it, haven't you?"

Slowly she nodded. "Once, from a distance. But when I asked Wally about it, he just told me that it was a secret—a big surprise for the opening of the park."

"And you didn't inquire about it again?"

"No." As she read David's disapproval, Faye's eyebrows drew together. "Wally loves surprises. He's always doing that sort of thing. Why should I try to spoil something that gives him so much pleasure?"

David rested his balled fists on his hips. "There's no reason to get defensive."

"Isn't there? Then why are you grilling me like this?"

"I'm not grilling you. I'm asking questions because I'm having trouble understanding your attitude. Didn't you see the barbed wire and the armed guards? Didn't those things make you wonder?"

"No, I didn't see them, as a matter of fact," she retorted. "I told you, I only saw the fence from a distance and through the trees."

The corners of his mouth compressed. "Shall I tell you what I think? I think there's something shady going on and that your uncle is behind it."

Faye gaped. "What? What are you talking about?"

David described the telegram he'd found in Gaffey's desk. As he talked, he saw what looked like a guilty flush suffuse Faye's features.

In reality, she was thinking of all the things that had been bothering her lately—Wally's increasing forgetfulness and both his and Roy's strange, secretive behavior. On top of all that there was the man in the gray car who'd been hanging around. Could there be something to David's accusation? No, she simply couldn't believe ill of her uncle. There had to be a reasonable explanation for all these things.

"That telegram could mean anything," she pointed out. "Wally's a very rich man. This wouldn't be the first time he's spent a million dollars. And," she added, her own expression darkening with suspicion, "what were you doing poking around in his desk drawers, anyway?"

David's temper began to boil. Was she accusing him of trying to rifle her uncle's desk? "I was looking for an envelope, but that's not the point."

Faye's hands clenched. "What *is* the point? You've been criticizing Wally and his methods from the moment you got here. Why you ever agreed to work for him in the first place is beyond me."

He'd agreed because of his absurd attraction to her, but David wasn't going to say that. Instead, he stared down at her frostily, waiting for whatever she was going to hurl at him next.

"You know what I think?" she snapped.

"No, but as I stand before you waiting to find out, I'm breathless with anticipation," he said in an acid tone.

Ignoring his sarcasm, Faye plunged ahead. "You're jealous."

"Jealous?"

"Yes, you even admitted it once to me. You said Wally was doing what you'd always wanted to do yourself, but couldn't because you were too poor. You're jealous that he can build a place like Wilderness Worlds and you can't, so you spend every spare moment finding fault—just blindly looking for reasons to dislike him."

David ground his teeth. "Faye, I didn't fabricate that telegram or the barbed-wire fence or the guard waving a gun in my face. You're the one who's blind. You're so blinded with loyalty to the man that you refuse to see what should be obvious to everyone. He's getting senile. He's not able to make intelligent judgments. And he's perfectly capable of dragging you and everyone else connected with this place into an unholy mess."

As Faye glared at the man who'd been her lover only a few hours earlier, a dozen disjointed thoughts ran through her head. Did he actually mean what he said, she wondered. Or was he just looking for an excuse not to have to see her again—provoking an argument with these ridiculous accusations so he could justify walking out of her life without a backward glance? That must be it, she thought, and tightened her fists as if they could protect her from the twisting pain the realization sent stabbing through her.

Heatedly David pressed on. "Well, I can't afford to have my professional reputation compromised. Since your uncle isn't here to accept my resignation formally, I'm going to give it to you informally." He stalked down the steps until he was standing level with her.

Trembling with hurt and anger, Faye looked up at him. "Good," she snapped when she could see the pinprick black centers of his icy gray eyes. "I'm delighted to hear it."

"I'll put a written version in the mail tomorrow."

"Fine and dandy. Now you can go back to Baltimore and your precious Grace with a clear conscience, can't you?"

"Faye..."

But instead of staying to hear any more, she turned her back, marched up the stairs and slammed into the house.

David stood by the step a moment longer. Then, with an oath and a black look at the still peacefully slumbering Missy, he strode back to his car.

DAVID'S LONG DRIVE back to Baltimore that afternoon was sheer hell. Beach-bound traffic jammed the roads, and the first serious heat wave of the season turned the inside of the Volvo into an oven. To complete his misery, all during the three-hour trip a merciless headache battered his temples. *I'm a doctor. Why don't I have any aspirin with me,* he asked himself when he finally wedged his vehicle into a tight parking space near his apartment building. Wearily he extricated his aching body from the automobile's sizzling interior. Then, head bowed, he slouched toward the pile of brick he'd been calling home lately.

Once in the foyer, he almost didn't bother to check the mail. But then, shrugging, he unlocked his box and pulled out the pile of envelopes and advertising circulars that had collected inside it. He didn't even see the foundation letterhead until he was inside his apartment and had dumped the mail on the kitchen counter. Then it jumped out at him. *Oh my God,* he thought, *the grant!*

With leaden fingers he slit the long, formal-looking envelope and withdrew the letter inside. He didn't need to read more than the first congratulatory paragraph. He and Grace had been awarded the grant.

The news should have made him happy. His visiting semester was almost over at Hopkins. All he had to do now was write a letter of acceptance, call Grace and pack his bags for England. It was the perfect escape from what had become an impossible situation at Wilderness Worlds. But instead of feeling relieved, he felt ill.

With a groan, David dropped the letter as if it had a burning fuse attached to it. Turning, he jerked open a cupboard, took out a bottle of Scotch and poured himself a stiff double shot. After a quick gulp that burned all the way down to his stomach, he refilled his glass and took it out to the living room. There he dropped down on the couch, rested his elbows on his knees and began to massage his temples with his free hand.

How had he gotten into such a hellish mess, he asked himself. When he'd come out here this winter, things had seemed pretty clear-cut—teach on the East Coast for a few months, accept the grant if it came through, then maybe do some consulting work in India that he'd been approached about. It all added up to the kind of life he'd been leading for years now, the kind of life he wanted—interesting work, no long-term commitments, plenty of travel, freedom. It should have sounded good. Why didn't it?

David raised his glass and took another swallow. He knew the reason, of course. It was Faye—Faye and her crazy uncle. But mostly it was Faye. Maybe if he'd never made love to her he'd be able to take off for England now without any regrets. But the night they'd spent in each other's arms had changed things. Walking away from her this afternoon had felt all wrong. He knew he couldn't put an ocean between them—not yet.

David got to his feet and began pacing up and down the short length of his living room. Periodically he paused to look out the window, where evening shadows gradually darkened the busy city street below. What were his options? How could he refuse to accept the damn grant when Grace's career was involved? He had an obligation to her, too. Maybe they hadn't exactly been Romeo and Juliet, but they'd offered each other comfort—comfort they'd both needed.

When David finally stopped his pacing, the street outside his apartment window was strung with glowing street lamps. Turning away and with his mouth set in a decisive line, he pulled the phone book from a bookcase and searched through it. Then he dialed the airport.

"Ticket information," a pleasant female voice intoned.

"Can you tell me when the next flight leaves for San Francisco?"

"Certainly, sir." There was a pause. "That will be Mountain Airways and departure time will be at eleven tonight."

David glanced at his watch. He would have about two hours to pack and make any arrangements he needed. Digging into his back pocket, he got out his wallet and started flipping through his credit cards. "Book me on that eleven o'clock flight, please."

"YOU WERE THE LAST PERSON I expected to see when I opened the door to get the morning paper. You could have knocked me over with a feather." Still clad in her nightgown and bathrobe, Grace took out a cigarette and waited while David lit it.

"Yes, well I'm sorry I didn't call, but I'm feeling sort of strung out. I spent the night sitting up in a plane, so I didn't get much sleep." Straightening, he blew out the match and then stood rubbing a hand over his unshaven chin while he looked around Grace's tiny, fenced-in yard. After opening the door to him, she'd led him through the dining room and directly out to the patio. The garden was ablaze with roses and badly in need of some conscientious weeding. It hadn't changed much in the months he'd been gone, but he couldn't say the same for Grace.

There was definitely something different about her—and it wasn't the three or four pounds she'd added to her already generous hips. What was it, he wondered as he turned back to study her. On the surface, she didn't look much different. Beneath her comfortable pink robe, her womanly curves blossomed lushly. Her wavy brown hair spilled around her shoulders the way he remembered, and she still smoked too much. Right now she was regarding him warily and puffing away on her cigarette as if her life depended on it.

"When are you going to give that up?" he queried.

"Soon." She laughed nervously. "As a matter of fact, I haven't had a cigarette in almost two weeks. I was keeping these around just to prove to myself that I had the willpower to resist them."

David frowned. "I don't understand. Then why are you smoking now?"

"It was the shock of finding you on my doorstep, I guess. I needed something to do with my hands."

As David watched her stub the cigarette out, he suddenly realized that she was more on edge than he was. Her hands were actually trembling. He took a step toward the lounge chair where she perched. "Grace, what's wrong? I know it's early, but I figured I'd catch you before you went to the office. Have I come at a bad time?"

"You might say that." She laughed again. "David, why are you here? Is it about the grant?"

"Yes. I need to talk to you."

"That's funny, because I need to talk to you." She cleared her throat. "As a matter of fact, I was thinking of flying out to see you this weekend."

"Really?" What was the matter with her, he wondered. She was as uptight as a treed cat. But whatever her problem, it couldn't be as bad as the dilemma he faced. He pulled a chair away from the patio table and sat down on it. How was he going to break it to her that he wanted out of the grant? All night he'd been racking his brains to come up with a way to make sure she wouldn't lose her half of the award if he withdrew.

"David, will you hate me forever if I tell you that I've had second thoughts about our grant?"

"What?"

"David, I..." She clenched the arms of her redwood chair and shot him a strained look. "Something's happened that makes me think I don't want to accept. Now just isn't the right time for me to be spending a year in England."

David was dumbfounded. But before he could say anything at all, he was further distracted by the creak of the glass door sliding open. As he looked behind him, he expected to see one of Grace's college-age daughters. Instead, a tall, balding man peered around the drawn curtain. The lower half of his face was obscured by a sand-colored beard and he wore a bathrobe and pajama bottoms. His long, thin feet were bare.

"Everything okay out here?"

Even more disconcerted, David looked from the casually dressed stranger back to Grace. Normally the epitome of aplomb, she had turned an incandescent tomato-red.

"Everything's just great," she muttered. "David, this is Mark Benson. Mark, my friend David O'Neill."

"Pleased to meet you," Mark said with a thin smile. "Grace has told me a lot about you."

"Same here," David replied a bit unsteadily. He was having trouble suppressing a roar of laughter. For suddenly he understood Grace's discomfiture.

"Well," Mark continued, looking down at his bare toes and then grinning sheepishly, "if you don't need me, I think I'll go take a shower."

"I don't need you," David told him with a perfectly straight face.

"Yes, do go ahead and shower," Grace chimed in.

When Mark left, David turned back to look at his former lover. "Nice guy."

Grace's cheeks were still flaming, and David mused that it was the first time he'd seen her embarrassed. It was actually quite appealing. For a moment she looked almost girlish.

"Well," she declared belligerently, "he *is* a nice guy. And you might as well know I'm going to marry him."

David was even more astonished. "You are?"

"Yes." She lifted her hands level with her generous bosom and pressed her palms together. "He loves me, really loves me. And I'm not getting any younger."

In the revealing morning light, David suddenly saw Grace as though for the first time. As far as he was concerned, she would always be a handsome woman. But it was true that she could no longer be described as young.

"Grace, I thought you weren't interested in marriage," he said gently.

She sighed and let her hands drop to her lap. "Well, I thought it was true. But Mark has made me realize that I was just saying all that because I knew it was what you wanted to hear." At David's startled expression, she added, "Oh, David, sometimes I think you really don't know what a hunk you are. When we first met you were such a doll—bright, good looking, great in bed—and younger. I didn't want to frighten you off. And you would have run the other way if I'd said that I wanted more than just a fling—now wouldn't you?''

David stumbled over his response. He knew she was right. But the realization didn't make him feel particularly good about himself. And he was also experiencing real concern for her. "Grace, are you sure about this?"

She smiled. "About marrying Mark? Oh, yes. He's not like you. When we go to a party, I don't have to worry about other women trying to take him away from me. He's a dear, sweet man who makes me happy. And I love him. But, oh David, I feel terrible about the grant." She gazed at him with worried brown eyes. "I know how hard you worked putting it together. Can you ever forgive me?"

David's face relaxed into a slow smile. "Yes, Gracie, I can forgive you. As a matter of fact, I have a confession to make myself. You're not the only one who doesn't want to leave the country."

It was a strange day and one that David would always remember. After Mark showered, he came out, gave Grace a proprietary kiss on the nose and left for work. When he was gone, she fixed a pot of coffee and while she and David drank it, they talked. As if it had all happened to other people a long time ago, they discussed their defunct affair. "It wasn't going anywhere," Grace pointed out. "Really, we were just using each other."

"Sounds pretty cold," David said ruefully.

She reached across and gave his hand a friendly squeeze. "Oh, David, you were never cold. And you were never unfair, either. From the first, you made it clear what you wanted, and what you didn't want. I think I'll always be your friend, and I hope that no matter what happens you'll still be mine." She hesitated. "You've met someone else, haven't you?"

"Yes," he admitted. "Yes, I have." And as he said the words, he realized that he wanted nothing more than to get on the next plane back to Maryland so that he could apologize to Faye and tell her how he felt.

It was another twenty-four hours before David's return flight landed in Baltimore. By that time he was so exhausted that when he got back to his apartment he fell into bed and didn't come to life again until early the next morning. But as soon as he'd showered and had his morning coffee, he called Faye. When she didn't answer her phone, he almost gnashed his teeth with frustration. Where could she be at eight in the morning? The office at Wilderness Worlds didn't open until nine.

After spending the next hour wearing a trench in his living room carpet, David dialed the office. "Miss Prior?"

"Oh, is that you, Dr. O'Neill?" she asked breathlessly. "Thank goodness! I've been trying to get you!"

"You have? Where's Faye?"

"She's in Alaska."

"What!"

"Yes, she had to take some important papers up to Wallace. And wouldn't you just know it! Now that she and Wallace and Roy are all gone and I'm here by myself, we're having a terrible problem with Kong and Daisy Mae. Won't you please come right away and see what's wrong with them?''

CHAPTER ELEVEN

"ROY, WHAT'S WRONG?"

"What are you talkin' about? Nothin's wrong."

While Roy steered the rental station wagon out of Juneau's new international airport and onto the highway, Faye sat next to him in the passenger seat frowning. Despite what he'd just said, she knew that something was amiss. True, since her angry parting with David she'd been depressed. But the sense of foreboding that had weighed her down all during the flight to Seattle and then on up to Juneau had nothing to do with that. And the moment she'd seen Roy her anxiety had increased.

"This valley certainly makes a spectacular setting for an airport," she said in an attempt at normal conversation. "I've never seen anything quite like it." The guidebook she'd consulted had explained that Juneau was accessible only by boat and airplane. Now she could see the reason. Surrounded by mountains, glaciers and water, the Alaskan capital's roads all terminated in natural barriers.

"Yeah," Roy retorted, "I hear the place is fogged in half the time. You're lucky your pilot didn't scrape you off on Mount Juneau."

Despite his cocky remark, Roy's eyes wouldn't quite meet hers, and his jerky, distracted driving made her worry that they might have an accident. It was impossible to look around and enjoy the gorgeous scenery while he was dodging in and out of traffic.

"What's the big rush? Why don't you just stay in one lane?" she queried. "We're going to have an accident if you keep on this way." Losing David made it seem as if life wasn't worth living, but Faye wasn't ready to give up on it entirely.

"Is that Wally's briefcase?" Roy asked, ignoring her complaint and braking sharply to avoid a slow-moving vehicle.

Faye put a hand out to steady herself against the dashboard. "It's right here."

"You didn't look inside it, did you?"

"Of course not. Wally asked me not to unlock it, so I didn't."

"Good."

Pushing a strand of windblown hair out of her eyes, Faye reflected that maybe she should have disobeyed her uncle's orders. His sudden, half-hysterical request that she drop everything and fly to the other end of the continent with the leather briefcase he'd left on top of his desk certainly seemed peculiar. Aloud she asked, "What's so important about this thing that I had to bring it personally? Why couldn't I have just sent it by express mail or courier?"

"The old man doesn't trust the mail, and the papers inside it are real important to the deal he's trying to pull off up here." Roy yanked at the steering wheel. "Sure beats me how he could have left them behind in the first place. But then he's forgetting everything these days."

That was true, Faye admitted to herself. She chewed on a nail and thought of David's cruel words about Wally: "He's getting senile. He's not able to make intelligent judgments." She'd resented him for saying such things. Yet she couldn't stop worrying that there might be a grain of truth in what he'd said.

"How's the deal with the bear coming along?" she asked.

"Huh, what bear?"

Faye shot him a startled look. "What do you mean, 'What bear'? Why, the one you came up here to buy, of course."

"Oh, that." Roy's pale skin pinkened. "Coming along just fine."

As Faye sat scrutinizing his sharp profile, it suddenly came to her that he was lying. What's more, he was going to kill them both if he kept driving like a maniac. "Roy, for heaven's sake," she snapped, "stop weaving in and out of the traffic like that." She looked back at the pickup they'd narrowly missed and then her eyes widened. About fifty lengths behind it she caught sight of a familiar face. "My God!"

Roy's head swiveled like a puppet's. "What? What is it?"

"Nothing. Will you keep your eyes on the road, please!"

His knuckles showing white on the steering wheel, he stared straight ahead through the windshield. "What did you see?"

"I—I think I saw a driver who looks like that guy who's been hanging around Wilderness Worlds. But it couldn't be him, of course."

To her amazement, Roy demanded, "Are you sure? Take another look and see if you can recognize him."

"Roy, we're in Alaska. It couldn't possibly be the same man I saw in Maryland."

"Look anyway."

Frowning, Faye peered through the back window. "I can't see him that clearly now. He's moved farther back."

"But he's still following us?"

Faye rolled her eyes. What was wrong with Roy, anyway? "He's still behind us, if that's what you mean."

Abruptly Roy swerved the station wagon onto a side road and accelerated through a red light. "Hey!" Faye yelped in protest as her body was slammed against the door handle. But instead of slowing, Roy pressed even harder on the gas pedal and roared through another traffic light before squealing onto a narrow side road and then into an alley where he pulled up sharply behind a liquor store.

"Are you crazy!" Faye screamed at him. She was clinging to the back of her seat.

"I wanted to lose that car. It didn't follow us, did it?"

"Of course not! Only a lunatic would have tried to follow us. You're lucky we didn't get killed or arrested."

At the word "arrest," Roy blanched. "I had to lose that tail before I took you to Wally's motel."

"Tail?" Now Faye was worried not only about her uncle's mental condition, but about Roy's as well. "You can't possibly believe that it was the same guy. We're about as far away from Maryland as you can get and stay on the same continent."

"Okay, maybe he wasn't the same guy, but he could have been from the same agency."

"Agency?" Faye's jaw dropped.

"The CIA, the FBI—who knows?" Roy muttered unhappily.

A chill ran up her spine. "Roy Hubbard, we're not going any farther until you tell me what's going on."

"I can't tell," he whined. "Wally made me promise not to."

"I don't give a damn what Wally made you promise. If you don't tell me this minute, I'm going to take whatever is in this briefcase straight to the police." She tapped the leather case on her knee.

Roy reached for it, but Faye held it out the window and out of his grasp.

"You can't take that to the police," he cried with a haunted look. "If you do Wally will be arrested."

Now Faye went pale. "For God's sake, Roy, tell me what this is all about."

He chewed on his knuckles, his nostrils flaring as he breathed noisily in and out. "All right, you win." Slumping back in his seat, he let his hands drop limply against the steering wheel. "All right, all right," he repeated, "we're in big, big trouble. And you know what? I think this time good old Uncle Wally may not be able to get us out."

"TALK ABOUT your male chauvinist pigs," David muttered. He eyed Kong, who glared sullenly back. "You've made Daisy Mae sick, do you realize that? Stealing her food, not letting her near the drinking water, being so damn nasty and high-handed with her. Well, now your girlfriend has been taken away from you for a while. We'll see how you like that."

Kong didn't like it at all, and he'd already made his displeasure clear. When Daisy Mae had been removed to another part of the ape house he'd screamed and carried on like a two-year-old deprived of its favorite toy.

With one last backward glance at the glowering young gorilla, David left the ape house and crossed behind the lion cages to the office. There he found a distracted Miss Prior. She was bent over an open file drawer sorting frantically through manila folders and muttering to herself. Her glasses had slipped down her nose and several of her curls stood on end as if she'd been tugging on them. "Oh dear, oh dear," she chanted under her breath. "Where could it be? I was sure I filed it under M."

When David shut the door with a click, she half-turned and peered anxiously at him as if he'd caught her reading a forbidden novel. Then her sharp features relaxed a fraction. "Oh, there you are, Dr. O'Neill. I've been so overworked I hardly know what I'm doing. Really, it's not fair of Wallace to leave me all alone here. Everything, just everything, has gone wrong. And now I can't find a contract I need to copy."

"Some days are like that," David agreed. "Daisy Mae hasn't exactly been having a good time of it lately, either."

Clucking, Miss Prior shut the file drawer and scurried back to the chair behind her desk. "What is wrong with that Kong, do you think? Daisy Mae seems like such a sweet-natured creature. Why is he treating her so badly?"

"It's an adjustment problem. I think eventually they'll settle down. For now I've separated them."

"Oh?"

"Yes. I've put Daisy Mae in next to Violet, which is a good idea in any case. It will give her an opportunity to see another ape mothering her child."

"Yes, I suppose so." Miss Prior looked faintly embarrassed. "You know, when I called you I'd forgotten all about your resignation. Faye did mention it before she left."

"Did she?" What else had she said, David wondered. Obviously Faye hadn't quoted any of his parting remarks to Ruby Prior. The secretary looked puzzled, but not unfriendly. Knowing her devotion to Wallace Gaffey, David figured she'd probably throw her typewriter at his head if she knew what he'd had to say about her boss.

"Dr. O'Neill, I hope you don't mind that I called you? I was desperate, and I didn't know who else to contact."

"Don't worry about it. It was all a mistake, anyway."

"A mistake? Oh, I hope you mean your resignation. Wallace thinks so highly of you."

David was trying to frame an answer that made sense—to himself as well as to the secretary—when the phone rang.

"Faye, dear," Miss Prior exclaimed a moment after she'd taken the call. "It's delightful to hear your voice."

Not bothering to pretend that he wasn't listening, David stepped toward the desk. Suddenly he was jealous of Miss Prior. He wanted to be the one hearing Faye's voice, and he wanted it so badly that he almost snatched the phone out of the gray-haired secretary's hand.

In the next instant a frown replaced Miss Prior's smile. "What is it, dear? What's the trouble...? I don't understand you." She covered the receiver with her hand and glanced across at David. "There's something wrong," she said in a stage whisper. "I can't understand what she's saying."

David reached over and seized the phone and pressed it to his ear. "Faye, this is David. What's the trouble."

"David? Oh God! David, you were right."

"What?"

"I can't talk about it on the phone, but there's something..."

Her voice trailed off, and he thought he heard a smothered sob. His fingers tightened around the coiled telephone cord, crushing it out of shape. "Faye, are you in some sort of trouble?"

"You might say that." All at once her voice sounded calmer.

"Can I help?"

"I don't know. I don't know if anyone can help."

He released the mangled cord and raked taut fingers through his hair. "Is there anything more you can tell me?"

Across the breadth of the continent, her laugh tinkled like breaking glass. "Only that you were right, and I should have listened to you."

Her words made his mind race. Then, decisively, he flattened his free hand on the desk. "Sit tight. I'll hop the next plane and be there as soon as I can."

"Oh, David..."

"Just give me instructions where to meet you." Grimly he listened and made notes on a piece of paper that Miss Prior had slid across to him. When the conversation was ended, he handed the receiver back to the secretary. "You heard."

"Yes. What's it all about?" Behind her glasses she was blinking rapidly and there was a terrified look in her pale blue eyes. "Wallace isn't sick, is he? Alaska is so far away. Oh, I knew I should have packed warmer clothes. But he kept insisting that it was summer. I shouldn't have listened. I should have done what I knew was best."

As he registered her frightened babble, it suddenly dawned on David just how deeply the woman cared for her boss. Why the old girl was actually in love with Gaffey.

Sympathetically—because David was beginning to understand just how that felt—he reached across and patted her scrawny shoulder. "As far as I can tell, he's not sick. I'll know better when I get there. But in the meantime, I'm afraid you're going to have to keep on holding the fort."

FAYE STUCK HER HANDS deep in the pockets of her new pale pink windbreaker. Accustomed as she was to Maryland's heat, she'd been unprepared for cool weather and had been forced to stop on the way to the airport to purchase the jacket. June was actually spring in Alaska. Tulips bloomed and the highs were in the fifties and sixties.

Head down, she listened to the loudspeaker's announcements about incoming flights. She knew she should stop her nervous pacing. She was calling attention to herself with it. But she couldn't seem to keep still. It had been that way from the moment of Roy's revelation. She hadn't slept a wink last night, and if she'd managed to force any solid food down this morning, she had no memory of it.

Once again Faye stopped to squint past the security point. According to the voice on the loudspeaker, David's plane had landed. Tired-looking people toting briefcases and garment bags were beginning to straggle up the concourse. At any moment she ought to see him.

Then, miraculously, there he was. Like everyone else on his flight, he looked weary. A lock of brown hair grazed his forehead and a faint shadow darkened his jaw. He wore lightweight tan slacks and loafers. A white shirt open at the throat and rolled up at the sleeves contrasted with his firmly muscled, hair-dusted forearms. He'd slung a sport coat over one shoulder, and his left hand gripped a sturdy leather bag.

As he strode past the security check, Faye felt like rushing forward and throwing herself at him. Ever since their night together and the argument that had capped it, she'd been one big ache compounded of loss and confusion. Even through this horrible mess with Roy and Wally, she'd kept thinking about David—remembering how it had felt to be in his arms and wondering if she'd ever have that pleasure again. It didn't seem likely—not after the manner in which she'd sent him away, not knowing that he had another woman. When she'd called Ruby Prior, she'd been stunned to hear his voice on the other end of the line—stunned, and despite everything, very, very relieved.

David had spotted her now. Steadily he closed the distance between them, his gray eyes fixed on her face. "You look exhausted," he said when he stopped in front of her. "What's been going on here?"

Faye plucked at one of the buttons on her new jacket. "You don't look so hot yourself."

He laughed briefly. "No, and with my complicated case of jet lag, I don't feel so hot, either." As if he had no doubt that Faye belonged to him, he appropriated her arm and guided her firmly toward the exit. "Let's get out of here and go someplace where we can talk."

"You don't need to claim any luggage?"

"Negative. I always travel light."

Yes, she thought, as they headed for the exit. Despite the proprietary way in which he was steering her toward the doors, he was a man who didn't like to be burdened, and he'd made that fact very clear. What was his reaction going to be when she laid Roy's story on him?

Once in the Toyota she'd rented, David looked out the side window while she threaded the little car through airport traffic. "Spectacular setting," he commented as he eyed the mountain barriers surrounding them.

"Yes. Our motel is near the Mendenhall glacier. It's a mile and a half wide and has a two-hundred-foot face. We can drive up and look at it if you want."

"Faye, I've been here before and I'm not interested in seeing the sights. I've come to find out what's been happening."

She shot him a sideways glance and replied in a strangled voice. "I know and I'm grateful. I really am. After the way I talked to you before, I feel like a complete fool."

"Do you want to tell me about it now?"

"No. Roy's supposed to meet us where we're staying. I think he'd better be in on this."

David frowned, but his only comment was a terse, "All right."

When they pulled into an unprepossessing motor lodge a few minutes later he made no comment about that either, but Faye saw his expression. She knew he was wondering why a millionaire like Wallace Gaffey would book rooms at such an undistinguished place instead of at one of the colorful hotels in downtown Juneau. She would have wondered that herself if she hadn't already known the reason. With a sigh, she switched off the car's engine and turned toward her passenger. "I'd better tell you now. Wally and Roy are booked under the names Howard Simpson and Gary Barker. I'm Margaret Simpson and I've registered you as Paul Reese."

David's brows shot up. "Is that necessary?"

"To be honest, I'm not sure whether it is or not. Roy and Wally wanted to do things that way, and I decided it would be best to humor them." She ran a finger along the edge of the seat. "As a matter of fact, Wally doesn't know you're here."

He gazed wordlessly at her, and Faye wondered if she looked as pale and sick with worry as she felt. When she'd left for the airport this morning, she'd done her best to dress attractively and mask the signs of her sleepless night with blusher. But as David looked at her with those clear, uncompromising eyes of his, all her little self-protective pretenses seemed useless and even ridiculous.

Exactly why had he offered to come, she asked herself. Was it out of a sense of duty because he'd slept with her and thought he owed her something? Or could she hope that it was because he felt more for her than he was willing to admit? But he hadn't heard the story yet. Faye sighed. When he did, she wouldn't be surprised if he turned around and took the next flight back to Seattle.

"You spend altogether too much time humoring that uncle of yours," David said.

"I'm beginning to think you may be right." Faye opened the door to get out of her side of the car. "Do you want to freshen up before we have this discussion?"

"No."

"Then let's go to my room and get it over."

"Anything you say."

A few minutes later she led him into her nondescript motel room. Sparing no more than a glance for the cheap furnishings, he tossed his jacket and case on the brown-and-orange-striped bedspread and then stood looking at her, his hands on his hips. "Faye..."

She didn't know what he wanted to say, whether it was a question about Wally or something more personal, but suddenly her heart began to race. She quickly crossed to the phone. "I'll see if Roy's back."

When she heard the maintenance chief's voice on the other end of the line, she wiped her forehead with relief. Roy hadn't been pleased about David's joining them. "What's that guy horning in on this for?" he'd complained. "What do you think he can do?"

"I don't know," she'd answered. "But Dr. O'Neill has been around. He knows more about this sort of thing than we do. Maybe he can suggest a way out of it."

Roy had snorted his disdain and disbelief, and now he repeated himself. "So lover boy's arrived," he sneered. "What do you want me to do about it?"

Normally Roy seemed impervious to the feelings of others. Yet there were isolated instances when his perception amazed Faye. How had he guessed that there was something more than gorilla management between her and David? Was it in the expression on her face whenever David's name was mentioned?

Lord, she hoped not! She hated to think of herself as being so transparent. Aloud, she told Roy, "I want you to come over here and let him know what's going on."

"And if I don't?"

"Then I will, and I can't be responsible for what happens after that. You're in this just as deep as Wally is."

"And so are you, little girl. Have you thought of that?" Roy flung back at her before slamming down the phone.

Minutes later there was a thud on the door and when Faye opened it a sullen-looking Roy stood outside. He wore his usual jeans and T-shirt. But he'd exchanged his baseball cap for a broad-brimmed leather hat trimmed with a pheasant feather. "I picked up this headgear today," he informed her as he tipped it back at a jaunty angle. "Like it?"

"Very attractive," she told him as she stood to one side. Actually she thought he looked ridiculous in it.

He swaggered in and ran an unfriendly eye over David. "Hiya, Doc."

"Hello, Hubbard."

Faye felt like screaming with impatience. "Roy, please tell David what you told me."

Roy's lip curled. "Then maybe he better sit down."

"I think we'd all better sit down." Decisively she pulled out the desk chair for Roy, indicated the armchair for David and then perched on the bed. When they were all settled an uneasy silence ensued.

Faye glanced at David, who was waiting grimly, and then turned to Roy. "Are you going to tell him, or do I have to?" she warned.

"All right, all right." Roy focused on a point three feet below the overhead fixture and began speaking in a monotone. "Well, the long and short of it is that Wally wanted a panda for the opening of Wilderness Worlds and what Wally wants, Wally gets."

Out of the corner of her eye Faye saw David's jaw slacken. Wait until he heard the rest of it, she thought.

"So anyway," Roy continued, "he latched onto a scheme to have one smuggled out of China."

"You can't be serious," David exclaimed.

Finally Roy addressed him directly. "I wouldn't kid you, Doc. This is real serious stuff."

David turned to Faye. "When did you first find out about this?"

"Just yesterday. You have to believe me. I didn't know a thing."

"She's tellin' the truth," Roy confirmed. "Me and the old man kept it a big secret. Well, we had to. No one could know until we'd pulled it off, and it was supposed to be a surprise."

There was a brief period during which nobody spoke and Faye could hear David breathing. "Does this have something to do with whatever's being built behind that guarded fence?" he demanded.

For a moment Roy looked blank. Then he nodded. "Yeah. That's supposed to be the panda house." His laugh was brief and nervous. "Wally even had some bamboo planted near the construction site. He didn't want anyone to see it before he was ready to open. Figured they might catch on to what it was intended for and blow the whistle."

Again David was dangerously silent, and Faye held her breath anticipating his next reaction.

"So far this sounds totally crazy," he finally bit out. "It would be impossible to get a panda out of China. They're too closely guarded."

Faye couldn't keep herself from stepping in. "Wait until you hear the rest of it. Wally actually financed a secret expedition into China."

"You're joking!"

Unhappily she shook her head. "The plan was for a team of men to leave East Pakistan and travel by mule and on foot across As—" She looked at him questioningly.

"Assam?"

"Yes. Wally actually showed me the route on a map last night, but my geography isn't all it should be. They were going to skirt the foothills of the Nyenchen—" Once again she hesitated.

"The Nyenchentanglha Mountains are in Tibet," David supplied. "I suppose that theoretically it's possible that once around them an expedition could reach panda country. But practically speaking, it's out of the question."

"The guy who approached Wally with the scheme didn't think so," Roy chimed in. "Of course, he didn't exactly come cheap, either. The old man's paying a cool million for this teddy bear."

For a long uncomfortable moment David simply looked at Roy. "And just how was this panda supposed to be spirited out of China?"

"Wally told me the plan," Faye said, wanting to come between some of the obvious friction the two men were generating. "They were going to bring it back into Pakistan, dye it a dark color and then smuggle it out as a low-value brown bear."

"Brilliant," David snapped. "I'm beginning to feel as if I've stepped through the looking glass into Wonderland and the Red Queen is shouting 'Off with their heads!'"

Roy flushed. "Off with whose head? Listen, O'Neill, you laugh but Baker must have pulled it off. He says he's got the bear."

"Then he's lying," David shot back. "There's no way that anyone could have smuggled a panda out of China." Suddenly his eyes narrowed. "Baker? Are you telling me that Gaffey worked this deal with a man named Morton Baker?"

"Yeah, that's the dude."

"My God!" David ground his teeth. "I might have known."

"Known what?"

Faye looked from Roy to David. "Just who is this Morton Baker?" Last night she'd asked Wally, but his answer, like most of his statements, had been vague. It had practically broken her heart to listen to him, and she'd been forced to admit to herself how badly he'd been failing during the past year.

"Morton is a renegade white hunter who's also a con artist." David turned back to Roy. "How much money has Gaffey already paid this man?"

"I don't know. A half a million, maybe."

David whistled. "Well, he can kiss it goodbye."

Roy looked outraged. "Whaddya mean, kiss it goodbye?"

"I meant exactly what I said. You might as well tell me the reason you and Wally are here. Are you meeting Baker?"

"Yeah," Roy muttered. "Wally is supposed to pay him another quarter mil, and make arrangements to

get the panda delivered. He left the money in a briefcase on his desk back at Wilderness Worlds. That's
why he had to get Faye to bring it up here personally."

"You mean your boss is paying Baker in cash?"

"That's the only way he would take it."

As she listened, Faye began to feel light-headed. On
the plane she'd never for a minute dreamed that she
was carrying a quarter of a million dollars in cash.
What if the security guard had checked the case to see
what was inside? "They're supposed to meet the man
on the tenth," she supplied in a weak voice.

David stood and consulted the calendar on his
watch. "Two days from now."

Looking up, she saw the pulse ticking at his temple
and cleared her throat. "There's something else you
should know."

"What?"

"For the past month or so there's been a guy hanging around Wilderness Worlds asking questions. Yesterday Roy thought we were being followed."

"Who does he think was doing the following?"

"How should I know?" Roy mumbled sullenly.
"Some government spook, maybe."

Exasperation etched David's face. "I wouldn't be
surprised. If the State Department got wind of this
deal they'd have kittens." He struck his open palm
with his balled fist. The impact made a sharp noise in
the little room, startling both Faye and Roy. "How
could Gaffey imagine for a moment that he could hire
a crook like Baker to bring a stolen panda into this
country? If he succeeded it would create an international incident. I can just see the headlines. The
Russians would have a field day. It would infuriate the

Chinese, embarrass the American government and ruin Gaffey."

Roy went pale. "What about me? I was the go-between."

"Then you could wind up behind bars right along with your boss. And so could Faye if she has anything more to do with this," David added. He turned back to where she sat, clenching and unclenching her hands. "Faye," he urged in a low earnest voice, "believe me, the smartest thing you can do is wash your hands of this. Call the airport and book yourself on the next plane headed east."

She stared back at him, her eyes burning while a monster headache began to pummel her temples. "Leave Wally? But David, I couldn't do that."

"Yes, you could," he insisted. "You had no part in this situation, and take my word for it, you want no part of it now."

"I can't just leave."

"No, she can't," Roy loudly agreed as he hopped off his chair. "I'm not going to take the rap all by myself. If the Feds get hold of this, I'll say that Faye gave Wally just as much help in the scheme as I did."

David swiveled and eyed Roy as if he were something he'd just found growing in a petri dish. "Don't overwhelm us with chivalry, Hubbard."

"It's every man for himself, and don't give me the fish-eye that way, O'Neill. I'll say you were in it, too." He shook his fist.

Ignoring Roy's histrionics, Faye focused all her attention on David. This had to be one of the worst moments of her life, and she hated what she was about to do. But if she had to beg, she would. "Please," she said in a low, pleading voice. "I can't leave Wally. I have to help him. I know I have no right to ask, but won't you stay and help, too? Oh, David, please..."

It was a long moment before he replied, and as Faye waited for his response, her nerves seemed to tie themselves into knots.

"Yes," he finally said. "I'll stay. Who knows, maybe if we put our heads together we can figure something out."

CHAPTER TWELVE

AFTER AN HOUR of edgy debate, Roy, Faye and David managed to agree on one thing. If there was to be any chance of extricating Wally and themselves from this mess, they would need his cooperation. Somehow, they had to talk him out of his crazy scheme.

"It's not going to be easy," Faye warned, her eyes once again clouded with worry. "He adores intrigue and he's in love with the idea of having his own panda."

"Well, that's one love match that isn't going to bear fruit," David commented dryly. "He has to be convinced of that. And right now I'm in the mood to do some serious convincing. Where is he?"

Wally's room was just two units down from Faye's, but when she ran to knock on his door, he wasn't in. "He's probably not back from lunch yet," she told David upon her return. "We'll have to wait."

"All right."

"Not here," Roy muttered. "I got things to do."

"And I could use a wash," David commented. "Think I'll take the time to unpack and get settled." As he spoke, he opened the door to let Roy out and then followed with only a brief look back. What he had to say to Faye would have to wait for a better time.

Maybe a hot shower will make me feel a little better, he told himself after he located his room. But a few minutes later as he stood letting hot water pelt his travel-weary body, he was anything but soothed. It wasn't just this tangle with Wally.

Seeing Faye waiting for him in the airport, looking so pale and frightened and so damn pretty had hit him with unbelievable force. He was furious with Wally and Roy for dragging her into their idiotic scheme. Not that she couldn't cope. It seemed as if she was perpetually surprising and impressing him with her inner strength. He had to admire the way she'd handled herself and Roy this afternoon. And for that matter—the way she'd handled him, too. She was quite a woman.

"And she deserves better, dammit," David said aloud. Faye Johnson deserved a man who could protect her from this sort of nonsense—a man who could make her happy, a man who could share his life with her.

Sharply David shut off the taps and stepped out of the shower stall. As water dripped from his muscled torso and down his sinewy legs onto the tile floor, he reached blindly for a towel and then peered through his water-clumped lashes into the clouded mirror. The gray eyes looking back seemed to mock him. "Well, David old boy," he muttered, "where do you fit in? Any chance of you being that guy?"

IN HER ROOM a few doors down, Faye paced nervously. What was going to happen next, she kept asking herself. The ring of the telephone distracted her and when she picked it up her hand flew to her mouth.

"Wally? Where have you been?"

He sounded defensive. "Just out walking around and getting some fresh air. This is really a beautiful spot. You should get out of that room and do some sight-seeing."

"Sure." Faye tucked a strand of hair behind her ear. Wally couldn't fool her. He might pretend to be full of confidence, but she was certain that he was beginning to have his doubts about this whole venture. Indeed, that was probably one of the reasons why he'd wanted her in Juneau at his side, she speculated. He needed reassurance. Well, he wasn't going to get it today, she thought grimly. "Uncle Wally, Dr. O'Neill is here."

"O'Neill? What's he doing in Juneau?"

"I asked him to fly up. Could we come and see you now?"

There was a long pause. "What did you want O'Neill up here for?" Wally questioned suspiciously.

"I can't talk about it on the phone. Can we come and see you?"

After a brief silence, he grudgingly agreed and Faye sighed with relief. Depressing the dial tone, she rapidly punched out David's room number. "He's back," she said when she heard his deep baritone.

"All right. I'm just getting dressed. Give me five minutes and then we'll tackle him together."

"David, he's an old man—an old man with a dream. He wasn't trying to do anything evil. You won't be..." Her voice trailed off.

"I won't be nasty," David replied, and for the first time since he'd arrived she could hear a hint of humor in his voice. "Faye, I promise I'll be as diplomatic as I'm able. But somehow that uncle of yours has to be made to realize that this is folly."

She nodded. David was right, of course. But then he usually was. It was she who'd been making dumb mistakes all over the place lately. "Okay. See you in five minutes."

"Five minutes. I suppose we should round up Hubbard on the way," he added unenthusiastically.

"I suppose."

David was right on time and, to Faye's vast relief, when they confronted Wally, David was as gentle as he'd promised to be. While Roy remained little more than a sulky presence in the background, David was the soul of tact. Knowing his temper and what he really thought about the situation, she had to admire the patient manner in which he outlined the reasons why Wally must abandon his scheme.

At first the old man tried to deny those reasons. But David was firm as well as gentle and simply wouldn't be put off. And Faye observed that despite her uncle's attempts to defend his actions, there was a bewildered, half-frightened look in his faded eyes. As she watched and listened, she realized that she'd been right. Behind the bluster, he was uncertain about the decisions he'd made. *It must really scare him,* Faye thought with a painful little twist in her chest. *He's probably never doubted himself before in his life.*

"From what I know of Morton Baker," David was saying across from where Wally hunched on the edge of his bed, "he's too smart a cookie to take six months of risks for a million when he could get half that much for free by doing nothing. There's no reason for Baker to live up to his end of the deal. I think he's going to take the next installment and disappear."

When Wally tried to protest, David leaned forward and added pointedly, "For all you know, he hasn't done anything with the money he's got from you so far, and if he clears out now you can't very well go to the police screaming fraud."

It hurt Faye to see the way her uncle seemed to shrink into himself. "All right," he admitted unhappily, "I see your logic. I guess it wasn't such a good idea to think I could get away with bringing a panda to Wilderness Worlds. But I can't just forget about it and go home. I'm supposed to rendezvous with Baker on the tenth. He's going to phone early tomorrow and let me know the spot. Baker's a very tough character. If I don't show up with the money, there's no telling what he might do."

"He could blackmail you."

Wally paled. "I don't know why I didn't think of it before, but you're right, O'Rourke. I'm in a hell of a position."

David put his hand on the old man's sagging shoulder. "Listen, if we go about this the right way, maybe he won't get the chance."

Wally looked up hopefully. "What do you mean? Have you got a plan?"

"Yes, I think I do." Suddenly a grin flashed across David's rugged features. "Baker won't get the chance to blackmail you because as soon as money changes hands between the two of you, he'll be arrested."

"Whatcha got in mind?" Roy demanded from the corner where he slouched.

But David only shook his head. "I don't have it all worked out yet, but I think I'm on to something. Just leave it to me."

Both Roy and Wally pressed David for more answers, but he remained firm and told them to wait until tomorrow. When they realized they weren't going to get any more out of him, the meeting broke up,

Wally claiming that he needed a nap and Roy mumbling something about going out for a beer. David headed back toward his room. But just as he was putting the key in the lock, he heard the soft thump of lightly running feet and Faye came up behind him.

"David, thank you. You were wonderful," she exclaimed a little breathlessly.

He turned, taking in with a stab of pleasure the delicate pink in her cheeks, the jade sheen of her eyes. "I want to do whatever I can to help." He left out the "you," which should have ended that statement. "And I'd like to put Morton Baker behind bars where he belongs."

"Do you really have a plan?"

"I think so."

"But you're not going to reveal it to me?"

"I'll tell you all tomorrow. In the meantime—" he glanced up at the lowering afternoon sun "—there are a few calls I have to make. When I'm finished with those, I'm going to be ready for a good meal. Do you have any plans for this evening?"

"Nothing in particular. Last night I ate with Roy and Wally. But they can certainly manage on their own."

"Then would you have dinner with me?"

Two days ago Faye would have refused. After finding out about his friend Grace, she'd made the painful decision that Dr. David O'Neill was a lost cause and the only smart thing to do was stay clear of him. But this was a different time and a different place and once more the rules between them had shifted. How could she say no when he'd just gone so far out of his way to help her? Refusing to think about the other woman in David's life, Faye nodded. "Yes, I'd be pleased to."

As she walked back to her room, she unconsciously rubbed her palms together while she tried to sort through her jumbled emotions. Uppermost was relief, relief that Wally was listening to reason, relief that David had taken charge. Welling up behind that was a spring of hope, and not just about retrieving Wally and Wilderness Worlds from the brink of disaster. Maybe it was dumb, but she couldn't help feeling that there might still be some chance for her with David. *Just being in the same room as he is, breathing the same air, hearing the same sounds makes me feel good,* she admitted to herself. *Oh God, just how deeply have I fallen in love with him?*

As she let herself into her room, she decided not to grapple with that question. It wasn't a case of the answer eluding her. She knew it, all right. But she didn't want to have to deal with it—not yet.

When David stopped by to pick her up, Faye was ready. She'd bathed and changed into the only dress she'd brought with her, a mint-green cotton shirtwaist with a swingy skirt, breast pockets and button-cuffed dolman sleeves. She'd cinched it at her waist with a leather belt in a darker shade of green that matched her shoes. A white linen blazer she'd had the forethought to bring along completed the outfit.

Except for a crisp shirt, David hadn't changed clothes but somehow he'd managed to get his slacks pressed. Something else was different about him, too, she noticed. He no longer looked angry and tired. The gray eyes that gave her an appreciative once-over held a secret sparkle, and there was a spring in his step that she didn't remember from before.

"You look as if you've had good news," she commented as he escorted her out to the car.

"I have."

"Care to let me in on it?"

"No. Right now what I care for is a good dinner. I'm still on East Coast time, you know, and I'm starving."

David had reserved a window seat at Yancy Derringer's. Decorated in natural wood surfaces that hearkened back to Juneau's gold rush era, the restaurant had a colorful location at the Merchant's Wharf. Diners could look out on the harbor with its sea lions and passing seaplanes, small boats and cruise ships.

After Faye and David had ordered drinks and their meals, he leaned back in his seat and gazed across at her.

"I've just remembered. When we had dinner together before, it was at a harbor."

"Yes," she said, thinking back to the evening when they'd eaten at the marina in Oxford, and she'd told him the story of her teenage pregnancy. "That was certainly a very different harbor from this one. I've been intrigued with what I've seen of Juneau. I wish this were a vacation and I had time to explore."

David didn't respond in kind to her attempt at light conversation. Instead, he said meaningfully, "A lot has happened since that meal we shared in Maryland."

"Yes, a lot." Faye looked down at her wineglass. To what did he refer—that night they'd spent making passionate love? Or was he just thinking about Wally's predicament? She cleared her throat. "David, I know I've already thanked you. But I feel I must do it again. And I also need to ask you about the risks you're taking. When you warned me not to involve myself in this situation, all I could think of was my uncle. But what about you? Is there any chance of your jeopardizing your career or anything else by helping him?''

David's faint smile was wry. Any involvement in a mess like this could ruin his professional reputation and destroy a career he'd devoted his life to building. By rights he should report this situation to the authorities and then wash his hands of it. That he was embarked on another course of action altogether meant something that he'd known when he went to see Grace but that he hadn't been willing to admit—even to himself. If Faye Johnson widened those tiger-green orbs and asked him to jump over the moon, he would probably do it. Aloud he said, "Don't worry about my career. I can take care of myself."

She looked at him doubtfully and then began to thank him all over again. "I really appreciate—"

"Faye—"

His tone cut off her apology sharply, and she gazed at him, transfixed by the strange expression in his eyes. But just then the waiter brought their dinners and the moment passed.

While they settled down to eat their seafood they talked of inconsequential things. It wasn't until they'd finished their meal and were sipping their coffee and herbal tea that they got back to the subject at hand.

"I wish you'd tell me what your plan is for the meeting with Baker," Faye said. "I can't help but worry."

"About me, or about your uncle and Roy?"

Faye studied his expression, taking in the cleft in his chin, his straight, strong nose and eyes the color of water on an overcast day. It was odd how there were moments that you never forgot, and they weren't necessarily the most dramatic ones in your life. Swallowing painfully, she acknowledged to herself that she would never forget David's face as it was at this instant.

"David," she said earnestly, "now that I've had time to think, I feel guilty about involving you. I was so relieved when I saw you at the airport today, but now I almost wish I hadn't let you come."

"You couldn't have stopped me. Faye, I came because I wanted to see you."

"You did...?" Her voice faltered and she was suddenly conscious of a tightness in her chest.

"Yes. I'm the one who should apologize. That argument we had in front of your house was stupid."

"You can say that after what's happened?"

"I can, but your uncle wasn't really why we were angry with each other. We both know that, don't we?"

"Yes." She sipped at her tea, hardly tasting it. It didn't take a genius to know they'd quarreled after their lovemaking because in the light of day the fantasy they'd shared had fallen apart. At least it had for her. Oh sure, she'd wanted him enough to tell herself that she was a mature woman who could handle the uncertainties of a temporary love affair.

But in the moonlight their loving hadn't seemed temporary. When the sun began to shine again and harsh reality prevailed, she'd had to face facts. He was not a Prince Charming who was going to stick around to live happily ever after with her. What's more, he already had another woman. The news about Grace had shocked her out of her fantasy world.

"I need to tell you something." His words dropped into the silence that seemed to vibrate between them like a struck harp string. "My internal clock is even more messed up than you might think. When I caught the flight out here, I'd just finished getting off a plane from California to Baltimore."

"What?"

"After I left you that day on your porch, I drove back home and found that my grant application had been approved."

"Congratulations," Faye said woodenly.

"I turned it down."

She almost dropped her tea cup. "You what?"

"When I realized I didn't want the grant, I flew out to California to talk the situation over with Grace."

Faye stiffened again, but as David hurried on to describe his encounter with his former lover, she began to relax. When he told her about Mark Benson, his eyes twinkled with amusement. And so great was Faye's relief at hearing the news that he and Grace were finished, she came close to laughing out loud herself.

"But really, you don't mind that she was having an affair with someone else and that she's going to marry the guy?"

David shook his head. "I'm happy for her."

"And that grant? I know you wanted it."

"I did, but I don't anymore." David signaled the waiter.

While he paid their bill with a credit card, Faye sat trying to assimilate his revelations. What did it all mean? Could she dare to hope that he'd given up the grant and his lady friend for her? But why else would he have told her about his break with Grace? At that thought all the worries weighing her down seemed to drop from her shoulders.

When David escorted her out of the restaurant a few minutes later, Faye felt as if she were floating at his side. He wasn't going to leave the country, and now he had no other woman in his life but her. As she repeated these two glorious facts over and over to herself, she trembled with happiness. And she sensed the same kind of excitement radiating from David. Though he walked with his customary contained grace, there was a coiled readiness about him, as if at the slightest signal he could take off with a shout and race for miles.

"Were you ever a runner?" she asked out of the blue.

He shot her a surprised look. "Yes, as a matter of fact. As an undergraduate I ran hurdles. I was quite fast. Not Olympic caliber, but quite fast."

"I'm not surprised."

After another quizzical glance, he took her arm to guide her toward the car. The contact sent such an overpowering wave of euphoria washing over her that she actually had to repress the urge to laugh out loud. *He could pick me up and run with me,* she thought and brushed her fingers over the sleeve of his jacket in a light caress. At that moment everything about him attracted her, and she didn't even try to fight it. She was drawn to the animal heat coming off his taut body, to the healthy masculine fragrance of him. His vitality seemed to radiate toward hers. *If auras were visible,* she suddenly thought a little giddily, *David and I would be glowing like stars.*

Despite the heightened awareness that she knew they were both experiencing, his voice remained steady. "Is there any place you'd like to go? By the clocks around here it's still early.''

A few paces from the Toyota he stopped to wait for her answer. What should she tell him? Faye felt as if every cell in his body were on the alert for her words, just as every nerve in hers was attuned to pick up the signals he might choose to send.

"I haven't really adjusted to the time change, either, and it's been a long day. Back to the motel is fine.''

"God, Faye,'' he muttered and reached out to crush her to him. Then they were kissing, their lips moving against each other's mouths with a kind of desperation, their tongues entwined in a voluptuous exchange of moist, shimmering heat. She pressed her breasts against his chest and stepped in to him so that his hips cradled hers and instantly felt his response. When he'd taken all he wanted from her yielding mouth he framed her face with his palms and covered her soft skin with hard, urgent little kisses. Then, with a groan, he wrapped his arms around her so that her head was pressed to his heart. For a long, breathless moment he stood stroking her hair and looking up at the brilliantly starred sky.

"Let's go back to the motel,'' he finally murmured roughly.

"Yes,'' she agreed.

He released her and with one accord they turned toward the car. Quickly she settled into the passenger seat and he went around to start up the engine. In a thinly stretched silence born of their mutual desire, David threaded the car through Juneau's busy streets. Once at a traffic light, he pulled her close and kissed her fiercely, but there were no words. None were required. Faye felt both tense and boneless as she tried to support the weight of her need for him. And from the taut deliberation of his driving, she knew David's feelings matched her own.

In front of the motel, he turned toward her, his hands clenched on the steering wheel. "Faye, can I come to your room?"

"Yes, please."

No further discussion was required. With their arms wrapped tightly around each other's waists, they hurried across the grass to Faye's door. Next to it a lilac bloomed, filling the night air with an almost painful sweetness, and she suddenly realized that from this moment on the evocative scent would always make her heart contract. When they were inside her room and the door securely closed out the world behind them, they didn't bother to switch on a light. Instead, like lovers who had been parted by a catastrophe and then miraculously reunited, they fell into each other's arms.

Their embrace was even hungrier and more frenzied than it had been after they'd left the restaurant. The iron control David had called upon to guide them safely back to the motel snapped. As he covered Faye's face and throat with fervent kisses, his hands rediscovered her slender body, stroking down the length of her back to her rounded bottom, easing around to her waist and the curve of her hip and then caging the softness of her breasts.

Faye wrapped her own hands around his neck, rubbing her thumbs along the strong ridge of his backbone as she pressed herself into him. Muffled little sighs and groans filled the darkness. A moment later Faye and David pulled apart and began undressing each other. While she worked at the buttons on his shirt, he undid the front of her dress. When she'd loosened his belt buckle, he slid down the zipper on his pants and stepped free of them as well as his shoes and socks. At the same time she let her loosened dress drop to the floor and then slipped out of her panty hose and unhooked her bra.

Once again they came together, skin on skin, Faye's silken softness flowing against David's sturdily muscled strength. "Where's the bed?" he whispered when their lips had finally parted.

"Somewhere behind you." As she spoke, she guided him to where she thought it must be and they fell back on it, laughing softly as the mattress cushioned their tumble. But an instant later they were lost in another starved and endless kiss, laughter forgotten.

Almost no light filtered through the curtained window. It was so dark that all of Faye's other senses were doubly heightened. Her fingertips absorbed the texture of him, the satiny skin that rippled over muscle, sinew and bone, the furred chest and legs, the warm breath of him, the taste of him.

And miraculously she rediscovered her own body through the same medium. In the thick darkness it was only through David's infinitely sensitive touch that she seemed real to herself. Under his fingertips her flesh came to life, her lips bloomed beneath his mouth, her breasts flowered against his hands, their tips aching like tender furled buds.

She needed very little preparation to receive him, though she luxuriated in the fire that his caresses sent tingling through her and would willingly have hung suspended indefinitely in the heat of that electric communion. Yet when at last he came to her, filling her with himself, the moment seemed all she could desire. That he ultimately gave her even more, an incandescent fulfillment that left her spent and satisfied beneath him, seemed a sweet miracle. As he softly stroked her forehead and kissed her closed eyelids, she almost purred with pleasure.

For a long moment they lay in silence, their hearts beating. But finally Faye had to speak. "Oh, David, when you walked away that day I was afraid—"

"I know, I was afraid of the same thing. But we're together again. Let's just hold on to that."

"Yes." Her fingers twined in his and stayed there, even when he rolled to one side so that he could cushion her head in the crook of his arm and gently stroke her breast.

"It's so dark in here, I can't see you," she complained.

"Would you like some light?"

"This is a motel. We can't open the curtains."

"Trust me." He squeezed her shoulder and then slipped out of bed. A moment later he switched on the light in the bathroom and then closed the door to within an inch of the jamb so that only a thin thread of brightness filtered through. Suddenly the dark well into which they'd plunged themselves became shadowy and Faye could make out the shape of the chair in the corner and the bureau on the opposite wall. She could also see David as he padded toward her. Naked, he was as fine and beautiful a masculine animal as she'd remembered, and she couldn't help watching him with possessive pride.

An instant later he was beside her in bed, cradling her in his arms.

"You're a wonderful lover, David," she whispered.

"Thank you."

She knew she shouldn't ask, but she couldn't stop herself. "I suppose you've made love to a lot of other women."

He kissed her forehead. "Faye, right now I wish we were both seventeen and with nothing behind us except our innocence. But I can't offer you that. I'm thirty-five and there have been others."

While she lay silent beside him, he stroked her shoulder tenderly. Experience, he mused, what did it amount to? Until Faye, he'd thought he'd gone through it all—the mistakes that left you feeling nothing but embarrassment and a kind of emptiness, the skilled exercises between two people amiably intent on using each other. He'd even once imagined himself in love. Suddenly he brought his face close to Faye's and gazed at her with an unsettling intensity. "There's never been anyone in my life like you."

She looked back at him in wonder. "Not Grace?"

"No, never Grace."

"You've never—David, haven't you ever loved anyone?"

"Once I thought I did. But I was wrong."

"Why? What happened?"

The question brought a wry twist to his lips. "I didn't love her enough to give up my work, and she didn't love me enough to cope with my selfishness. I was gone as much as I was there, and she didn't like that—not that I blame her. We'd been living together for a year when I came home after three weeks of consulting at a zoo in West Germany to find that she'd moved her things out and left me a six-word note. 'This isn't for me. Sorry, Janey.'"

"Oh, David, that's too bad."

"Why? It happened years ago, and obviously it wasn't exactly an enduring passion for either of us."

Frowning slightly, Faye stifled the urge to offer more sympathy. Janey's desertion must have meant more than he was admitting if he could still quote her note, she thought. Faye could only guess at his real feelings and at what had actually happened. Maybe Janey had left him for good reason. After all, what would it be like living with a man whose work always came first—a man who was never there for you?

"I felt you shiver. Are you cold?" David queried and leaned over to tug the sheet up around them both.

"No," she replied, and not wanting to think about the question she'd just asked herself, she changed the subject. "What happened to your glasses?"

He chuckled. "They're somewhere in that pile of clothes we dropped on the floor."

"Yes, we were in an awful hurry," she admitted with a giggle, letting her fingers drift across his chest. "Better not step on them."

"No, I'll need to see what I'm doing when your uncle and I meet Morton Baker."

Faye sobered again. That was changing the subject with a vengeance, she thought. For a brief time tonight the world outside their window hadn't existed. Now once again it began to loom with threat. Sighing, she leaned back against the pillow. "David," she began tentatively, "a few days ago you told me you thought Wally was senile."

"I know. Faye, I should never have talked that way. I was just so angry I couldn't see straight."

"Yes, but after what's happened, I have to wonder. Do you think that's why he got involved in this crazy scheme—because he's getting senile?"

Echoing her sigh with one of his own, David put his folded arms behind his head and looked up at the ceiling. "I haven't given your uncle a medical examination and I'm no expert on aging, but forgetfulness and poor judgment are signs that there might be a problem."

"What are the other signs?"

"Loss of enthusiasm, lack of clarity in communications, restricted vocabulary, radical mood shifts."

"Wally doesn't suffer from any of those."

"No. My bet is that with observation and treatment, he'll be okay. He is getting older and he's got to learn to slow down a bit. When we're out of this situation, we'll get him to a specialist. I know a good one at Hopkins."

"'When we're out of this situation?' You make it sound as if there's no doubt."

Propping himself up on his elbow, David turned to look down at her. He wanted to lower his head and kiss her worried expression away. He wanted to whisper tender words in her ear and make love to her again. But talk of Wally and his problems had destroyed the mood for Faye, he judged. And though she might accept his attentions, if they made love now it would probably be a poor second to what they'd just experienced.

Regretfully he sat up and raked his fingers through his hair. "I suppose I should go."

"Oh, why?" Seemingly unconscious of her nudity, she sat up next to him.

"Tomorrow is going to be a long day, and I don't suppose you'd like Roy or your uncle to see me coming out of your room in the morning." As he spoke, he was hotly conscious of her naked breasts, so round and beautiful and only an inch or two from his bare chest. Despite his calm words and collected tone of voice, his loins began to glow.

"No," she agreed huskily, "but it's not really late yet. They'll be less likely to see you if you stay for another hour or two."

"Another hour or two?"

"At least," Faye said, reaching out to him and offering her lips.

He accepted her invitation and soon their bodies were meshed. Once again they sought and discovered ecstasy in each other's arms. And their quest was not—as David had feared—a poor second, but its own unique adventure with its own special kind of found treasure.

CHAPTER THIRTEEN

"DAVID?"

Faye stared at the vacant pillow on the other side of the bed and then, clutching the sheet to her naked breasts, sat up and looked dazedly around the room. Only her green shirtwaist abandoned on the motel's carpeted floor testified to their night of lovemaking. Sometime while she'd been asleep, David had dressed and left.

Still drowsy and, despite her disappointment over David's departure, feeling illogically content, she pushed back a lock of blond hair and glanced at the clock on the bedside table. It read eight, which meant she'd slept hours past noon by East Coast standards. Maybe she was adjusting to the time change. And maybe she'd better stop yawning and get out of bed, she told herself. David had promised to lay his plan before them today, and she was eager to hear it.

Flipping back the covers, Faye climbed out of bed. As she reached for her bathrobe, she was conscious of her nakedness in a new and exciting way. It was strange to be so aware of her physical self, she mused as she belted the garment around her slim waist. But she knew what had caused it. This was now the body that David had loved, that he had kissed and caressed and finally claimed, and that knowledge changed everything.

As she padded toward the bathroom, she was alive to all kinds of new sensations—the slide of her thighs against each other, the way the silky fabric of her robe felt against her breasts, the slight soreness that was the result of David's pleasurable attentions. Even the pressure of her feet against the nubby carpet was a heightened sensual experience.

Once in the bathroom Faye shed her robe, turned on the taps and stepped into the shower. Lifting her face up to the warm water, she smiled and thought dreamily of how it would be if David were with her—of the things he would do and say and of her response. Crossing her arms over her breasts, she closed her eyes and let her imagination take fire.

But Faye was too sensible to indulge in daydreams for long. Twenty minutes later, dressed in her pink slacks and shirt, she was feeling more alert and less romantic. Last night had been wonderful, but today was today and there were massive problems to be faced.

The first thing she did was sit down on the edge of the bed and dial David's room. When he didn't answer, she tried Wally's number and then Roy's. After drawing a blank on all three, she bit her lip. Were they out someplace together? And if so, where, and why hadn't they taken her with them?

She had hoped to run into one of the three men in the motel's coffee shop. But when she walked into the place there was no sign of them. Wally's rented station wagon, she'd already noted, was missing. Taking a small table by the window where she could keep an eye on the parking lot, she ordered a light breakfast of fruit and tea.

She had just drained her cup and was wondering what to do next when Wally's rental car pulled into the lot and her uncle and David climbed out. The grim expressions both men wore made her stomach tighten. While she hastily settled her bill, she watched them walk past the coffee shop. A moment later Faye caught up with them just in front of Wally's door.

"Where did you go? Why didn't you wake me?" she demanded as she hurried toward them.

"No need," Wally mumbled. He unlocked his door and pushed it open.

"But where have you been?"

David took her by the shoulders, guided her into Wally's room and then shut the door behind them. "We've been to the airport," he stated.

"The airport? But why?"

"Faye, Roy's gone."

"Gone? Gone where?" For a moment she didn't understand what David meant. Then she looked over at her uncle, who had plopped down on the edge of the bed and was sitting with his shoulders slumped and his head down.

"Hightailed it out of here last night," Wally muttered in a defeated tone that she'd never heard from him before. "I wouldn't have thought it of him. That boy was almost like a son to me."

Faye blinked. "You mean Roy got cold feet and left you holding the bag?" she asked furiously.

"So it seems," David commented dryly. "Most of his things are gone from his room and the records show that someone named R. Hubbard hopped a night flight to Seattle. I'm afraid we've seen the last of Roy for a while."

Faye's eyes went back to Wally. He looked absolutely crushed. His face was so drained of color that it was almost gray. Maybe it had been another piece of bad judgment but, for whatever reason, he'd trusted Roy and he'd been betrayed. Faye's anger spiraled. "The rat," she said through clenched teeth. "Wait until I get my hands on him. I'll wring his scrawny neck."

"If you ever catch up with him, I'll help you," David offered. "But in the meantime, we have another problem to deal with. The airport wasn't our only stop. Early this morning your uncle was instructed to go to a certain phone booth to take a call from Morton Baker."

"What happened? Did he speak with Baker?"

"Yes." David crossed his arms over his chest and leaned against the door. "Unfortunately, the plan has been changed. Wally and Roy are supposed to meet Baker tonight at sundown."

"Tonight? But will that give you enough time for this scheme of yours?"

"I think so. I hope so." David began to pace back and forth between the door and the end of the bed where Wally still slumped. "I've contacted a friend in Alaska's wildlife service. At one time Baker was behind a polar bear poaching operation, so they'd like the chance to get their hands on him. It will have to be a hurry-up job, but I think there's still time to spring a trap."

"What sort of trap?"

After Faye sat down in the nearest chair, David hunkered in front of her, took her hands and explained that Baker had instructed Wally to meet him at a deserted dock in a cover off the Gasteneau Channel, the waterway separating Juneau from Douglas Island. "The place is pretty inaccessible. From the nearest road it's a two-mile hike through a muddy rain forest."

Faye was aghast. "But Wally can't go hiking."

"Baker understands that," David assured her. "We'll have to hire a boat."

"Then you'll be going with Wally?"

David nodded. "Disguised as Roy."

"Disguised as Roy!"

Chuckling, David got to his feet. "Shouldn't be too difficult. All I need is a T-shirt and a baseball cap."

Faye was too upset to appreciate his attempt at humor. "This is beginning to sound dangerous. Why must you disguise yourself as Roy?"

"Because he's the one Baker has been dealing with and expects to see. Anyone else would make him suspicious."

"But you don't look like Roy."

"Our height and coloring's not so different, and as far as we know Baker's never seen Roy up close. It shouldn't be a problem. You must realize that I can't let Wally do this by himself."

"No," the old man exclaimed behind them. "I don't want to have to find this place on my own."

Faye reflected that since her uncle got lost driving to Baltimore these days, he probably didn't have a hope of ever finding the obscure dock David had described. "Just what do you expect to happen at this meeting?" she asked.

"I'm hoping that when I hand over Wally's money to Baker, he'll be arrested. It should work, but it's going to take some doing to get it all set up." He consulted his watch. "In fact, I should start on it now. There are a million things to be done."

Faye stood and grabbed at his hand. "What can I do to help?"

"Nothing."

"Nothing?"

He gave her fingers a squeeze. "You expressed an interest in sight-seeing. Why don't you visit the Alaskan State Museum? It has a terrific collection of Indian, Russian and pioneer artifacts."

"You're not serious."

"I am. If you don't want to play tourist, you can keep Wally company this afternoon and make sure he's okay. Otherwise, the best thing you can do for me is not get involved in this."

"But..."

The expression on David's face offered no room for argument. "Please, I'm going to have enough on my mind. I don't want to have to worry about you, too."

But what of me, Faye thought as she stared back at him. *I'm going to be worried sick.*

A moment later David prepared to leave. "I probably won't be back until late this afternoon," he warned the two of them as he opened the door. "So don't expect me. Wally, get a good rest. It's going to be a long evening."

When he was gone, Faye turned to her uncle. "Well, you heard him," she said, doing her best to keep the anxiety she felt out of her voice. "And you do look tired. Maybe you should lie down for a while."

"Maybe I should," he answered wearily. "I didn't get much sleep last night." With a groan he stretched out on the bed.

Faye drew the curtains and then gently propped his grizzled head on a pillow and spread a thick plaid blanket over him. As she gazed down at his lined face, she said in as cheerful a tone as she could command. "I'll go tell them at the office to make sure you're not disturbed, okay?"

"Okay," Wally agreed. "But don't go just yet. Sit and talk with me a little, will you?"

"Sure." She gave his hand a pat and then drew a chair up next to the bed and settled into it. "What would you like to talk about?"

"You. I've been worried about you." Wally grimaced apologetically and then closed his eyes. "I'm sorry I dragged you into this thing."

He looked so tired and pale lying there, Faye's heart went out to him. "You haven't involved me. You heard David just now—he's not going to let me do a thing."

Wally's hands fretted with the fringe on his blanket. "Well, I'm glad for that, and I'm glad he's here. That's something else I need to thank you for." Suddenly he opened his eyes and fixed her with a piercing look. "Something going on between you and that young man?"

Faye opened her mouth to reply, but words momentarily eluded her.

"Don't deny it," Wally chided. "I may be an old ᴵ, but I'm not blind yet. I see the way the two of ᴼᴼk at each other. O'Reilly can't take his eyes off long. And you're the same. Are you in love ?"

ᵈ question toppled what was left of her "Yes," she heard herself say. "I'm afraid

"Why, 'afraid'? Something wrong?" Wally's hands stilled and his gaze grew sharper.

"David's not the marrying kind," she mumbled.

"He tell you that?"

"Yes," she admitted wistfully.

"Then I suppose he believes it, but there's no reason why you should."

Faye's eyes widened.

"Take some advice from a crusty old bachelor who's been there. If a woman wants a man she should get out her traps and chain him up by the ankle."

"But if a man isn't going to be happy tied down..."

"Pish." Wally's laugh sounded rusty. "A lot of men aren't smart enough to decide for themselves what's going to make them happy. I wasn't. Now you take Ruby Prior. She's been mooning after me for more than a quarter of a century. And there was a time when, if she'd insisted on it, she could have had me. But like a fool, she didn't insist, and look what's come of it," he declared irritably.

Faye stared. "What?"

"She's a dried-up old prune and I'm a lonely old bachelor with no family and no one to care about me."

"That's not true. You know perfectly well that we all love you."

"It's not the same. Probably none of this foolishness over a panda would have happened if I'd had a sensible wife to talk me out of it."

He might be right about that, Faye reflected, though Wally was certainly stretching things to blame Ruby Prior for his own poor judgment.

"Your O'Shea isn't getting any younger, you know," the old man continued. "There'll come a day when he'll be tired of the gypsy life he's living and sorry he's alone. But by then it'll be too late. Listen to me, my girl.'' Under shaggy gray brows, Wally directed a fierce glare at her. ''If you really love him and have any starch in your backbone, you won't let that happen.''

So saying, the old man dropped back on his pillow, closed his lids and fell silent. But Faye knew he wasn't really asleep. For several minutes she gazed down at him, her green eyes narrowing as she mulled over his words. ''Wally,'' she suddenly said, ''do you have the instructions for how to get to this place where you and David are supposed to meet Baker?''

He opened one eye. ''Why are you asking?''

''Because I think I ought to know where it is, in case something should go wrong with your plans.''

''Oh, I suppose,'' Wally muttered. His hand slipped beneath the blanket and Faye heard the crackle of paper as he struggled to reach into his pocket. A moment later he produced a crumpled envelope. After handing it to her, he rolled over on his side and tugged the plaid blanket up around his shoulders. While Wally's breathing evened out into sleep, Faye sat reading the instructions he had scribbled. Then she put them down on the table, switched off the bedside lamp and tiptoed outside.

Back in her own room she counted out her traveler's checks and then grabbed the keys to her rental Toyota. Her next stop was the motel office where she left word that her uncle was not to be disturbed and asked directions to the nearest store that sold hunting goods. Then she headed for the parking lot.

Twenty minutes later she pulled up in front of a small row of shops. Thorner's Outdoor World, she read as she got out and directed her steps toward the one with display windows filled by dome tents, bowie knives and sleeping bags.

"What can I do for you?" a bearded young man inside the store queried when she approached the cash register.

"You can show me a good pair of hiking boots, a compass and a rifle," Faye replied.

DAVID DIDN'T GET BACK to the motel until around four. Faye was in her uncle's room when he tapped on the door. She opened it and then gave a startled squeak. Instead of the polished leather loafers, tailored slacks and immaculate shirts he normally wore, he had on ragged high-top sneakers, faded blue jeans, a T-shirt depicting a frothy mug of beer under an open red-and-black checked flannel shirt, and a feathered hat like the one Roy had been sporting for the past two days. With his eyes hidden behind prescription sunglasses, David could almost have passed for a less stringy version of the runaway maintenance chief— except that on David the hat was sexy, where on Roy it had been absurd.

Grinning with satisfaction over his disguise, David came into the room. Three gracefully contained strides and the difference between him and the other man was even more apparent to Faye. The muscular, well-knit body beneath that getup was nothing like Roy Hubbard's. Nevertheless, she smilingly congratulated him on his transformation and so did Wally.

"I see you two have been keeping yourselves busy," David commented, eyeing the remaining half of a large pizza, which sat on the middle of the bed in an open cardboard box.

"We got hungry," Wally explained. "Stomach's still not quite used to the time change, I guess. Have a piece. It was just delivered a few minutes ago."

"All right, thanks." David reached down for a slice and a paper napkin. "Actually, I haven't had anything to eat since breakfast."

"Why not?" Faye asked as she watched him devour the cheese and tomato concoction. There weren't many men disguised in sunglasses and a leather hat who could look good while wolfing down pizza. But David did, she reflected—at least to her.

"Too busy," he volunteered between bites. "Had a lot of running around to do, arrangements to make."

"And are those arrangements all made?" she asked anxiously.

He nodded and then glanced at the clock next to Wally. "We have to get going pretty soon. In half an hour we're supposed to pick up a boat in Juneau. From there we'll motor over to this cove south of town. That will put us on the dock Baker described in plenty of time."

While Wally changed into a pair of soft-soled shoes, David ate two more slices of pizza. Faye sat on a chair in the opposite corner of the room, watching and thinking. For all their nonchalance, she was certain that what David and Wally were about to do was dangerous. This Morton character sounded like a ruthless international outlaw. A hundred things might go wrong when they met and tried to trick him. If David imagined he could leave her sitting here just twiddling her thumbs while he risked his life and her uncle's, he had another think coming, Faye told herself.

"Are you sure there's nothing I can do to help?" she asked when the two men were ready to leave.

David shook his head, and Wally, looking pale but resigned, did the same.

"Just stay put and keep your fingers crossed," David said with a faint smile. He took off his sunglasses and for a moment his clear gray gaze lingered on hers, speaking to her in a language she wasn't sure she fully understood. Then he and Wally were gone and she was left alone in the motel room with nothing but the ravaged remains of a cold pizza to keep her company.

With her gaze fixed on the clock, Faye waited for ten full minutes. When that time was up, she leaped to her feet, let herself out of her uncle's room and headed for the parking lot at a fast trot. Once there, she glanced around. Wally's station wagon was gone, so he and David were on their way to pick up their rental boat. As she strode across the lot to her own automobile, she checked her watch. Tempting though it might be to speed, she'd have to drive at a sedate pace, she told herself. Since she'd be following David and Wally into Juneau, she couldn't take a chance on overtaking them.

As quickly as possible, Faye threaded her car through the city's traffic and then followed the main coast road out as far as it went. When it came to an end, she killed the Toyota's engine and got out to survey the situation. Ahead lay a thick forest. According to Wally's instructions, if she hiked through it for two miles and her compass didn't fail her, she'd come out at the place where David and her uncle were going to rendezvous with Baker.

Faye glanced up at the sky. All day it had been a clear blue, but now gray clouds were moving in. What if it started to rain? She hadn't brought any rain gear and neither had David or Wally. Shivering, she opened

the car door and sat down sideways on the seat to don
the boots she'd purchased earlier. When they were
laced over her cotton slacks, she zipped up her pink
windbreaker, checked her compass and stuffed it in
her pocket along with a box of cartridges. Then she
took out the gun she'd hidden under a blanket in the
back of the car and hefted it.

Faye's father had taught her how to use a rifle.
Nevertheless, as she rested the unloaded weapon
against her shoulder she didn't feel good about carrying it into the forest, and she certainly hoped there
wouldn't be any occasion to fire the thing. She only
wanted to find the dock and then hide behind a tree
and watch. When she was sure that everything was
going according to plan and that David and Wally
were okay, she'd turn around and hike back. With
luck, she'd arrive at the motel before they did and no
one would be the wiser.

About half a mile into the forest the sun disappeared completely and a slow drizzle started. Hunch-
ing her shoulders, Faye thought about David and her
uncle. What were they doing now? Had they reached
the dock yet? David would have to take off those sunglasses. He would look ridiculous wearing them in the
rain. But if Baker had never seen Roy up close, that
shouldn't matter. Indeed, by the time she got there, the
whole transaction might be over. Faye doubted it,
though. Baker had said sundown, and there was at
least an hour and a half of daylight left. And despite
the forest's uneven, muddy floor she was making good
progress. Luckily she'd found a trail, so she was almost certain of being headed in the right direction.

If Faye had been hiking for pleasure, she would
have made frequent stops to admire the beauty sur-

rounding her. Pine was the evergreen tree that grew wild on Maryland's flat and sandy eastern shore. This magnificent stand of Alaskan fir and cedar that seemed to stretch for mile after rolling mile all around her was a new experience. Like everything she'd seen in this part of the world it had a distinctively regal and rugged beauty. The pungent fragrance of cedar perfumed the damp air, and the mist rising from the muddy ground seemed to intensify the green of the thick fir boughs lifting their shaggy arms skyward. But there was no time to appreciate the scenery. Faye's eyes remained on the trail for fear she'd leave it, and when she wasn't looking at the ground she was studying the compass clutched in her palm or glancing at her watch.

As she strode along over the rough terrain, her heart beat heavily inside her chest. But she knew it wasn't due to the rugged exercise. She was terrified of what she would find when she finally came out in the open at this dock. Even though she knew she'd never really had him, she was terrified of losing David.

Oh, please, she thought, *don't let anything happen to him. Let him be okay.*

It was another full hour of hard hiking before the trees began to thin, and Faye, damp and cold from the drizzle and thick mist that now blanketed the forest floor, had begun to despair of ever finding Baker's mystery dock. But finally through the fog she heard the sound of water lapping and caught glimpses of something beyond the looming evergreens.

Cautiously she made her way over the muddy terrain. When she saw the outline of what looked like some sort of structure in the distance and heard the faint echo of angry voices, she stopped walking and listened intently. What was going on up there? Whatever it was, it didn't sound friendly.

Dropping down on one knee, Faye reached into her pocket to withdraw the cartridges she'd stored. Then, with fingers made clumsy by fear, she began to load the gun. But that was as far as she got. Suddenly she heard running feet hammering the ground directly behind her.

"Oh, no, you don't," a gruff voice snarled. Before she could move a heavy weight hit her from the back and sent her sprawling facedown into the cold mud.

CHAPTER FOURTEEN

"THAT MUST BE IT," David commented as he turned the small open boat toward the shore.

"Looks like the place," Wally answered glumly.

As the boat putted toward the broken-down old dock, David cursed himself for not thinking to bring rain gear. Minutes after they'd set off the sky had clouded up and started dumping a chill drizzle on them. The old man looked wet and miserable, and David didn't feel so great himself. What's more, he'd had to remove the sunglasses and replace them with his regular ones, which made him less confident about his disguise. But, he reminded himself, Baker had never seen Roy, except possibly from a distance when he was dropping cash at a pickup point.

Since there was nothing to be done about the success of his impersonation now, he dismissed the problem and concentrated on the wooden structure looming up in front of them.

"Looks as if it might have been used by commercial fishermen," Gaffey commented.

"What makes you think that?"

"See the pile of boxes at the far end? They were probably for icing fish."

"Well, that's something you would know more about than me," David admitted as he eyed the shoreline. He had to admire Baker's cunning. Since the rickety dock extended at least seventy yards into a deserted cove, he and Gaffey would be visible to anyone who wanted to look them over. What's more, except for the ramshackle pile of old wooden boxes, the dock offered no protection. David shivered as he realized what that meant. If something went wrong, he and Gaffey would be sitting ducks.

Throttling down the motor, David eased in and then tied up. After he'd helped the old man onto the shaky wooden structure and handed him the briefcase, he leaped out himself and consulted his watch. "I guess it wasn't such a good idea to get here early," he admitted ruefully. "We've got at least half an hour to wait in this rain."

Gaffey shrugged. "If I end up with double pneumonia, I'll only be getting what I deserve for making all this trouble."

At one time David might have agreed. Now he patted the old man's shoulder and tried to reassure him. Strangely, he was beginning to feel almost as protective toward Wally as Faye did. The man's intentions really were good. He just needed a helping hand to make sure he never again got into the kind of difficulties they faced now.

"You're sure your friends are going to step in at the right time?" Gaffey queried.

"That's the plan. Now we'll just have to wait and see if it works."

The old man tapped the leather briefcase that held the money he would be giving Baker. "Well, I'm set to do my part."

Nodding, David dug his hands into his jeans pockets. He was grateful for the leather hat, which was keeping the rain out of his eyes, though the jaunty feather, he suspected, was losing some of its jaunt in the wet.

"I feel sorry for Faye," Wally commented.

David shot him a questioning look. "Why?"

"She's not the type to sit on the sidelines happily. Must be tough alone in that motel room wondering what's going on. She's probably crazy with worry."

"At least she's safe," David replied gruffly. "That's the important thing."

"There are more important things in life than being safe."

David slanted his companion another look. "What are you getting at? Is there something you want to say to me about Faye?"

"Only that I may be old and I may be foolish, but if you hurt her, I'll come after you with an army."

David laughed sharply. "I believe you."

"You'd better," Gaffey replied pleasantly. "Not that I'm not grateful for your help in this thing. I am. But Faye's happiness isn't a price I'm willing to pay for it."

"Faye's happiness is important to me, too," David muttered.

"How important?"

David eyed his interrogator. "I'd cut off my hand before I'd hurt Faye," he said quietly.

"Does that mean you're not going to run out on her?"

"What if I told you that running out on her might be the kindest thing I could do?"

"Then I'd say that you were a gutless coward," Gaffey declared flatly.

Their terse conversation was interrupted by the thrumming of a motor, and they both turned to stare out at the water. A vessel in the distance seemed to be pointed their way.

"Baker?" Wally whispered.

"Could be." David pulled the hat down low over his forehead and took off his glasses. He'd be meeting Baker blind, but since Roy didn't wear glasses, neither should he, David thought as he slid the silver frames into his breast pocket. "Maybe we should walk up a little closer to the end of the dock."

Wally agreed and they made their way along the narrow, half-rotted walkway. All the while they kept their eyes nailed on the boat. It had turned into the cove and was close enough so that David could see two men on it. They were swathed in yellow slickers, their faces obscured by rain helmets. The one in the rear throttled down to a crawl and the small craft approached the dock obliquely. As David felt himself being scrutinized, the flesh beneath his soaked clothing grew even clammier.

"Taking their time about it," Wally muttered.

"Yes," David answered shortly.

Finally the intruder boat pulled up to the dock with its bow facing out to the channel. The man at the helm slowed the boat even further, but didn't turn the engine off. While it purred in hushed menace, his colleague slipped a line over a piling and clambered up onto the dock. Once there he straightened and faced them—a wedgelike figure in his protective yellow camouflage. "Gaffey?" he said.

David stared with narrowed eyes. Was this the notorious Morton Baker, he asked himself. The man was standing about twenty feet away. His fisherman's rain helmet covered most of his face so that all David could see was his eyes. But there had been something familiar about his voice.

When Wally finished identifying himself, the presumed Baker reached beneath his slicker and drew out a wicked-looking handgun. "I hope you don't mind," he clipped. "But one can't be too careful in this business."

"Is that really necessary?" Wally protested.

Ignoring him, Baker focused on David. "Roy Hubbard, I presume."

"Yo," David muttered, keeping his head down and wishing his vision were better.

"All right, Hubbard, take the old man's briefcase and open it up for me. I want to see what's inside."

There was something infinitely sinister about the manner in which the gunman leveled his pistol. With quiet efficiency, David relieved Wally of the case, set it down on the dock at their feet and unsnapped it so that the numerous stacks of hundred-dollar bills inside were clearly visible.

After a moment, the gunman nodded and David shut the case back up again.

"Leave it there," the man instructed when David started to pick up the container. "And both of you," he added, "put your hands on top of your heads."

As David straightened, he followed instructions and so did Wally. Gaffey was doing all right, David thought, shooting him a quick, concerned glance. He appeared pale and worried, but so far he was handling himself well. It was beginning to look as if they were going to get through this thing okay. After all, Baker had no reason to harm either of them. All he wanted was the money. Soon he'd have it and take off and then their part would be done.

"Where's my panda?" Gaffey demanded, getting into his role.

The gunman snorted. "Don't worry about a thing, grandpa. Your teddy bear is safe and sound." He turned back to David. "Okay, Roy, I have a little job for you, and if you do it right we can all go back home to our suppers safe and sound. I want you to bring that briefcase to me." When David started to lower his hands, Baker shook the pistol at him and snarled, "Not that way. Keep those hands on top of your head."

"Then how—"

"With your feet. Just use your two feet to nudge it down my way. And be damn careful. I wouldn't like to see you knock that much money into the drink and have to go diving in after it."

No, David thought, struggling with his temper. At that moment what he wanted to do was knock the briefcase into Baker's teeth. Feeling like an utter idiot and wishing he could take a swing at the jerk, he began to shuffle toward the end of the dock, pushing the case in front of him with the rubber tips of his sneakers. But as he moved steadily closer to Baker, it wasn't just the absurdity of what he was doing that bothered him.

There was something very familiar about the man giving the orders. David wished he had the use of his glasses and could see more clearly, because it wasn't just Baker's voice. Now that he was closer he could get a better look at his eyes. David had seen those eyes somewhere before. What was even worse, they were staring back at him with the same dawning recognition.

"Stop right there! You're not Roy Hubbard."

David froze. He was still five or six feet away from Baker—too far to make a flying leap for his gun. The man would have plenty of time to shoot him and then Wally.

"Take off that hat. I want to get a better look at your face."

Slowly David removed the leather hat. While he stood bareheaded in the rain, there was a spine-tingling silence.

"Well, as I live and breathe. If it isn't Dr. David O'Neill. And here I thought I'd seen the last of you."

It wasn't until he heard his name spoken that David realized with a gut-churning sensation where he'd seen the man in the yellow slicker before. He'd met him in Africa and had had a drink with him in the hotel bar about a week before the elephant-poaching incident. His name hadn't been Baker then. He'd called himself Webster, Donald Webster. He'd lied about that, of course. Indeed, David now guessed that Baker had struck up the brief acquaintance to pump him for information and get an idea of whether or not he could be bribed. When he'd found that he couldn't be, Baker had arranged to have him bushwhacked.

"Jump him!" Wally cried.

Baker tightened his grip on his gun. "Just try it," he snarled. "I've got this thing aimed right at your belly. And Gramps gets it after you. Stay right where you are, O'Neill!''

Suddenly a shout from the woods distracted them both. David turned his head, and what he saw made him go pale.

"Oh, my God!" Wally moaned.

A burly man dressed in green fatigues and toting a rifle was marching a slight figure up onto the dock. The chill breeze whipped at her short blond hair. At this distance David couldn't make out her face, but he recognized the pink jacket and slacks. It was Faye.

"Look what I found in the woods, boss," her captor shouted. "When I jumped her, she was loading ammo into this rifle."

Baker must have had a man staked out behind the trees all this time, David thought. But what had Faye been doing there? The news that she'd been caught loading a rifle boggled his mind.

"What's this, O'Neill?" Baker hissed. "Did you bring along a cheerleading section?" Not waiting for an answer, he turned his attention to Faye. "Bring Blondie up here," he told his henchman in a sinister tone. "There's room for one more in the boat."

David's heart lurched. They were going to take Faye and the money with them and use her as a hostage. Who knew what they might do with her once they were away free? As Faye and her captor drew abreast of him, he gave a sharp kick that sent the briefcase slamming into Baker's feet. The gun fired and David's ear burned. Ignoring the bullet that had just sung past his head, he pushed Faye out of his path and leaped at her jailor. Luckily the man was caught off balance. David's blow toppled him off the side of the dock and into six feet of water.

"Set up, Sam! Cast off!" Baker yelled.

David didn't even look back. Wally had already grabbed Faye's wrist and was scrambling with her toward the shelter of the pile of boxes. David took off at a run in the same direction, and a moment later all three of them crouched behind the fishy-smelling wooden barrier.

Fifty yards away the water seemed to thrash as Baker picked up his half-drowned colleague. The air at the far end of the dock thickened with their shouts and curses, but there was no more shooting, and moments later the boat containing the three men and Wally's leather briefcase raced out of the cove and into open water.

"But he's getting away with the money," Faye exclaimed. "Shouldn't we have tried to stop him?"

David shook his head and put a restraining hand on her shoulder. "No. There's really nothing we can do except wait here."

"Wait for what?"

"Yes," Wally seconded. "For what?"

David held up a hand for silence and squinted out toward the channel. "Listen."

At that instant shots echoed explosively over the water. "That's what I was waiting to hear," David said with satisfaction. "Baker's being picked up with the briefcase."

"By who?" asked Faye.

"The state police. He's wanted on charges here, and if Wally testifies that Baker tried to extort money from

him in an illegal animal-smuggling scam, Baker will be
sent to prison.''

"But won't that make Wally look bad?"

"Not if he agreed to the scheme because he wanted
a notorious international poacher caught redhanded
and jailed." David shot Wally a sharp look. "That was
your motive, wasn't it?"

Wally blinked several times in rapid succession.
"Why...why yes...of course." He passed a hand over
his eyes and laughed ruefully. "You don't really think
a smart old coot like me would be dumb enough to
imagine he could get away with smuggling a panda
into the country, do you?"

"Of course not," David said with a grin.

"Very clever," Faye admitted. "But what about the
man in the gray car, the one who's been hanging
around Wilderness Worlds?"

"What about him?"

"Well, Roy seemed to think he might be connected
with some government agency."

"He might have been," David agreed. "But if Wally
was just trying to catch a criminal and wasn't really
going to go through with the panda-smuggling
scheme, that ought to take care of any concern the
State Department would have in the matter."

"So the story is going to be that all this time Wally
was just trying to fool Baker into getting himself
caught." Faye shook her head. "You know, Dr.
O'Neill, I remember thinking when we first met and
you tricked Kong that you had the makings of a con
artist. Now I'm sure of it."

David only laughed. "If you'll think back, Kong
was the one who tricked me—and you. I have to ad-

mit that for a while there this plan looked as if it was going to backfire even worse than the doped banana.'' As he spoke he appraised Faye, taking in her torn and dirty clothing and the smears of mud that daubed her face and clumped her hair. She wasn't merely dirty, he thought, she looked in need of medical attention. She was pale, and a long angry scratch zigzagged her cheek. David reached out to lay a gentle finger on it and queried ruefully, ''Did you get that when I pushed you away from the creep with the rifle?''

When she nodded, he shook his head. ''I'm sorry.''

''No reason to be sorry. You saved me.''

Suddenly David's expression shifted into one slightly less tender. ''What in hell were you doing out in the woods with a gun?''

''It's a long story.'' And one Faye didn't feel up to telling him just at the moment. She glanced over at her uncle. Wally had borne up quite well under all this, but she knew that reaction would soon set in. ''Let's save it for later, shall we? Right now I think we'd better get back to Juneau where it's dry and warm.''

''Yes,'' David agreed with a nod, ''and where we can get some information. I'd like to know how this all turned out.''

TWO DAYS LATER Wallace Gaffey's Lear jet banked to avoid the mountains sheltering Juneau's fog-shrouded airport and then headed southeast into the night. Inside the luxurious private aircraft, Faye and David relaxed on a comfortably upholstered couch. Immediately after takeoff Wally had retired to his private sleeping quarters.

"Alone at last," David said as the old man closed the door behind him.

"Yes," Faye agreed. All at once she felt a bit nervous. The past forty-eight hours had been so event-filled that she and David had had no opportunity for private conversation. This was really their first time alone together since Morton Baker's capture. What would they have to say to each other once they got past the obvious, she wondered.

Though Faye hadn't been able to talk much with David, she'd been thinking about him a lot. In fact, when she'd realized that Wally's problem was going to be satisfactorily resolved, her relationship with David had once again become the main focus of her thoughts. And that relationship, Faye had to admit, was still a maddening enigma. Yes, during the stressful time in Juneau they'd become lovers again. But what had their intimacy meant? She knew what it signified for her, but she wasn't at all sure about David.

He stretched his long legs out and leaned back against the velvety padding with a sigh. "You never did tell me that long story of yours," he pointed out. "Just what *were* you doing out in the woods and where did you get that rifle? I thought you promised me you were going to stay safe in the motel room."

Faye crossed her legs. "I never promised. I couldn't stay there, David. I was too worried." Briefly she told him how she'd purchased the rifle. "Purely as a precaution. I never intended to use it." Then she described her long trek through the rain forest and her subsequent capture.

When she finished, David shook his head. "You could have been seriously hurt."

"But I wasn't, thanks to your quick thinking."

He gazed at her for a moment, and though his gray eyes smiled, his mouth was a straight line. "Thank God," was all he finally said. Then he shook off the solemn mood, got to his feet and wandered over to the Lear jet's well-stocked bar. "It's been quite a weekend."

"Certainly has," Faye agreed. "Everything worked out exactly as you said it would. There was no panda, so all the time Baker only intended to cheat Wally."

"An expensive lesson for your uncle," David answered, "but at least this way, after he testifies at Baker's trial, he'll get some of his money back. Meanwhile, Baker and some of his thugs are safely locked up out of harm's way. I know that won't stop the poaching that's going on in animal preserves all around the world, but it may give some of the endangered animals a bit of a breather." David reached for a cut-glass decanter of Scotch and then hesitated and looked back over his shoulder. "Can I get you a drink?"

"A glass of sherry would be nice."

As he turned back to the bar, Faye cleared her throat. "You really feel very strongly about that, don't you?"

"About what? Getting us a drink?"

"No." She laughed. "About protecting endangered animals."

David picked several cubes of ice out of a silver bucket and dropped them into a tumbler. "Yes, I always have. I think it's a cause worth devoting one's life to." Holding the sherry bottle in one hand for a moment, he paused to stare off into space. "The world will be a poorer place when elephants and rhinos and gorillas have gone the way of the dinosaurs. Unfortunately, unless something radical is done soon, that day isn't far off.''

"Wally feels the same, you know."

He turned toward her. "Your uncle's commitment is a little different from mine. But you're right about his motives. It's just that his methods aren't always what they should be."

Faye sighed. "Poor Wally. I wonder what he'll do with that panda house he's been building in secret."

"We'll find some other use for it." Holding a small stemmed glass of pale sherry in one hand and his Scotch on the rocks in the other, David strolled back to the couch.

"We?" Faye shot him a quizzical look. "Does that mean you'll be coming back to Wilderness Worlds?"

"Well, I did think I had a job there." He sank down beside her and proffered the sherry, which she accepted without taking her eyes off his face. "At least, I hope I have a job there," he continued smoothly. "My visiting semester at Hopkins is almost over, and I have to earn my living somehow."

Faye clenched the stem of her glass. "You really meant it about not accepting that grant?"

"Of course I meant it." He swirled the cubes in his tumbler until they clinked merrily. "As a matter of fact, yesterday Wally reopened his offer of a full-time position at Wilderness Worlds and I accepted."

Faye almost spilled her sherry. "You did?"

"Yes, I did."

Faye knew she should have been delighted by this news—and she was. But she also felt panicked.

David's expression was faintly disappointed. "You know, all day I've been looking forward to telling you about this. I was hoping you'd be glad. But you look…" His eyes continued to search hers. "You look upset. Is something wrong? Don't you want me there on a regular basis?"

"It's not that. It's—" Faye took an overlarge gulp of her sherry. Eyes watering, she put the drink down on the low table in front of them and waited for the burning sensation in her throat and chest to subside. This was a critical moment, she realized, and she had to make a decision. There were things that she and David had to get clear between them. If their relationship was ever to go the way she wanted it to, now was the time for honesty. But what if that honesty meant losing him?

When she felt able to speak, she said very carefully, "David, why have you made this decision? Being the vet at Wilderness Worlds has got to be a lot less glamorous than some of the other things a man with your credentials could do. So what's in it for you?"

Obviously puzzled by her reaction, he looked at her for a moment before answering. "Actually, I think working at your uncle's place is going to be very rewarding. Yesterday while Wally and I were waiting at the police station, we had a long talk. He's willing to give me a lot more freedom at Wilderness Worlds than I had before. With his financial backing, I think we could accomplish some interesting things, and I'm excited about the prospect. But Faye, you must know what's really behind my decision to stay on."

"No, I don't," she answered. "You'll have to tell me."

David set down his own glass. "All right," he said, "I'll tell you in the way I've been wanting to ever since we made love in that motel room. Faye, it's been a very frustrating forty-eight hours."

As he spoke, he reached for her. And before she could summon up the presence of mind to resist, she was in his arms. His lips on her were warm and strong and tasted faintly of Scotch, and as her hands curled around the reassuring strength of his shoulders, she couldn't stop herself from kissing him back with all the urgency and longing that she possessed. When had she ever been able to control her response to this man? From that first moment when she'd been Kong's prisoner, it had been David—David with his steady gray eyes and surefooted grace who'd really captivated her.

"We shouldn't be doing this," she managed to say when at last he pulled away. "Wally..."

"Wally's fast asleep. And besides, after the kiss you just gave me, you can't pretend that you don't want another." While he smiled down into her flushed face, David's hand stroked her back and then crept up under her loosened shirt. His sensitive fingertips on her bare flesh made her shiver, and not because she was cold.

"But he might wake up. Oh, David—" With a little cry, she buried her face in his chest and clung to him.

Puzzled again, he frowned even as he wrapped his arms around her protectively. "Faye, what is it? What's wrong?"

"We have to talk," she said in a muffled voice.

"Now?"

"Yes, now." She lifted her head and gazed up at him, a half-frightened look in her long-lashed green eyes. Then, curling her hands around his muscular forearms, she held herself stiffly away from his body and said with an effort, "David, I can't let you take this job under a false impression. What did you think it would be like between us once you were working at Wilderness Worlds full-time?"

His brow furrowed more deeply. "What was it going to be like?"

"Yes. Did you plan to give up your apartment in Baltimore and get yourself a place in Haverton?"

"Well, not exactly. I'd thought I might come to live with you." Though she was holding him at arm's length, his hand still rested on her shoulder. He squeezed it gently. "There's room in your house for two, don't you think?"

"Of course there is." At that moment Faye ached to wrap her arms around his waist and say no more. But she knew that if she wanted to respect herself, she had to resist that temptation. "And I want to have you live with me, very much," she continued. Then she swallowed. What came next wasn't going to be easy, yet the words had to be said. "But not as my lover, David. As my husband."

He blinked. "Husband?"

"David, Haverton is a small place. I couldn't have a live-in lover."

His eyebrows jerked up. "Surely...Faye, this is not the Victorian era."

"Eras don't make much difference on the Eastern Shore. I couldn't live that way surrounded by people who've known me since I was a baby."

He made a rusty sound in his throat. "All right, then I could get my own apartment. We could be discreet."

"Discreet is not what I want." Though it was no longer necessary, her hands still gripped his forearms tightly. "David, you once told me that you're not the marrying kind. When I made love with you that first time, I pretended to myself and to you that it didn't matter. Well, this time let's both be honest. I'm not a sophisticated lady like your Grace was. I *am* the marrying kind. I'm in love with you—too much in love to be willing to settle for an affair. Tell me the truth, how do you feel about me?"

During the electric silence that ensured Faye was suddenly vividly aware of the throb of the Lear jet's powerful engines bearing them aloft and the strangeness of the moment. She and David were confronting each other in a tiny silver capsule that was flying through the night at least a mile above the earth. It was like a dream except that the emotions between them quivered with harsh reality.

"You know how I feel about you, Faye. I adore you," he finally said.

"I'm not sure what 'adore' really signifies. Do you love me?" While she waited for his answer, she stared into his gray eyes, trying to divine the struggle behind them. At that moment she was convinced that he cared. Why was it so hard for him to admit the fact?

"Yes," he answered. "I do. I love you so much I'd risk just about anything for you. But Faye, I'm just not sure that marriage to me would make you happy."

She cocked her head, still studying him, still trying to understand what fueled his fear of commitment.

"Tell me something, David. What's the most dangerous thing you've ever done in your life?"

As he returned her steady regard, his brows began to slowly elevate. "I don't know. A job like mine involves risks."

"I'd really like to hear you answer my question. Won't you please think about it?"

"All right." He shrugged. "Maybe it was the time at Whipsnade when I had to get a cub away from an enraged male black bear. Or maybe it was a few years later when I was studying sharks and a Great White broke through my cage. Both of those were very near things."

"You amaze me."

"What do you mean?"

"David, you're not afraid to face bloodthirsty sharks and enraged bears. But the thought of loving a woman and making a commitment to her terrifies you, doesn't it?"

There was another tense silence and then he chuckled. "You're forgetting something. Whether or not it scares me, and it does, I do love you and I've admitted the fact."

"But the commitment part is more than you can handle?"

He picked up his Scotch and downed what remained. When the glass was empty he said, "I don't know, Faye. It's a big decision. I know that marriage isn't a happy dream. It certainly wasn't for my mother and father. It would kill me to see what we have turn sour the way it did for them."

"It would kill me, too. But I'm willing to take that chance, because I want to build something with you."

She sighed and looked away, focusing on the night outside the airplane's tiny portholes. "I suppose that while I'm being honest, I might as well be completely honest."

"There's more to come?" David queried warily.

"A lot more." Gathering herself up, she confronted him again. "I don't just want to marry you, I want to have a family with you."

"A family? You mean children?"

She nodded. "And not just one or two, either. David, I want lots of children. You remember what you once said to me about my being the kind of woman who should live in a big old house filled with kids and dogs and cats? Well, you were right, only I want gerbils and guinea pigs, and maybe even an ant farm, too."

"An ant farm, too?" He shook his head.

Something in his tone made her smile through her seriousness. "Have I frightened you to death?"

"Not to death, sweetheart, but close."

He didn't look particularly frightened. Encouraged, she said, "This isn't a large plane, but if you want to get away from me, you could sit on that sofa opposite the bar. I'd understand."

He put his head back against the couch they were both on and smiled. Then he drew her close to the warmth of his body. "Faye," he said, stroking her hair tenderly, "when I saw that creep dragging you up the dock, it was the worst moment of my life. Not even your ant farm could terrify me the way that did."

"You were afraid for me?"

"Afraid for you and afraid that I'd lose you. I don't want to ever lose you. But I've been a pretty determined bachelor for thirty-five years now. I need a little time to adjust. Will you give me that time?"

She looked up at him trustfully, her green eyes shimmering like wet emeralds in her small face. "Of course I will."

"It won't be long."

"I know it won't."

Instead of answering, he kissed her. And this time, as his lips moved against hers, the kiss was gentle with promise.

CHAPTER FIFTEEN

"OH, I'M SO HAPPY that Wallace has finally stopped smoking those nasty cigars and started taking vitamins. Now that he's eating and sleeping right and getting healthy exercise he's like a new man. Why, he hasn't forgotten his wallet or misplaced his glasses in almost three weeks." Miss Prior leaned forward and whispered, "He's invited me out to dinner tonight. What do you think of that?"

"I think it's about time," Faye answered forthrightly. "You've been his mainstay for years. I'm glad he's gotten around to noticing the fact. And—" she leaned forward and winked "—I hope you're going to wear something sexy and knock his socks off."

"Sexy! Me?" Miss Prior made a you've-got-to-be-kidding! gesture. Nevertheless, as she turned back to her typewriter her pale blue eyes sparkled in a way they hadn't for years.

Smiling, Faye picked up the order forms she'd just collected and headed for the door. Lately there had been a lot to smile about. Since their return from Juneau a month earlier, Wally had allowed himself to be examined by a geriatric specialist at Hopkins. The doctor had put him on a strict regimen that Miss Prior had made sure he stuck to. Already his improvement was noticeable, and he was almost like his old self.

Though he and Faye would have to go back to Juneau to testify at Morton Baker's trial, their lawyer assured them that because Wally had been instrumental in the infamous poacher's arrest, he had nothing to fear.

David and Roy Hubbard would also be testifying at that trial. Two weeks ago Roy had shown up in the office looking beaten. After apologizing abjectly, he had asked for his old job back and Wally had given it to him. Faye was glad, because though Wally hadn't exactly greeted Roy's return like that of the prodigal son, she knew he'd missed the wayward maintenance chief. And somehow Wilderness Worlds wasn't quite the same without Roy's cantankerous presence.

Every apple needs its worm, Faye thought with a shake of her head. As she walked down the path toward the ape house, she had to dodge a wheelbarrow loaded with bricks and several workmen carrying buckets and heavy tools. With the official opening of Wilderness Worlds only five days off, last-minute preparations had reached an almost frantic level.

When Faye reached the ape house, she walked around to the moated outdoor area. As she approached the fence, David, who'd been leaning on it, turned and beckoned. "You're just in time."

"In time for what?"

"Come on over and take a look."

She hastened her step and a moment later stood next to him, letting the sun warm her back through her thin cotton blouse. "Oh, for heaven's sake!" she exclaimed.

On the other side of the moat, the large grassy enclosure contained a sturdy, naturalistic jungle gym, various other climbing and swinging toys and a huge slide. Kong and Daisy Mae were playing on the slide, pushing each other down it with great glee and then wrestling at the bottom.

"They look like a couple of kids," Faye commented.

"Big kids in furry gorilla suits."

She laughed and then glanced over at a sunny spot nearby. "Violet's doing pretty well, too."

"Yes, she is."

The young mother was cuddling her baby, cooing at it while she held it to her breast. Every now and then she cast an indulgent look over at the antics of Kong and Daisy Mae. But she showed no interest in joining them.

"I guess Violet is too mature for that sort of thing," Faye speculated. She returned her attention to the adolescent couple gamboling on the slide. "It's wonderful to see them playing together so well. I was worried there for a while."

"So was I," David admitted, dropping an arm lightly around her shoulder. "But I figured it was just a matter of time. Kong had been alone so long, it was bound to take him a while to adjust to the idea of taking on a future mate and eventually turning into a family man. But as you can see, he's coming around."

Faye slanted David a sideways look. Did he realize how ironic his statement was in view of their own situation, she wondered. A lot had happened since they'd come back to Wilderness Worlds—Wally's improvement, Roy's return, the Herculean amount of work everybody was putting in to get the animal park ready for its opening. But as far as Faye could see, not a lot that was positive had developed in their relationship—at least not from her point of view.

"What do you think the turning point was between Kong and Daisy Mae?" she queried. "When did he start being nice to her?"

David withdrew his arm from her shoulder and clasped the top of the iron fence with his hands. "Oh, I think that dates from when I separated them. Taking her away was a really good idea. It made him appreciate how much he liked having her around."

"You really think so?"

"I'm certain of it. A little deprivation went a long way."

"Interesting," Faye said aloud. Under her breath she muttered, "Now why didn't I think of that?"

She *had* thought of it, of course. That night on Wally's plane when she'd confronted David about their love affair she'd meant to keep the physical part of their relationship on hold until he made some sort of decision about whether or not they had a future together.

At first David had seemed to respect that. Ten days ago he'd finished the last of his assignments at Hopkins, given up his apartment in Baltimore and moved into a couple of rooms for rent above a garage in Haverton. For the past week he and Faye had worked together closely. And though the atmosphere between them had been taut with feelings barely held in check, he'd treated her like a friend and respected colleague. He'd said nothing more about his original proposal to move into her cottage. Was his tacit withdrawal from their love affair only temporary, Faye wondered. Was he just thinking things over the way he'd told her he needed to do? Or did his silence mean that he'd lost interest?

Last night that question had been answered. After work David had invited her to stop by and take a look at his rooms. When she'd seen them Faye had been appalled.

"David, they're so small and dingy. Isn't Wally paying you enough so that you can afford a nicer place to live?"

He'd been amused. "Sure, but I have better things to do with my money. Besides," he'd added when he'd seen the worried look on her face, "where I live has never mattered much to me. Compared to some of the places I've hung my hat, this is the Taj Majal."

Nevertheless, as Faye looked around the dark, cheaply furnished little rooms, she'd been disturbed. After all, she had denied the man she loved the comfort of her home. She'd done it because she wanted him to realize that he couldn't live without her. But still, she felt guilty.

Her remorse had taken the form of inviting David back to her house for dinner where she had made him her favorite stir-fried vegetarian lo mein. And despite his jokes about her dietary habits, he'd eaten the meal with every appearance of relish. Afterward he'd uncorked a bottle of wine he'd brought along.

Just as on a previous occasion, they'd clinked glasses and looked into each other's eyes as they sipped. It had been a month since they'd last made love, and Faye had spent sleepless nights longing for him and wondering if she was a fool to deny herself the pleasure of being in his arms.

Inevitably when their wineglasses were drained, they had begun to sip from each other's lips instead. One thing had led to another, and they'd wound up in her bed. It had been a memorable night. David had made love to Faye with a passion and tenderness that left her breathless.

But the next morning as she'd lain awake while he slept contentedly at her side, she'd stared up at the ceiling and told herself that she'd committed a strategic mistake. By yielding to her desire for him had she made herself just like his other forgotten lovers? How long before she slipped into being just his colleague and bedmate? And when that happened, what was to keep him from growing tired of her? Loving David as she did, she didn't think she could bear having him bid her a fond but firm farewell when he found someone new or was offered a job he liked better than the one he had at Wilderness Worlds.

Now as he stood smiling across at the fledgling family of apes, she shaded her eyes against the hot summer sun and cast him a long covert glance. She hadn't yet weakened enough to invite him to move in with her the way he'd originally suggested. And he hadn't asked. But she knew that if he did she couldn't hold out much longer.

How could she when she adored this tenderhearted yet tough and maddeningly elusive man? Just standing close to him like this made her tremble with longing. She wanted to reach out and touch the corded back of his strong hand, lay her cheek against his sunbrowned forearm and drink in the vital fragrance that clung to his skin. She wanted to give him her life. If only she could believe that he wanted to give her back some of his in return.

David glanced at his watch and then up at the piercing blue sky. "Almost lunchtime. How about going for a picnic with me?"

"A picnic?" Faye was taken aback. Somehow David didn't strike her as being the picnic type.

"Yes," he said in his deep voice. "It's a gorgeous day, and we've both been working nonstop since we got back from Alaska. I think we should play hooky for an hour or two."

He was right about the perfect summer weather, Faye thought glancing around her. Temperatures were in the high eighties and there wasn't a cloud in sight. Suddenly she found David's suggestion irresistible.

"Where will we get the food?" she queried. "Do you want to stop back at my place?"

He shook his head. "No, it's all packed and ready."

"It is? Where?"

"At the spot where we're going to have our picnic."

"What spot?"

"You'll see." He took her hand. "Come on. Time is precious on a day like this. Let's not waste any more of it."

"But where are we going?" she questioned again as he led her toward the parking lot and his car.

"Trust me. It's a pretty place I've discovered out near the river. I think you'll like it."

"I didn't know you'd done any exploring around here."

"Well, I have." He waited for her to settle in her seat and then started up the engine and backed out of his space.

When they passed through the gate, Faye sighed. At least she didn't have to worry about the man in the gray car anymore, she thought. Through David's highly placed friends they had learned that Bob Selden was connected with the State Department and that he'd been hot on Wally's trail. But now that the case had broken in a way that could do the United States no harm internationally, he'd dropped out of their lives.

Fifteen minutes later David guided his automobile onto a country road, and a hot breeze thick with the early-July incense of grass and pine and the faint dankness of nearby lapping water fanned Faye's cheek. She knew the area around Haverton. He was heading toward a part of the river where several nice old houses fronted on a little tree-shaded inlet. But it was all private property. There weren't any public picnicking spots that she was aware of around here.

Yet when she glanced over at David, he was driving along, smiling to himself as if he were enjoying some special secret, so she supposed he must know what he was doing. Maybe he'd made friends with one of the landowners out this way and had been given permission to use their property.

Deciding that this must be the case, Faye closed her eyes and leaned back against the padded headrest. As always when she had time to think lately, her mind turned back to the puzzle of her love affair with David. Was it wrong to want him to make a commitment to her? Would it be wiser to simply live for the day? *Trouble is,* Faye thought, *I'm just not comfort-*

able living that way. I need a future as well as a present.

Recently she'd had a conversation with Wally on the subject—one that made her frown every time she recalled it, as she did now.

"Just what's going on between you and that young man?" he'd demanded.

"I don't know," she'd answered. "Nothing, I guess."

"Nothing!" Wally's thick eyebrows had beetled. "Don't try and sell me that, young lady. Anyone with eyes can see the two of you are crazy about each other. When are you going to stop wasting time and make it legal? Time you presented me with a grandniece or nephew."

Though Faye had kept her voice calm, her face had reddened. "Wally, I told you before that David isn't the marrying kind."

"And I told you that's a lot of horse manure. Do you want me to have a talk with that young man and put the fear of God in him?"

"Oh, no!" *That's all I need,* Faye thought as she begged her uncle not to interfere. If Wally started badgering David about his intentions toward her, he'd probably run for his life, and she'd never get the chance to sell him on domesticity.

"Harumph!" Wally commented, eyeing her very much askance. "You remember what I told you about Ruby?"

"I remember."

"She had her chance years ago, and she muffed it. I may, out of the goodness of my heart, give that woman another opportunity. But even if she doesn't mess up this time, we will have lost a lot of good years together. Don't you go and make the same mistake.''

"Wally, believe me, I'm trying not to,'' Faye had replied a little desperately. "But David can't be pushed, and he has his own ideas on the subject.''

"Well, where's your gumption? Don't accept his ideas. Sell him yours instead. And just to give you an edge, let me tell you something.'' Wally had leaned forward, his brown eyes sparkling conspiratorially. "Faye, honey, I'm getting old. Who knows how much longer I'll live.''

She had put her arm around his shoulder. "Don't talk that way. You have a lot of good years left.''

"Maybe. Maybe not. Anyhow, except for you I have no close family, and I want you to know that one day this place will be yours.''

"Mine?'' Faye had been flabbergasted. "You mean you're going to leave me Wilderness Worlds?''

"Yes, and if O'Grady has the good sense to marry you and make you happy, it'll be his, too. What do you think of that for a dowry? He'll have his own private animal park to play with. I know how crazy he is about preserving endangered species. So if nothing else will make him see the light where you're concerned, that little piece of information ought to do the trick.''

Faye had simply stared. By telling her his intentions, Wally had put quite an ace in her hands. Should she use it? Did she want to? She knew better than he what it would mean to David to actually own his own preserve. But did she want him so badly and have so little pride that she was willing to try to bribe the man she loved into marrying her?

"You're supposed to take a nap after the picnic, not before it." Her eyes popped open and she saw David's face inches from hers. He was smiling tenderly and something about the light in his clear eyes made her heart flutter.

Repressing the impulse to throw her arms around his neck, she said, "I was just thinking."

"What about?"

"Oh, I don't know. Just things." She straightened in her seat and looked around. David had pulled the Volvo off the road and up a gravel drive flanked on either side by tall privet hedges. "Where are we?" she asked.

"At our picnic spot."

"But this is someone's private property, isn't it?"

He nodded and slipped the car back into gear. "Yes, but don't worry. I have permission to use it."

As the car crunched forward over the gravel and rounded a bend, Faye glanced around curiously. "Oh, how beautiful!"

"Like it?"

"Oh, yes!" A two-story gray stucco house had come into view. Dating from somewhere around the turn of the century, it was solidly grounded in a nest of overgrown greenery including dogwoods, hollies and tall yews. A thick wisteria vine covered one wall and next to the brick path that led to a small veranda, a thicket of blooming roses rioted around a sundial. This was the back of the house, Faye realized. The front must face the water.

Under the shade of a towering oak, David turned off the engine. "Would you like to get out and look around?"

"I'd love to. But are you sure the owners won't mind?"

"I'm certain. As a matter of fact, they aren't even here today. We have the place to ourselves."

"That's wonderful," Faye exclaimed as she got out.

David went to open the trunk and took out an old army blanket.

"Where did you meet these people?" she asked when he joined her. "I know who lives in most of the houses around here, but not this one."

"The Selwyns are a retired couple," David answered. "Nice people, but now that they're getting on in years they're finding the upkeep on this place more than they can handle."

"I guess I can see that." The garden really did need some attention, Faye thought as David led her through it. If it were hers, she would get out the pruning shears. As they passed a bed of hosta her fingers fairly itched to pull out the weeds pushing up around the delicate white lilies. Yet almost everything about the place delighted her. She breathed in deeply, inhaling with pleasure the heady fragrance or roses mixed with the faintly bitter scent of boxwood.

When David walked right up to the rear porch, Faye hung back. "We're not going inside, are we?"

"We have to if we want our picnic. Our lunch is waiting for us in the kitchen."

"Goodness, you must be very close friends with these people."

"Not exactly," he said, inserting a key in the lock. "It was a special arrangement."

There was something peculiar about this, Faye thought. As he took her hand and urged her forward,

David kept looking at her in a strangely intent way. What was going on? But once inside she forgot her misgivings. The kitchen was almost as charming as the garden. "Oh, look at that blue tile on the counter! And a stained-glass window over the breakfast nook— how pretty!"

"The appliances are old," David said. "And the cabinets need to be replaced."

"Oh, no," Faye protested, rubbing an exploratory finger along the edge of one drawer. "You're right about the appliances, but if these cabinets were mine, I'd just refinish them. Under all that paint I bet they're solid oak."

"Could be." David had crossed over to the small refrigerator and with his back to her was filling a basket with chilled drinks and wrapped sandwiches. When he spoke his voice was oddly muffled. "Why don't we walk through to the front. There's a gorgeous view of the water from the living room."

Faye felt a little strange about making so free in someone else's house. On the other hand, she was itching with curiosity to see the rest of it. With no more than a faint protest, she allowed David to guide her down a narrow hall. The living room was smaller than she'd expected, but it was cozy and charming. And from its many-paned windows the river, shaded by drooping willows, really looked as if it belonged in a nineteenth-century English landscape. Out on the lawn a few yards from a small dock there was even a white gingerbread gazebo.

"I thought we'd have our lunch down there," David said.

"Sounds great. Lead the way."

With a faint smile, he shifted the basket of food to his left hand, wedged the blanket under his arm and opened the door so that he could usher her onto the front lawn. After taking her hand with his free one, they strolled down toward the water.

As they walked, Faye savored the warmth of David's strong fingers twined with hers and asked herself again if she should tell him about Wally's intention to bequeath Wilderness Worlds to her. The trouble was that she didn't know how he would react. Would he think she was trying to buy him and get angry? Or would the knowledge that he would one day have his own animal preserve be all it took to wring a commitment from him? And was that something she could live with herself? It was so hard to know what to do.

As David spread out the blanket on the grass, she gazed out over the river. In the center the sun streaked its surface with flickering gold. Closer to shore the slowly moving bottle-green water reflected graceful images of the willows, which trailed their lacy branches into it like drooping dancers.

This would certainly be an idyllic scene for a marriage proposal, Faye thought. But how would she feel if David asked her to marry him only after she'd bribed him with his heart's desire? *She* wanted to be his heart's desire. And anyway, she wasn't even sure that Wally's bequest would be enough to keep him tied to a backwater place like Haverton. David was used to going anywhere he wanted in the world with no constraints. What made her think that she and an Eastern Shore animal preserve would be enough to tie him down? Oh, why had she fallen in love with such an unobtainable man?

Still fretting silently, she helped him spread their food out on the blanket. In addition to two chilled bottles of mineral water and a half-carafe of white wine, there were egg-salad and ham and cheese sandwiches, several kinds of fruit and a large plastic container of coleslaw.

"This looks very good," Faye commented. "Quite a spread! I didn't know you were so domestic."

"I'm not. I ordered most of it from the diner. I'm still not sure what you will and will not eat, so I had them pack a variety."

Smiling to hide her troubled thoughts, Faye unwrapped an egg-salad sandwich. "This is fine. Anyway, in a setting like this you couldn't go wrong. I would have been happy with nothing more than an apple."

He gestured around them and then back at the house. "Do you really like it?"

"Of course. I'm jealous of these Selwyns. I'd like to own this place myself."

As he opened one of the mineral waters, David glanced at her under his lashes. "Actually, the Selwyns want to retire to Florida. I'm thinking of buying their property."

Faye couldn't have been more astonished. Convulsively she swallowed the large bite of egg salad she'd just taken and promptly choked on it. While David looked on in concern and then began vigorously slapping her back, she gasped and sputtered for a good thirty seconds. When her coughing spasm had finally subsided, she gazed at him through watery eyes.

"Are you all right?"

"Yes," she croaked.

"You worried me."

"Me, too."

"That was quite a reaction you had to my news."

"Well, that was quite a piece of news." Faye cleared her throat and then flattened her palm against her chest and breathed in and out carefully. When she was sure she could speak safely, she said, "David, does this mean that you think you're going to stay for a while?"

He gave her another one of the strange looks he'd been directing at her ever since they got here. "Yes, if you haven't changed your mind."

"What do you mean?"

He hooked a thumb back toward the house. "If you think it's big enough for an ant farm and you're willing to live in it with me."

Fortunately this time Faye didn't have her mouth full. Nevertheless, she didn't try to speak, either. All she could do was stare back at him round-eyed. What was he trying to tell her? Could this possibly be the marriage proposal she'd been longing—and scheming—to get?

"Faye," he said, reaching out to take her hand, "I love you. I knew that before Juneau. I just didn't know what kind of a husband I'd make and I was afraid of failing you. But you've given me the time I needed to realize that I could never leave you and that you're the person I want to spend the rest of my life with."

"You can't? You do?"

He nodded. "You were right, you know. I am a coward. I wasn't afraid to face charging lions, but the thought of loving someone enough to commit my life to them terrified me. I've resolved that. But what about you? Are you really brave enough to take me on?"

Faye cleared her throat again. "David, are you asking me to marry you?"

Suddenly, his gray eyes were filled with longing. "Faye," he said, "I'm begging you." With one sweep of his hand he scattered the food that blocked the way between them. In the next instant her body was crushed beneath his and he was propped up on his elbows leaning over her and staring earnestly down into her flushed face and glowing green eyes. "I adore you. I adore everything about you, and I don't think I could face an existence without you. If you sent me away now, I'd shrivel up and die."

"But David," Faye managed through the happiness that was all but paralyzing her, "I'm not going to send you away." There was no chance of that, she thought, and a radiant smile suffused her features. No chance at all. "I love you," she told him simply and reached up to put her arms around his neck and draw him close. "I love you, I love you! If you'd tried to leave me I would have stowed away in the trunk of your car!"

A long time later they finished their lunch and then sat propped up against the trunk of a willow alternately kissing and planning their future.

"Does this mean I've condemned myself to a lifetime of herbal tea and fruit pancake breakfasts?" David teased.

"It depends on how hard you resist my efforts to tempt you into healthy eating habits."

"I've never been good at resisting your temptations," David replied huskily, and there was another long silence as they kissed each other hungrily.

"Remember, I do want lots of kids," Faye said at last and nuzzled his neck.

"What do you mean by 'lots'? Won't three or four do?"

"I don't know. We'll just have to see."

He laughed and planted a kiss on her forehead. "All right, as long as I get to be in on the early planning stages."

"Oh, you'll be included in every stage, especially the first one. How do you feel about dogs and cats?"

"I feel fine." He ran his finger lightly over her lips. "I draw the line at tarantulas, though. No pet tarantulas."

"We might have a child who is a budding entomologist."

David sighed. "Yes, I suppose we might." He glanced back over his shoulders. "Shall we have a look around the upstairs to see if there's an appropriate bedroom in which to conceive such a prodigy?"

Faye grinned. "Yes, I think we should." She had decided to wait before giving him Wally's news. They had enough to think about now. And what if David wasn't interested in Wally's gift, and wanted to leave the Eastern Shore? In that case she would go with him, of course. It was all very simple. As long as they were together, that was what counted.

After another lingering kiss, he helped her to her feet. For a moment they stood staring toward the shady old house almost as if they could see their future waiting there in front of them. Then, arm in arm, they walked toward it.

Harlequin Superromance

COMING NEXT MONTH

Six exciting series for you every month... from Harlequin

Harlequin Romance
The series that started it all

Tender, captivating and heartwarming...
love stories that sweep you off to faraway places
and delight you with the magic of love.

Harlequin Presents

Powerful contemporary love stories...as individual as the women who read them

The No. 1 romance series...
exciting love stories for you, the woman of today...
a rare blend of passion and dramatic realism.

Harlequin Superromance
It's more than romance...
it's Harlequin Superromance

A sophisticated, contemporary romance-fiction
series, providing you with a longer,
more involving read...a richer mix of complex plots,
realism and adventure.

Harlequin
American Romance™
Harlequin celebrates the American woman...

...by offering you romance stories written about American women, by American women for American women. This series offers you contemporary romances uniquely North American in flavor and appeal.

◆

Harlequin Temptation™
Passionate stories for today's woman

An exciting series of sensual, mature stories of love...dilemmas, choices, resolutions... all contemporary issues dealt with in a true-to-life fashion by some of your favorite authors.

◆

Harlequin Intrigue™
Because romance can be quite an adventure

Harlequin Intrigue, an innovative series that blends the romance you expect... with the unexpected. Each story has an added element of intrigue that provides a new twist to the Harlequin tradition of romance excellence.

Harlequin Books·

PROD-A-2

If **_YOU_** enjoyed this book,
your daughter may enjoy

Romances from

CROSSWINDS

Keepsake is a series of tender, funny, down-to-
earth romances for younger teens.

The simple boy-meets-girl romances have
lively and believable characters, lots of action
and romantic situations with which teens can
identify.

Available now wherever books are sold.

ADULT-1

ATTRACTIVE, SPACE SAVING BOOK RACK

Display your most prized novels on this handsome and sturdy book rack. The hand-rubbed walnut finish will blend into your library decor with quiet elegance, providing a practical organizer for your favorite hard-or soft-covered books.

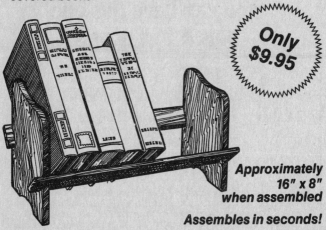

Only $9.95

Approximately 16" x 8" when assembled

Assembles in seconds!

To order, rush your name, address and zip code, along with a check or money order for $10.70* ($9.95 plus 75¢ postage and handling) payable to *Harlequin Reader Service*:

Harlequin Reader Service
Book Rack Offer
901 Fuhrmann Blvd.
P.O. Box 1396
Buffalo, NY 14269-1396

Offer not available in Canada.

BKR-1A

*New York and Iowa residents add appropriate sales tax.

Can you keep a secret?

You can keep this one plus 4 free novels

FREE BOOKS/GIFT COUPON

Mail to **Harlequin Reader Service**®

In the U.S.	In Canada
901 Fuhrmann Blvd.	P.O. Box 609
P.O. Box 1394	Fort Erie, Ontario
Buffalo, N.Y. 14240-1394	L2A 5X3

YES! Please send me 4 free Harlequin American Romance® novels and my free surprise gift. Then send me 4 brand-new novels every month as they come off the presses. Bill me at the low price of $2.49 each*—a 9% saving off the retail price. There are no shipping, handling or other hidden costs. There is no minimum number of books I must purchase. I can always return a shipment and cancel at any time. Even if I never buy another book from Harlequin, the 4 free novels and the surprise gift are mine to keep forever.   154 BPA BP7F

*Plus 49¢ postage and handling per shipment in Canada.

Name   (PLEASE PRINT)

Address   Apt. No.

City   State/Prov.   Zip/Postal Code

This offer is limited to one order per household and not valid to present subscribers. Price is subject to change.   MSAR-SUB-1B